DISC

Into The Shadows - The Fever
A Spy Novel

Michael Brady

Published by Waldorf Publishing
2140 Hall Johnson Road
#102-345
Grapevine, Texas 76051
www.WaldorfPublishing.com

Into The Shadows - The Fever, A Spy Novel
Book 1

ISBN: 978-1-68419-256-4
Library of Congress Control Number: 2016957016

Dedication

For the men and women who operate in the shadows and those who wonder about them.

Sira Fortress, Port of Aden, Yemen – October 2, 2014, 9:30 PM

Into the Shadows he went. The passage leading from the rear office of the Khan Shipping Company was narrow and dimly lit. Dust began rising into the air as his feet struck onto the hard-packed dirt.

After descending for approximately fifteen meters, Michael Brennan drew his weapon and peered around the corner. Standing at the entrance of the bunker were two guards carrying AK-47 assault rifles. Inside the shelter sat his target along with two other men. Their weapons rested vertically alongside old wooden chairs.

Imagery from a low earth orbit satellite provided the intelligence necessary to plan his entrance. Traveling by a small boat to the Sira fortress, Michael found a narrow opening in the rocky outcroppings one hundred meters from the remote building. Anchoring the craft, he slipped into the frigid waters and rapidly swam ashore. Al Qaeda in the Arabian Peninsula (AQAP), also known as Ansar al-Sharia, one of the world's deadliest and most sophisticated terror organizations, was about to lose its chief financial officer, Hossam al-Banna.

Michael quickly spun around the corner and placed two rounds into the chests of the astonished guards. He sprinted ten more meters, stormed into the bunker and finished off the last two remaining sentries. The audacious act stunned the Al Qaeda leader who never reacted.

"Hossam, I have been looking for you for a long time," said Michael.

He pushed one of the dead men off the chair and now sat across from his target. Michael squarely pointed his weapon at the man.

"I have been expecting someone like you. MI6, NSA, CIA or something else?"

"Does it matter?"

"I suppose it does not. May I call my family to say goodbye?"

"First, I want to know the bank you're using in Zurich. What is the name and account number?"

"I cannot give you that. I simply oversee the collection of cash, tax revenues, and other sorts of financial matters. Someone else has that information."

"No. You have it. Our drones intercepted a call you made last week. You told Khalid you would transfer funds to Zurich right away. Do you want to speak with your family or not? You have ten seconds to decide."

Hossam understood the situation confronting him. The man had lifeless eyes and just killed four of his loyal guards in under ten seconds. Nearly four decades of jihad were ending. He decided to remain quiet and stare into his assassin's eyes. He had one final act of defiance left in him.

Hossam's time expired. Michael anticipated the man would not turn against the organization he co-founded. His file, transmitted over encrypted software by CIA, indicated Hossam's capture in Afghanistan and subsequent imprisonment from 1983 until 1985. There, military forces from the Soviet Union held the young rebel in horrific conditions ripe with rats, disease, and limited rations. He did not break despite the harsh interrogation techniques employed by his captors.

Michael squeezed the trigger. The bullet entered Hossam's forehead, and he slumped forward in his chair. Hossam al-Banna's jihad was over.

He quickly returned to the to the boat, fired up the single engine and made his way to the hotel in Aden. A short update to Langley was in order.

Hossam is dead. Unable to collect financial requirements regarding Zurich. Awaiting guidance.

The following morning Michael received a message from CIA headquarters in Langley, Virginia. They were terminating his mission in Yemen. The National Security Agency (NSA) successfully penetrated Hossam's computer in downtown Aden. An earned vacation for Michael Brennan awaited the long time non-official cover (NOC) intelligence officer.

Uwais al-Qarni Mosque, Ar-Raqqa, Syria – October 30, 2014, 4:45 PM

Inside the executive conference room of the Uwais al-Qarni Mosque, the nearly two dozen individuals filed in and found a chair. Experienced combatants from years of insurgency, they were also violent killers. Their victims included Sunni Muslims, Shiites, and Christians, western aid workers, homosexuals, reporters, and children. These men all knew one thing, *death*.

After sharing experiences from recent battles with Syrian and Iraqi armed forces, men of the Islamic State (IS) intelligence and military councils convened and waited for their leader to arrive.

The silence became ominous.

Abu Bakr Shirazi arrived as scheduled. He was an imposing figure. Standing at over six feet tall, he walked with a steady purpose while commanding respect from his loyal fighters. He was, after all, battle tested who earned his fierce reputation fighting US soldiers in the streets and deserts of Iraq.

A loyal follower of Usama Bin Laden, he sought to fill the void missing after Bin Laden's death in 2011. To do so, he carefully constructed a series of coordinated attacks throughout Iraq that terrorized Iraqi citizens and strained the resources of a young and unpopular Shia government. History had given Shirazi an opportunity.

Today's meeting would include recent developments in northern Syria, particularly with the troublesome Kobani issue. Kobani, also known as Ayn-al Arab, a city in the

Aleppo government and along the Turkish border, was under siege.

Though relentlessly pounded with short-range artillery and mortars for months, sections of Kobani held. As a result, countless numbers of refugees were crossing the border into Turkey. This stressed the humanitarian efforts of the Turks and emergency supplies were running low.

Islamic States' continuous attack had stalled, jihadi faithful were dying, and Kurdish opposition was holding.

Their commander wanted to know why.

"What has happened in Kobani?" asked the group's leader.

"We've had to withdraw into the surrounding villages and rural areas to escape enemy air strikes," said a hesitant yet confident young commander.

Coalition air strikes, conducted mostly by American drones, also known as remotely piloted vehicles (RPVs), were having their desired effect thought one fellow commander. The Americans, and their coalition allies, were achieving tactical success and now forced a major offensive to stall.

Shirazi sat motionless for a few seconds. His eyes stared at the young commander, clearly disappointed in his response. Yet he knew his young commander's assessment of the situation was correct.

Hassan Akbar, only twenty-nine years of age, had nearly captured Kobani just days before. Shirazi thought he made the cogent tactical decision. More personnel losses by precision guided missiles such as the GBU 38 Joint Direct

Attack Munition (JDAM) were no longer acceptable, despite the cause.

"What can we do to support the resumption of operations in Kobani?" asked Shirazi.

"I need three hundred more fighters from the Aleppo region. Allah willing that should be enough for a victory," said Akbar.

Shirazi knew redeploying these fighters would burden strategic efforts near Aleppo. Nidal's proposal was undesirable.

Shirazi, and everyone else in the room, recognized the tremendous capabilities of western forces; particularly drones. Not only were these flying "machines of death" capable of destroying his forces on the ground, their intelligence, surveillance, and reconnaissance (ISR) capabilities meant it was nearly impossible to move or communicate without detection.

However, his forces could disperse within the local population and communicate through couriers. Detection was then nearly impossible assuming support existed.

"Can we spare three hundred fighters from Aleppo?" asked Shirazi as he turned to one of his top leaders.

Nidal Qureshy, one of Shirazi's fiercest and senior commanders, only replied, "We cannot."

Nidal's tone and demeanor angered Hassan who could do nothing but listen. His leader was in charge, and any unwarranted input would simply be ill prudent.

"If we divide our forces, the Syrian regime will see an opportunity to stage more aggressive counter attacks. We cannot afford to lose the revenue and support within Aleppo," added Nidal.

Shirazi knew this was intolerable and turned to Hassan. "We need other options. I expect them at the next council meeting."

Hassan stared toward Nidal and showed his displeasure. His penetrating eyes said so, and a discussion with the senior commander would come later.

The council then proceeded to update Shirazi on all sorts of topics including public administration, propaganda operations in Europe and North America, and recruiting efforts. Council participants provided a brief summary due to time considerations.

The Sahel and Maghreb regions in Africa received particular attention where rampant poverty and lack of government control provided greater opportunities for recruitment. The caliphate needed funding and motivated individuals willing to give their lives in support of the Caliph. Expansion gained from eighteen months of brutal fighting throughout Iraq and Syria could not stall.

A spectacular attack was necessary, thought Shirazi to himself. His mind wandered for the rest of the meeting.

Soon after short discussions of oil production, the council concluded its thirty-minute meeting. Meetings such as these were routine but kept to a minimum due to such a gathering of key leaders. Despite meeting mostly in Mosques and other holy places, they were risky to the senior leadership and just one successful precision air strike, gained from real-time intelligence, could wipe out the council completely. The only men remaining in the room were Shirazi, his two personal armed guards, and leader of the intelligence council.

Shirazi turned to his senior intelligence officer, a wicked and former advisor to the late President of Iraq, Saddam Hussein.

"A spectacular attack against our enemies must be planned and executed soon."

The intelligence officer, who Shirazi trusted implicitly, simply nodded and spoke softly.

"I will have something for you in a day or two, Caliph. An attack no one has ever attempted nor will anyone expect it. If successful, it will bring our enemies to their knees and crush their will to oppose the Caliphate."

The man would not disappoint his commander. Events thousands of miles elsewhere prompted the imagination of the spymaster and ruthless killer.

Kenema, Sierra Leone – November 1, 11:30 AM

The smell of death in the air was pervasive. At a nearby remote village, eighty miles north of Kenema, Sierra Leone, another body needed removal. Today's casualty was a forty-three-year-old farmer infected with the Ebola virus.

Ebola, also known as Ebola hemorrhagic fever (EHF), first originated in 1976 in Nzara, South Sudan. The first outbreak there killed one hundred and fifty-one people while infecting nearly three hundred others. It took the world health organization (WHO) medical teams six months to end the destruction in Nzara.

The deadly virus, transmitted from infected wild animals and bats to humans, can kill a person in as little as a week. Without hydrating the patient, death is near certain. Once a human being is infected, he or she can transmit the disease to others through body fluids. Body fluids include mucus, sweat, blood, breast milk and even tears.

Ebola had found its way to the Kenema district.

Despite the ongoing efforts of doctors without borders and other leading non-governmental organizations (NGOs), Ebola was ravaging the countryside. Today marked the thirtieth victim near Kenema since the outbreak began just a few months ago.

Manjo, a well-educated member of the village, was devastated. His father was a tribal elder of the village and a man he aspired to be. Watching him go from a vibrant working farmer to one slowly dying the past few days took its toll on the young son. All he could do was wait for the black SUV used to transport the dead.

It arrived. Two men, dressed in protective masks, scrubs and latex gloves exited from the rear of the vehicle. The driver, a young woman in her thirties, named Lucee, soon joined them. She knew there would be anxious villagers asking why no one arrived earlier. Nothing could bring the lifeless farmer back to life despite their cries for help.

"Good morning everyone. I am Lucee Ba with MSF. Where is the man who died?"

Lucee was a new employee for Doctors Without Borders. Based in New York City, and also known as Medicins Sans Frontieres (MSF), this group was at the forefront of a bitter war between man and nature. MSF was determined to wipe out the disease despite losing several of its leading doctors and nurses in recent weeks.

The sudden loss of life around the Kenema region, coupled with reports from across West Africa compelled Lucee to join the organization. She could no longer sit by and watch the disease ravage her fellow West Africans.

"He is inside, over there," said an elderly man as he pointed to Manjo's hut.

"When did he pass?" asked Lucee as her colleagues entered the hut and began carefully removing the corpse.

"Early this morning, he died in his sleep."

"Has anyone touched the body?" asked Lucee.

"Yes, his wife and daughter-in-law."

Lucee's task now was to convince the villagers that touching the dead, though customary in Sierra Leone, would only place them at further risk. Tradition had to go by the wayside to prevent further contagion.

"I know the traditions of touching your loved ones who pass. I share the same custom. Many of you know what Ebola is and what its symptoms are. However, touching the dead body of a family member or friend can spread the disease. I urge you to stop doing this until we are sure the virus has passed. Where are the man's wife and daughter-in-law?"

"Still inside."

Lucee requested they come outside and join her. The two grieving caregivers reluctantly agreed.

"I am deeply sorry for your loss. Have you been with him for long?"

"Yes, we both spent several days by his side," said the distressed widow.

"How are you feeling?"

"Tired and sad, of course. Angry too. Why did you not come earlier?"

"We came as soon as we heard. I am sorry. Are you feeling ill?"

"No. I just want to sleep."

"There is a chance you may have caught the disease. May I take you and your daughter-in-law to the hospital for observation? If you are sick with Ebola, we have treatment and care available."

"My home is here, and hers too. We will not leave."

Lucee pleaded with the woman.

"Ma'am, if one or both of you have the disease, you risk infecting the entire village. Do you want to take such chances?'

"We do not have it. Now be gone."

Lucee realized the woman had made up her mind.

"May we disinfect your home?"

"Yes, but do it quickly."

Lucee's two colleagues returned to the hut and began disinfecting everything inside including the walls, all its contents, and front steps.

"I am truly sorry for your loss, Ma'am. Please contact us if you or your daughter-in-law begin feeling ill."

Lucee soon entered the vehicle and began the slow forty-three-mile trip back to the mortuary. The sheer distances and isolation of many villages, coupled with poor roads and infrastructure, led to many long drives and reflection. Lucee asked herself what more she could do to help these and other villagers. The questions, she thought, kept repeating, but her brain was short of answers.

This ride back to Barma would be no different.

As Lucee and her co-workers left, Manjo stood gazing into the distance. He was angry, confused, and frustrated by his fellow West Africans for not arriving sooner. Maybe his father would be alive. Maybe if the disease were contained earlier, he would be alive. Questions, thought Manjo, which needed answering. He needed time to think and the next few days would challenge his values, his father's legacy, and his soul.

Langley, VA – November 1, 11:25 PM

Deep inside the headquarters of the Central Intelligence Agency (CIA), computers were processing data at their usual high rates. Megabytes of data were flowing through the facilities using a variety of optical equipment including transceivers, wave-ready network systems, and fiber laser engines.

Sarah, having arrived a few minutes earlier, sat comfortably in her chair, alongside four other emergency operations officers. Would tonight be any different from previous nights this week, she thought? Probably not.

After reviewing ongoing and mostly routine reports from the previous shift at the emergency operations center (EOC), Sarah settled in for the evening. Communications checks with various government agencies, utilizing numerous forms of encrypted and secure communications, were complete. Things appeared routine.

Surprisingly at 12:43 am, a flash priority message arrived in her inbox. Operation Kallinikos was the source and requested an immediate response. It had been months since Sarah received a high priority message such as this. Moreover, protocol dictated confirmation within ten minutes.

Operation Kallinikos derived its name due to historical events, which occurred in the Hellenistic period. In approximately 230 B.C., King Saleucus II Callinicus would name his growing city Kallinikos. It later became al-Raqqa in 640 A.D. CIA often named its most sensitive operations based on historical events. Operation Kallinikos would be no different.

Standard procedure for Sarah required nothing more than *"ack receipt, message forwarded to DO. Verified by DO EOC."* Next order of business was to call her boss, Doug Weatherbee, deputy director of the operations directorate at CIA. Sarah and her colleagues never really enjoyed making these calls but did not mind waking up the boss when flash traffic entered the EOC.

"Sir, this is Sarah, we have flash traffic from operation Kallinikos. Message authenticated and ready for transmission."

"Send it over, Sarah," said Doug groggily. "I'll be in shortly."

As Doug awaited the message over his encrypted cell phone, he slowly sat on the bed and placed the glasses over his drowsy eyes. As the message began to arrive, Doug's attention quickly shifted to his phone.

He could not believe what he was reading. Time to get to the EOC right away he thought. The last time he received a similar message, a suicide bomber killed forty-eight Iraqi citizens in Baghdad while nearly two hundred others were injured. He was determined to foil whatever plot his enemy was planning, no matter the cost.

Montclair, VA – November 2, 6:30 AM

Michael Brennan awoke. After a long night's rest, coupled with the company of a beautiful, confident and intelligent woman, Michael felt invigorated. A lengthy vacation in Belize just two weeks earlier, he felt rested and prepared for the next assignment, whenever that would come.

His line of work demanded patience, meticulous planning, violent execution, and trust. Extended periods of rest and mental relaxation were the norm. After his latest assignment in Yemen, where he spent four long months, he had earned it.

After a healthy breakfast consisting of eggs, toast and chilled orange juice, and chit-chat with Laura, it was time for her to leave. They both relished each other's company the previous night and genuinely enjoyed how the relationship was progressing. After several dates, intimacy had finally arrived. Both were pleased thus far.

Laura kissed Michael on the cheek and said she looked forward to dinner in a few days. She would be back in D.C. after a short visit to New York. There would be an investment conference focused on emerging software platforms. The theme would be predictive analytics. Some of the hottest start-ups, big industry heavyweights like Microsoft, Apple, IBM, and government agencies would be there. One such agency would be the Intelligence Advanced Research Projects Activity (IARPA), under the Office of the Director of National Intelligence (ODNI).

IARPA had been at the forefront of innovative technology since its inception in 2006. From metadata collection techniques to predictive analytics and everything in between relating to intelligence activities, IARPA was at the forefront. The agency had formed when the NSA's Disruptive Technology Office (DTO), the NGA's National Technology Alliance and the CIA's Intelligence Technology Innovation Center converged. The purpose of these "teams of wizards" were clear---acquire technology that will give the United States intelligence community (IC) advantage over its adversaries. In New York, it would be Dr. Peter Breckenridge and his team from ODNI leading the charge on predictive analytics.

After Laura had left in her fiery red Lexus RX 350, Michael began to clean up. He would soon change into some triathlon gear and go for a long ride. Whenever Michael was between assignments, a healthy dose of training and extensive workouts is what he needed. Assignments in remote parts of the world could not accommodate his training regime, nor would he have time anyway. The preparation he put into physical training would ensure he was ready for any assignment. The secondary effects of a chiseled and toned body that projected confidence, success, and attitude always helped while on assignment or out. This time, Laura would enjoy his body for however long their relationship would last or in whatever direction it would move.

Today's brick workout was short. It would include a thirty-mile bike ride followed by a nine-mile run. Michael wanted to reduce the bike ride to have energy for his run later in the afternoon. The rides were always beneficial as Michael had the opportunity to reflect on his life, his decisions, and the man he became.

The crisp Virginia air moved through Michael's lungs. He felt alive, focused, and content. Early into the ride, Michael remembered how he wanted to leave high school and help transform the world. Any difference, he figured, was better than nothing. He was, after all, a product of the Reagan era in the 1980s. Ronald Wilson Reagan, the nation's fortieth President of the United States, vowed to defeat the Soviet Union, the greatest threat to American democracy and freedom the world had ever known. Michael and countless other men and women whose faith in America was unwavering would answer Reagan's calls. Their fight would be enduring, costly, and necessary.

Michael chose to enter college at The Citadel located in historic Charleston, SC. The Citadel, also known as The Military College of South Carolina, was deeply rooted in military tradition and service. The location was ideal, and Michael wanted to prepare himself for military service. America, he thought, needed fighting men and women who would preserve America's democracy and challenge those nations or rogue actors who threatened it.

Into his groove and settled on the bike after just 20 minutes it came. Vibration from the phone located inside his rear jersey pocket meant one thing. Langley was calling, and this ride was likely over.

CIA Headquarters, Langley, VA – November 2, 1:30 PM

Michael arrived at CIA HQ as directed by Anne Conterres, the executive assistant to Doug Weatherbee.

"Good afternoon Mike," said the usually cheerful Anne. "Doug is waiting to see you."

Inside Michael went. Doug's office was typical of senior executive servants within the government. Plush with a walnut and cherry wood desk, paintings of former CIA leaders, countless degrees and certificates hanging from his walls, and President Obama's picture behind him, Doug was a bureaucrat, thought Michael. Also, he loathed these meetings. Operations reports could provide most of the information he needed anyway.

"Afternoon Mike. Sorry to have called you in so quickly; know you're on leave."

"No problem, Doug. What's the situation?"

Doug proceeded to tell Michael about the flash message received by the EOC the night before.

"Operation Kallinikos is our effort to penetrate the Islamic State. For nearly twelve months now, a high-level source from Mossad has provided us good intelligence. Mossad is actually running the source and brought us aboard when the joint operation began."

Doug's description of the operation was a result of renewed efforts by Mossad and CIA to improve joint collection and targeting of high-value targets (HVTs) around the world, mostly terror groups in the Middle East.

Despite the public tension between President Barrack Obama and Prime Minister Benjamin Netanyahu, a resurgence of radical Islam forced the leaders to put aside their political differences and focus their strategic resources on terrorism. Their attention remained on Al Qaeda and Hezbollah respectively, but the sudden rise of Islamic State made both leaders nervous.

"Last night the source sent a message stating that Shirazi had discussions with his senior intelligence officer where he instructed him to devise a spectacular attack. We have no further information as of now."

As usual, Doug's initial brief to Michael was nebulous with few specifics. Conversations like these were the norm in the human collection business, at least on the front end of an operation. Vague information such as this was useless. Only credible and actionable intelligence concerned Michael, he thought to himself.

"I want you to travel to Israel immediately, meet with Mossad, and prevent whatever attack Islamic State is planning. Anne will fill you in and provide the op report."

Short and sweet. That is how Michael preferred these office calls. Nevertheless, he often wondered why Doug and others at CIA summoned their officers for mission briefs. It simply was not necessary, Michael thought, as anything useful was included in the operation report.

After departing Doug's office, Michael received his file from Anne. A one-terabyte capable thumb drive would allow Michael to upload files onto his laptop at home, study whatever information was available, and prepare himself for the trip to Jerusalem.

Highly secure thumb drives issued to non-official cover (NOC) officers such as Michael were standard. In fact, Michael's thumb drive included a fingerprint id scanner. Therefore, only Michael could use the drive on his personal computer or other electronic devices. This was the preferred method used by the Directorate of Operations (DO) for a variety of reasons.

Data breaches and cyber intrusions were becoming commonplace due to the fragility and vulnerability of wired networks. Despite the technological advancements of encrypted software, routers, fiber optics, modems and other sorts of communication devices, true cyber security had not been realized.

Nearly all information collected from various intelligence agencies used satellites and secure wired and wireless networks to move information. However, human intelligence collection required a greater fabric of security. Moreover, CIA determined years ago that sensitive clandestine human collection and other *black* programs would be off the grid. This reduced the likelihood of penetration by cyber hackers, rogue individuals and nation states.

However, in order to prepare a NOC officer before an assignment, he or she would utilize a self-destructive thumb-drive and study operational data on a remote computer. Of course, the computer would have sophisticated software to eliminate viewed data and automatically scrub itself after viewing. The only risk to this was if the officer was compromised leaving CIA and traveling to his or her residence. According to CIA, this was an acceptable risk during the preparation phase. Moreover, the fingerprint id scanner on the thumb drive added a layer of operational security.

"Good luck Michael. Stay safe and return in one piece," said Anne with a smile.

Michael then returned a smile and off he went to prepare for his journey to the *Holy Land*.

Tel Aviv, Israel - November 3, 2014, 5:48 PM

Michael's trip aboard Turkish Airlines flight 8 was a good one and ending shortly. The Airbus A330 was comfortable and allowed Michael some last-minute rest in preparation for his meeting with Mossad. Departing Washington, D.C. at 12 AM was never ideal, but it would result in an arrival in Israel at approximately 6:30 PM. The nearly seventeen-hour flight from Dulles International Airport to Ben Guirion International Airport in Tel Aviv included a layover in Ataturk airport in Istanbul, Turkey.

While in Istanbul, Michael had a few hours to kill and he chose to visit *Simit Sarayi*, a small cafe in the airport serving traditional Turkish pastries. Michael chose Cezerye, consisting of caramelized carrots, nuts and pistachios covered with grated coconut. Delicious he thought as he spent time reading the local newspaper and catching up on the political twists and plots that were in Istanbul.

Once off the flight at Ben Guirion, Michael was greeted by Aaron Tager, a longtime Mossad veteran and now deputy chief of the Collections Department within the shadowy organization.

"Mr. Brennan, welcome to Israel," said the middle-aged professional spy. "I have a vehicle for us. I will take you to your hotel."

"Thank you, Aaron," said Michael, as he could not wait to arrive and shower. He looked forward to sampling the local cuisine.

Michael's ride from Ben Guirion airport to the Rothschild Hotel was short. In the few minutes he and Aaron spoke, the two men mostly conversed in pleasantries, expected of intelligence professionals when operating in open environments. Aaron asked Michael how long he had served in the agency, why he joined and other trivial questions. He appreciated Michael's serious nature but quickly discerned the American's disdain for such discussions. A true man operating inside the shadows, he thought to himself.

The discussion and specifics of Operation Kallinikos would come in the morning at Mossad headquarters. Aaron would be back at eight in the morning to pick him up.

Upon exiting Mossad's vehicle, a friendly valet greeted Michael. The young woman, probably in her late twenties, took hold of Michael's luggage and promptly escorted him to the front desk. Once checked in, Michael arrived at his suite. A hot shower was in order followed by a hearty and delicious meal.

After dinner, which included green tea, Sambuca, and a baked cheesecake, Michael returned to his suite. It had been a long twenty hours of traveling; nevertheless, his hot shower and full belly meant the night was coming to end. Only one thing left to do, send Laura a short message.

Hi, Laura. Just wanted to send you a quick hello and best wishes while at the conference. Hoping to see you after your return. Enjoy the city. Michael

Iskenderun, Turkey - November 3, 8:50 PM

Along Turkey's Mediterranean Sea, near the beautiful seaport of Iskenderun, and the legendary Nur Mountains, Raif Demir checked his Facebook page. Most of the messages were trivial of course, just news feeds from "friends" he barely knew. However, one caught his attention.

Raif received the message at precisely 8:50 PM. The sender, a small cafe along Ataturk Boulevard in Iskenderun, known as Eroglu cafe, would be running its monthly specials beginning at 9 PM this evening. Like previous months, Eroglu would be offering its customers fifty percent off all drinks until 11 PM. Nights like these came along only once a month, and loyal patrons never knew the day or time beforehand.

The cafe's location along the palm-lined Mediterranean Sea made it an ideal spot for local residents. A perfect place for business outings, parties, or locals looking to surf the web utilizing Eroglu's free Wi-Fi; the location was stunning near sunset. Tonight, would be no different.

Outside seating at the cafe offered its customers beautiful evenings and cool breezes flowing from the Mediterranean. On a clear night, the moon radiated light off the water leaving customers breathless and hopeful the night would never end.

For Raif, the message was entirely of a different scope and nature. It meant he needed to be at Eroglu precisely at 11 PM to meet with his handler, a beautiful Turkish woman he met there approximately one year ago. Off he went, as the nearly one-hour drive meant he had little time to spare.

As with previous encounters with Elif, Raif hoped this time would be different.

Tel Aviv, Israel – November 4, 8:45 AM

Michael arrived at Mossad headquarters, went through the usual security protocols for visitors, and found himself sitting with Aaron in a large secure conference room filled with screens, laptops, PDAs, and various other individuals.

"Mr. Brennan," said the young man standing in front of the center projection screen, "today's briefing is on Operation Kallinikos, a highly sensitive program started nearly six years ago."

The young man, named Simon, proceeded to inform Michael of various aspects of the operation including the source, his history, and motivation for reporting the information. As Michael listened attentively, he recalled why Mossad, the most sophisticated and controversial spy agency in the world was the clear leader in Human Intelligence (HUMINT) collection. After all, their operations, many who have become public, were legendary.

Simon proceeded to brief Michael on various other logistics and communications details of the operation. Also discussed were the reliability and reporting methods of the source, both critical components to human intelligence collection.

In the human intelligence collection business, sources are only as good as their reliability. Mossad's source had proven reliable in previous reporting, and there was no reason to doubt the information was genuine this time.

Michael proceeded to ask a series of questions about the source.

"Why does the individual have such an important position within the organization? Why do you feel his reporting is still credible if you have not heard from him in nearly seven months?"

Simon stated the source had been with Shirazi since 2009 where he first met him while planning an attack in Mosul, Iraq. The source helped Shirazi plan the attack, coordinate for men, and even ended up taking a bullet for him in a firefight with local police forces.

"Has the source been with Shirazi since Mosul?" asked Michael.

The genius and forethought of Mossad were now on full display.

"Yes. He has provided frequent reports on Shirazi and the organization since then. And many terror attacks have been disrupted," said Simon.

Michael's first instinct was to ask himself why Mossad simply did not order Shirazi's execution. However, he quickly reminded himself that having a source inside the organization was more valuable. If Shirazi died, the organization would simply replace him with another and the source reassigned or killed. Keeping the source alive, in character, and reporting offered Mossad greater intelligence collection in the future.

Brilliant thought Michael and likely necessary for an intelligence agency whose sheer existence is to ensure the survival of Israel.

"What exactly did the source say?" asked Michael.

Aaron leaned forward and stated that Shirazi met with his intelligence officer and directed a spectacular attack.

"The plan will be submitted to him within a few days. We know nothing else," sighed Aaron.

Puzzled by Aaron's response, but clearly understandable, he asked Aaron where the attack would likely be directed.

"Our analysts suggest two courses of action. The first is a suicide bombing aboard a commercial jet heading into the United States. The second is a suicide bombing on American soil. Probably a major metropolitan city such as New York or Washington, D.C."

Intelligence analysts undergo rigorous training prior to their assignments. They develop multiple courses of action, also known as analysis of competing hypothesis (ACH), to operators during the planning process. This in turn allows operators such as Aaron and Michael to develop their own courses of action based on expected enemy behavior.

A red team analyst sitting across from Aaron, then spoke.

"There are many scenarios we envision, but we believe Shirazi will plan something his organization has not yet accomplished elsewhere. The possibilities are endless, unfortunately."

Michael thought to himself. This was useless information provided yet again by an intelligence analyst. Though he respected most analysts' motivation and intellectual capacity, vague predictions such as this annoyed him. How could anyone act on such analysis or information?

Michael turned to Aaron.

"Did the source indicate he would make contact again in a few days? Or are we in a wait-and-hear mode?"

"He will report to his contact as soon as possible. However, that information could be delayed by at least twelve hours due to reporting methods," said Aaron.

Michael thought to himself that twelve hours would be too long. What if the analysts were correct and ISIS directed its attack at the Homeland? His mind contemplated the horrific consequences of these and other similar attacks. A plane, if the hypothesis was correct, could already be airborne.

"I would like to meet your asset and remain there until the source reports. Can you arrange this Aaron?"

Aaron, anticipating Michael would likely ask, already cleared the meeting with his boss earlier in the morning.

With a few keystrokes, Aaron revealed Mossad's asset on his iPad.

"Iskenderun, Turkey. We'll arrange travel and provide specifics this afternoon." Michael's attention turned to the iPad. This face would not be difficult to memorize.

Iskenderun, Turkey - November 3, 11:00 PM

There she sat. At the end of the bar inside the inner section of Cafe Eroglu, Elif Turan waited. As usual, she enjoyed her glass of red wine and some peanuts to curb her hunger. A beautiful woman with long black hair in her mid-thirties, Elif was the perfect "false flag."

False flags, a method often used by Mossad, were human collectors (spies) who represented themselves from other nations or organizations. Mossad found this method of human intelligence collection effective and often necessary. In the Middle East and nearby regions, getting Arabs to spy for Israel was nearly impossible, despite the asset's political or religious views. Condemnation from family, friends or brutal regimes merely limited one's risk and tolerance from assisting the Israelis. The peril was not worth it, despite Mossad famously offering large sums of money for reliable information.

Elif became Mossad at an early age. Found in the slums of southern Lebanon by Israeli Defense Forces (IDF) during the 1982 Lebanon War, an errant mortar attack from PLO militants killed her entire family. At least that is what her schoolteachers told her in Tel Aviv years later. She never questioned her past; after all, she was highly educated, given immense responsibilities, and Jewish for as long as she could remember.

"Hello Elif," said Raif. "Nice to see you this evening."

Elif was her usual friendly self.

"Hi Raif, good to see you as well."

After the two went outside and found themselves a table, Elif was ready for her update. Monthly meetings between Raif and Elif were common. Most of the reporting focused on activity along the Syrian border. Raif had family fighting in northern Syria with members of the elite People's Protection Units (YPG).

"Aleppo has not been retaken," stated Raif.

According to his sources, Aleppo was too fortified. Coalition air strikes, though highly accurate, proved ineffective at eliminating Islamic State fighters from their defensive positions. Attacks would continue in the coming days, but without air support, his sources indicated taking Aleppo might be futile.

Elif listened attentively and asked Raif a simple question.

"Is there anything I can provide if air strikes continue to be unproductive?"

"Weapons. I've been specifically asked to inquire about anti-tank weapons like the AT-4."

The Soviet Union built and deployed the anti-tank four (AT-4) Spigot in 1970. According to its founders and designers, its real name was the 9M111 Fagot. The tube-launched system's maximum effective range was two thousand meters and built at the Tula Machinery Design Bureau in Tula, USSR.

With the collapse of the Berlin Wall and end of the Cold War in December 1989, Soviet military equipment was up for grabs. Anyone around the world with cash in hand was a prospective buyer. Terror groups, military despots, rebels, mercenaries, and Kings relished in the opportunities to purchase tanks, trucks, AK-47s, ammunition, or anything else they needed for whatever purposes. Only nuclear warheads and intercontinental ballistic missiles (ICBMs) seemed off limit.

"The AT-4 system is very hard to find Raif. And missiles are even more difficult due to limited stockpiles," said Elif. "What exactly will they need the systems for?"

Raif proceeded to inform Elif that Islamic State fighters were using captured tanks and armored personnel carriers from Iraqi and US stockpiles in the region. They were providing a substantial tactical military advantage in and around Aleppo preventing YPG offensive operations. Elif knew that Islamic State had acquired such capabilities but unsure of exactly how many.

"If we were to offer a dozen systems, could you deliver them to your contacts along the border?" asked Elif.

"I believe I can. But will the government pay for such systems knowing they will go to the YPG?"

"Leave that to me Raif. In the meantime, I'd like you to propose a plan on how you will move the equipment to your contacts along the border."

Raif pressed Elif further. He asked how she would acquire such sophisticated systems. It seemed odd she was willing to try considering the Turkish government had historically opposed the YPG. However, after a few more attempts, and sensing Elif becoming a bit annoyed, he stopped.

Next order of business for Raif was to discuss his fee for such an endeavor. As a smuggler of illegal goods ranging from western cigarettes to American jeans, bribes were necessary to move the equipment along the border. Moreover, the risk he would take was substantial. In addition, his contacts would need cash for the same reason.

Elif agreed and with a wink and a smile said, "The Turkish government will take care of you Raif. Payment will be generous."

After finishing their drinks and discussing social issues such as upcoming events in the city, the night was over. Both would part ways with much work to do.

Ar-Raqqa, Syria – October 30, 2014, 5:20 PM

Immediately following the IS military and intelligence council meeting, Hassan Akbar confronted Nidal Qureshy. Nidal knew it was coming.

"Why did you not support my efforts for three hundred fighters to take Kobani? We are so close. It is all I need to finally take the city and expand our operations. I would have paid them well after the siege."

Though Hassan's cash reserve was low, taxing the residents of Kobani would prove to be a worthy financial endeavor. If only he took Kobani.

Qureshy's fierce eyes gazed into Hassan's and he simply stated, "I cannot afford to lose them, and many will not leave the Aleppo region." Qureshy was right on both accounts. First, his Islamic State forces and those loyal to President Assad's military units were still battling for large portions of Aleppo. In addition, Free Syrian Army (FSA) backed rebel groups and Nusra Front fighters (Al Qaeda affiliate in Syria) were also battling for Aleppo. This chaotic battleground filled with dozens of belligerents defined anarchy. Also, caught in the crosshairs of all the waring factions were civilians who had few choices and staying alive meant submission.

Nidal went further. "How can I ask that many fighters to leave their homes and fight for Kobani? Kobani is full of Turks."

Nidal referred to the Islamic State's capacity to recruit local fighters when expanding their operations. Islamic State was achieving success recruiting foreign fighters, but the bulk of their forces were composed of the local population convinced to extend the caliphate to their neighbors.

Their strategy was simple – ferociously attack a target such as Aleppo with a small force of determined fighters, preferably with military training in the Iraqi or Syrian armies. They would then use local men to administer Sharia law and govern. It also included public executions for anyone who attempted to resist them. Beheadings were commonplace for those civilians living in towns and cities where the Islamic State made their advances. The tactic had played out well throughout Iraq and Syria thus far.

"Much of Aleppo remains in your control. Three hundred fighters for just a few weeks will make the difference, Nidal," said Hassan passionately. Nevertheless, Nidal would have none of it.

"Hassan. It will not happen. You must focus your attention and resources to recruiting fighters in and around Kobani. Allah Akbar."

Off Nidal went, escorted by several of his loyal lieutenants. Hassan was furious but clearly mindful he would not convince Nidal to change his mind. He needed to reach out to other commanders and convince them to send fighters. But how he thought to himself? He did not have the funds to pay them, their journey to Kobani would be perilous, and Shirazi may not even authorize the repositioning of fighters. The trip back to Kobani would allow him time to think but only for a short while.

Tel Aviv, Israel – November 4, 12:10 PM

Michael returned to the Rothschild Hotel and finished lunch with Aaron. After his successful meeting with Mossad, he only had a few hours before Aaron would return. Time to update Langley he thought and inform them of his pending departure to Iskenderun.

After his report to Langley, Michael turned his attention to Laura. It was clear to him he would not return in the next few days and needed to let her know. Laura was different and needed an explanation. Though he only knew her a short time, Michael wanted to see her again and see where their fates would take them.

His email was short.

Hi, Laura. Our factory in Jerusalem had a fire. Some of the workers were injured and production is going offline. Leaving for the airport soon and not sure when I will be back. It could be a few weeks. Hope to see you soon and looking forward to dinner. Please let me know how it went in New York. Michael

Michael now had just under two hours to prepare for his short flight. Time for a nap as his instincts told him this mission could be his most challenging and dangerous.

At 3:00 PM, Aaron returned to pick up Michael. Upon exiting the Mossad vehicle, Aaron updated him. He told him the plane would take him directly to Iskenderun and an agent would meet him at the airport.

"They will then take you to our secure facility in Iskenderun and update you with the latest Intel. There are a few files on board you can review in flight."

"Thanks, Aaron. I cannot thank you enough for the hospitality, the update, and support from Mossad. You have my word I will share everything from Langley with your contact in Turkey. Shalom, my friend."

The two men shook hands, and up the air stair ramp, Michael went. The trip to Iskenderun would be short and provide him an opportunity to review critical files with pertinent operational details while in Turkey. The Israeli Aircraft Industries (IAI) Astra 1125 business jet was now airborne.

Hatay Airport, Turkey – November 4, 5:40 PM

Approximately fifteen miles from Iskenderun, Michael's Astra 1125 jet landed at Hatay airport. Hatay was the nearest airport to Iskenderun and used extensively by Mossad when transporting personnel into Turkey. Operating under the guise of a jet supporting executives from the Israeli Electric Corporation, Hatay was the perfect entrance point into Turkey. It would be no different with Michael aboard.

"Welcome to Iskenderun, Mr. Brennan."

"Thank you, you must be Elif? Have you heard anything from Raqqa?"

The two walked briskly from the aircraft to the Mercedes GLK 350 SUV. Though Mossad used Hatay often, individuals within sight of the hangars, and terminal could always be Turkish Intel, Milli Istihbarat Teskilati (MIT). Unbeknown to Michael, a fuel truck operator nearly 300 yards away took a photo.

"Nothing from our contact. I am hoping for an update this evening. Let's get to the safe house."

Within an hour, Elif and Michael arrived at the safe house on the eastern side of Iskenderun. It was an unassuming location off Ataturk Boulevard along 18th Street.

Inside the safe house were two of Elif's associates. Both men appeared Mossad, but Michael could not be sure.

They might be local contractors, thought Michael.

"Mr. Brennan, we should hear from our contact in a few hours. I recommend you get some sleep. The room in the back is yours and should have what you need to shower and rest. I am going to pick up some coffee and return shortly. Any requests?"

"Thanks, Elif," said Michael, who was still feeling a bit of jet lag from his transatlantic journey. "I'll grab some sleep."

MIT Headquarters, Ankara, Turkey – November 4, 6:46 PM

Tadio Sadik sat at his computer. A junior intelligence officer with MIT, his first assignment was as a night watch officer in the Israeli counter-intelligence directorate. A lackluster position but expected of a new analyst within the organization.

He had to perform well, ensuring reports were properly cataloged and disseminated to the veteran analysts focused on Israeli activities inside Turkey. Additionally, his Directorate leadership would scrutinize his decisions when informing them of tactical data and real-time information from numerous sources throughout the country. He had to get it right each time if he wanted a promotion and placed onto an analytical team. There he would have the flexibility to think creatively without all the rules that come with night shift duties.

Milli İstihbarat Teşkilatı, also known as MIT, the National Intelligence Organization of Turkey, had a long history and reputation as a corrupt and inept organization. Its roots dated back to the end of the Ottoman Empire. For nearly seven decades, while undergoing several rebranding efforts, MIT mostly filled its ranks with relatives of current and former employees. Restructuring began in the mid-2000s changing this dynamic. Cultural change is necessary specifically when an organization loses confidence from the public. MIT had done that long ago.

Well into his shift, Tadio received a secure message from a source near Hatay. The source simply wrote, *this man may be an Israeli intelligence officer. He arrived this afternoon at Hatay airport shortly after 5:30 PM. Subject quickly entered a black Mercedes SUV, possibly a GLK 350 model. Attached is his photo along with the others.*

Tadio recognized the others, but the photo depicted a man not seen before. Utilizing his computer's facial recognition software, he uploaded the picture and launched the scanning feature.

After a few minutes, no matches existed within the MIT database. Tadio became curious as the subject entered Hatay using the established method by Israeli intelligence. After enhancing the quality of the photo, he ran it again. Nothing new.

Tadio picked up the phone and called his supervisor who still worked at her desk. A few minutes later, Dabria Uzun arrived.

Dabria, an officer with MIT since 2002, was the first female supervisor at the operations center in MIT history. Her brilliance as an analyst became legendary when she assisted with the apprehension of an Israeli spy in 2010.

While serving in an operations role tasked to support the External Operations Directorate, she also served with distinction in Yemen from 2011-2013. There, Dabria provided MIT valuable information on Al Qaeda Arabian Peninsula (AQAP) leadership and financial activities. In just two short years in Yemen, coupled with identifying a mid-level Mossad agent in Istanbul, her path to senior leadership within MIT was secure.

"Yes, Tadio. What is it?" asked Dabria.

"I received a report from one of our sources in Hatay. He sent us photographs of a group of individuals arriving in the country this afternoon. I did not recognize one of them. So, I ran his photo. Nothing. Here he is."

"Okay, send me the photo and contact the intelligence unit at national police intelligence and Interpol with an informal inquiry. Keep it discreet, Tadio. Maybe they will have something on him. I'll check with some of our associates in the west," stated Dabria as she began walking toward her office.

Tadio surmised Dabria's reference to the west likely included CIA, MI6, and BND with who MIT occasionally conducted joint intelligence operations. Western intelligence agencies often initiated them when high-value targets were in Turkey or just traveling through.

This was way above his paygrade, he thought. It was time to make some phone calls and execute Dabria's guidance. His first inquiry would be to the intelligence unit at national police intelligence.

While Tadio began collaborating with national police, Dabria sat down. She could not believe what she had seen. A secure phone call away from headquarters was in order, and would need to be initiated quickly.

Kenema, Sierra Leone – November 2, 8:45 AM

Manjo finally awoke. Nearly twenty-four hours after his father's death, it was time to get up. Still angry, he decided to leave his village and travel to Kenema. It was only a few hours' drive and the time away would do him some good, he thought.

Manjo, like everyone else in the village, was poor. Accustomed to a lifestyle that afforded few luxuries, Manjo's next task was to get his old pickup truck running again. He last used the truck five weeks ago while delivering a crop to the Kenema farmer's market and was concerned the battery might be low.

The truck's engine started and with a half of a tank of gas, he departed his village.

Manjo's trip to Kenema would be arduous due to poor road conditions. Paved roads did not exist in most places, another indication of Sierra Leone's weak economy and lack of infrastructure. Dirt roads were the norm for villagers living in rural areas.

The landscape was magnificent. Sierra Leone, a tropical climate with four distinct geographic regions, is a beautiful country ripe with natural resources and foliage. Manjo's trip included breathtaking views of several plateaus plush with dense trees; however, it offered little comfort. He cherished the countryside for as long as he could remember while accompanying his father to Kenema to sell the family's crops. He would now make the trip by himself until a child entered his life.

A few hours later, Kenema was in sight. He knew he was close as the garbage piled along the dirt road became more prevalent. Residents and those surrounding the city did not have access to efficient garbage disposal methods.

Nearing the outskirts, Manjo finally reached a paved road entering the northern part of the distressed city. As he drove, he thought a visit to the nearest Mosque might provide some inspiration and solace. He was Sunni Muslim by birth but rarely engaged in its practices.

Sierra Leone is predominantly a Sunni Muslim country. Some estimates indicate eighty percent of the population practice the faith. The religion entered its way into Sierra Leone in the early part of the 18th century and continued its growth despite British colonial efforts and the introduction of Christianity.

As Manjo entered Kenema, he recalled a non-denominational Mosque, common in many parts of Sierra Leone, near the farmer's market just a few blocks from his normal setting. Manjo had noticed a rise in the Sunni Muslim population in Kenema recently and wondered why. Today, he was determined to find out.

The Kenema Central Mosque was warm and inviting. Manjo entered as men gathered for their routine prayers. Manjo estimated there were fifty men inside. However, a Sunni Muslim by birth, and not versed in the practices of his faith, he was unsure what to do next.

In the distance, Sheikh Sahr Cissi noticed Manjo. He moved toward the stranger.

"As-Salam-u-Alaikum," said the Sheikh.

"Hello. My name is Manjo, and it has been a long time since visiting a Mosque. I am not sure what to do next," he said half-smiling and visibly uncomfortable.

After exchanging some pleasantries, the Sheikh asked if he would join him in his office. Manjo politely agreed.

After nearly an hour in the Sheikh's office, Manjo became restless. He genuinely enjoyed meeting the Sheikh and was grateful for his hospitality. An invitation to return the following morning was a pleasant surprise. However, he was unsure and thought the Sheikh was a little too intrusive.

As Manjo stood up, he asked the Sheikh one final question.

"Sheikh Cissi. Can you recommend some reading from the Quran to help me find peace?"

"Of course, Manjo. You may want to start with Quran 29:2-3 which reads, *Do men think that they will be left alone on saying 'We believe', and that they will not be put to the test? And certainly We tested those before them, so that God will differentiate those who are true from those who are false.*"

The Sheikh believed this was an appropriate verse to get him started. Manjo was confused and vulnerable. Little did Manjo realize the Sheikh's true intentions were to steer him toward a more radical way of thinking.

Mossad safe house, Iskenderun, Turkey – November 4, 7:00 PM

Elif returned from her coffee run carrying a hardened black briefcase and a bag full of local pastries and bread. She was unsure if Michael and her colleagues were ready for dinner as it was still early.

An upscale apartment in the center of Iskenderun offered Mossad an ideal location. Most residences in the building were affluent local businesspersons and shop owners. Security was good, but not overly elaborate. This reduced the likelihood of arousing nefarious individuals in the area.

Elif spent several hours at the small complex each week. This ensured surrounding residents knew her and found nothing out of the ordinary even when entertaining visitors. For all they knew, Elif was the owner of a thriving tourist business, which shuttled tourists to and from the Bagra fortress and Iskenderun Museum of the Sea, among other locales. Her clients included some of the top corporate leaders in the Middle East and celebrities from across Europe. Some of her best clients even stayed there instead of nearby luxury hotels, or so her neighbors thought.

From time to time, and after each client's trip ended, she would let the cleaning service come in. This added to the illusion that her trade was as a successful tourism operator.

Elif lived outside Iskenderun in the town of Arsuz, approximately twenty miles to the southwest and just two hundred meters from the coast. It was a majestic location and ideal for her. As a single woman, it was safe and since Mossad owned the property, a location where she always felt secure. It provided the ideal spot when she needed to relax and decompress from her dangerous duties.

Her property manager was a retired Mossad officer, who also served as a contractor there. It was also part of the retirement package for the former intelligence analyst, which included a suite on the sixth floor overlooking the Mediterranean. By all accounts to the outside world, the Erdinc Apart Otel condominium was an upscale location in the region serving those seeking a more rural environment than Iskenderun offered.

Michael entered the living room as he heard Elif arrive. He could not really sleep, but the quiet and dark room offered some much-needed mental relaxation, even if for only an hour.

The operation report from CIA just two days earlier, coupled with information from Mossad, was a bit much. Even spies feel overwhelmed from data at times. Memorizing safe houses, contacts, frequencies, and emergency numbers was no easy task.

After Elif and Michael had engaged in a few minutes of pleasant conversation, it was time. Elif directed her associates to leave the room and wait for her in the vehicle. These contractors, though trusted implicitly by Elif, did not have a need to know regarding some specifics of the operation. Mossad, like all other credible intelligence agencies, limited the access to information for security purposes. In this situation, the need to know was limited to just a handful of intelligence officers.

At 7:10 PM, Elif opened the briefcase. Inside was a secure laptop Mossad used for a variety of communication methods. Its military grade capability included secure web searching, using open sources and high-frequency communications, among other capabilities, including an incredible 528-bit encryption link with Tel Aviv.

"At seven-fifteen PM we'll open our chat and wait," said Elif. "My contact knows me as Ayse."

Michael looked into her eyes and gave a sign of approval as he sipped his Turkish coffee.

A few minutes after 7:15 PM, the first message hit.

Good evening Ayse. I only have a few moments.

Hello, Haris. What can you share?

Shirazi wants to attack America using a bio-weapon.

How and when?

I need to leave Ayse, too dangerous for me.

Can you provide specifics of the attack?

Not now, need extraction. Much turmoil here. Can you arrange to meet me along the border?

Probably, but what about the attack?

I will know more this evening and will tell, but only in person. Can you get me out of Syria?

Is the attack imminent?

No, but soon.

Michael leaned forward and asked Elif if she could get them across the border.

"I believe so Michael, but it may take a few days."

"Can you make it within forty-eight hours?"

Elif let out a deep sigh and nodded her head.

"Convince the source we can meet him in a designated location in two nights. It's your call where we extract him. I need to speak with him immediately," urged Michael.

Elif turned away and began to think. In just a few moments, she conducted intelligence analysis of her own and compared several hypotheses.

Elif had to make a significant tactical decision without formal input from Tel Aviv. Her tradecraft always permitted for substantial independent thought and action regarding her assets. However, this was a bit more complex due to the potential deployment of biological weapons.

The asset inside Islamic State was reliable, and their relationship existed for many years. Nevertheless, if he felt compromised or ready to leave, the parameters of the operation needed adjustment. Additionally, a successful biological attack against the United States would be devastating, regardless of the casualties. The psychological impact would be massive.

This development had the making of an international crisis and could jeopardize relations with the west.

She imagined if such an attack occurred what her superiors in Tel Aviv would think. Would they reward her for urging the asset to remain in place even if his intelligence was poor or the attack failed? Would they discipline her for sitting on intelligence to see if it was actionable? Worse, would her services as a Mossad agent abruptly end?

Not knowing the details of the attack or its potential magnitude, complicated the decision-making process further. However, the risk of delay was too great despite the complications of planning and executing an extraction in forty-eight hours.

In a few moments, her mind became clear. Elif turned back to the screen and began typing.

We will get you out of there in two days. Can you transmit again tomorrow evening?

Yes, thank you, Ayse. Till tomorrow.

Till tomorrow.

Michael turned to Elif. "What can I do to get this moving, Elif?"

"How about some AT-4 weapons that would go to the YPG in Aleppo?"

Without missing a beat or asking why, Michael simply asked, "How many do you need?"

"Twelve will do, and I have just the person who can move them. We will use the shipment into Syria as a way to extract Haris."

The two had little time to make the extraction work, but forty-eight hours was sufficient to plan the operation and secure the AT-4s. The job would be complicated but both were crafty and had contacts that could expedite this unforeseen chain of events. However, Michael and Elif needed to report to their respective headquarters soon. This was highly actionable intelligence requiring immediate reporting.

Elif left the safe house shortly after Michael assured her he could secure the missiles. Her first priority was to contact Raif. Tel Aviv would follow. Michael, on the other hand, would call Paul Hernandez, a longtime friend at CIA. He would be in a position to identify a stockpile of AT-4s and more importantly, help move them.

Ankara, Turkey – November 4, 8:20 PM

Dabria entered her apartment in the suburbs of Ankara. She reached into one of her drawers and pulled out an untraceable cell phone purchased just one month ago.

After dialing the number and finally connected, a deep voice answered.

"Hello, Dabria. It has been a while. Do you have something for me?"

"One of the men whose picture you sent me in September is here in Turkey."

"Where?"

"He arrived at Hatay this afternoon. I believe he may have traveled to Iskenderun."

"You know what to do Dabria?" asked Nasir.

"Yes."

"When can you do it?"

"Very soon, I hope."

"I will wait for your call Dabria. Goodbye."

Dabria's conversation with Nasir was short. It had to be. American drones collecting intelligence, while simultaneously hunting high-value targets for kill strikes, patrolled Yemen continuously. As the commander within Al Qaeda's branch in Yemen, Nasir was at the top of the list. He knew this all too well.

Evading a squadron of drones with shoot to kill orders required Nasir's sparing use of cell phones. Most communication methods with subordinates or assets were by way of the courier, a technique Nasir directed months ago. Nasir learned this through years of precision drone strikes delivered by American military forces. They killed hundreds of his fellow jihadists, and more were likely in the future, despite increased security protocols.

Couriers reduced the likelihood of operational compromise and detection. However, they were ineffective abroad. It simply took too long to move orders and instructions, unless, of course, routine financial transactions were the effort.

The electronic intelligence (ELINT) collection capabilities of the United States are massive. Satellites, drones, piloted aircraft, ground-based systems, and even unattended ground sensors will record anything they target, if deployed correctly. Each day, countless computers at the National Security Agency in Fort Meade, Maryland process terabytes of data received from sensors throughout the world.

Yemen is crowded with these sensors, and suffered its first drone strike in 2002. This occurred after President George W. Bush authorized the global war on terror in response to the September 11th terror attacks in 2001.

Dabria's next call was to a shadowy individual living in Adana, Turkey. Using the same phone, she dialed the killer's number, a contractor who MIT used in sensitive domestic operations.

"Kadir. This is Dabria. I have a contract for you. But it must be executed before the morning."

"That will double the price Dabria, who is the target?"

"An Israeli Mossad agent who just arrived this afternoon," said Dabria.

Dabria was unsure if the stranger was Mossad or how long he would remain in Turkey. However, a quick strike now using actionable intelligence gave her the best opportunity to accomplish her mission. She had to entice Kadir knowing his disdain for Jews.

Kadir thought quickly to himself. *An Israeli Mossad target? Now that would be a first.*

"Where?" asked Kadir.

"Drive west and into Iskenderun. I will send the address. He should be alone."

"That is what you told me in Istanbul a couple of years ago," Kadir reminded Dabria.

Kadir referred to a contract awarded to him in the summer of 2012. There, Kadir's target was a leading human trafficker in the country with links to the Serbian Mafia. Turkey had become the launch point for transporting victims from Eastern Europe into the Middle East; as Syria had simply become too unstable in recent years.

The individual ran a horrific and psychologically tormenting business, mostly exploiting young girls and children. Kadir enjoyed killing the man. Children were always off limits while Kadir earned his living as a contract killer for hire with MIT. He believed that no respectable criminal in his profession would exploit children for illicit activities or subject them to ghastly abuse.

However, when the time to kill the degenerate arrived, Kadir found him in the company of another woman. She was not a young girl, and Kadir assumed she was either a local prostitute or associate of the trafficker. After all, a man who engaged in the exploitation and sale of children could never have a relationship with a woman, Kadir thought to himself.

After deliberately entering the living room, lit by slow-burning candles, Kadir fired three rounds of hollow point 9 mm bullets into the man's skull. The target never knew it was coming. His companion would be next, though not part of the contract. A few seconds later, she lay dead.

Kadir could not allow her to identify him. In his line of work, no witnesses would remain alive. The risk of capture was too great. Poor intelligence from Dabria would contribute to the woman's death, an unfortunate victim of bad luck and circumstance.

Not at all pleased with Kadir's reference to Istanbul, she urged him to get moving.

"Payment will be made once I receive confirmation from the local police," said Dabria.

"Iskenderun is only two hours away. I will be ready by midnight," said Kadir.

The assassin became eager at the prospect of killing the Jew, who was not welcome in his beloved republic.

Berlin, Germany - November 4, 6:30 PM

While dining in the Matte district in Berlin, Paul Hernandez enjoyed his dinner from *Hugos*, a top French Mediterranean cuisine located on the fourteenth floor of the Inter-Continental Hotel. Joining him were his wife, Anna, and daughter, Alexis. As Paul devoured his *Saddle of Limousin lamb*, a menu favorite of local patrons, his cell phone buzzed.

"Paul, it's Michael. Can you go secure? This is hot." Paul quickly realized this was not a social call.

"I can, but give me a few minutes. I'm out having dinner with Anna and Alexis."

"Thank you, brother. On an operation now. Standing by." Click, Michael was gone.

Anna knew it was coming. Observing Paul's facial gestures, her husband of twenty years would be leaving soon. At this point of their marriage, she was numb to it. Married to the Chief of Station for CIA in Berlin meant rewards, but the occasional call ending dinner still annoyed her a bit.

Paul urged Alexis and Anna to remain. Anna did not need convincing. However, Alexis, a high school senior, was still getting used to her father's professional responsibilities. He assured Alexis he would be home within a couple of hours. They were very close, and tonight she wanted to play a new composition from the family's violin.

The violin drew Alexis at a young age. The daughter of a former violinist with the Berlin *Philharmoniker*

Orchestra, Alexis was a top student within the Orchestra Academy. The students enrolled in the program were some of the brightest young musicians recruited from throughout Europe. Anna and Paul's unwavering support over the years allowed Alexis to thrive. Paul could not be prouder of her.

Near the front desk of the Inter-Continental, the valet greeted him.

"Are you ready for your vehicle, sir?"

Paul handed him the ticket and a few minutes later his car appeared at the circular entrance of the upscale hotel. Paul then drove away in his Mercedes E350 sedan, a nice reward for CIA's top spy in Germany.

As soon as Paul sped off, he called his friend and colleague of nearly twenty-five years. Throughout their careers, the two men's paths crossed together in places such as Germany, Spain, and South Africa. Both men graduated from the CIA's national clandestine service (NCS) program in Virginia in 1991.

Paul graduated as an official cover operative, meaning he served CIA overseas in an official cover status. His first assignment took him to Berlin where he served as a trade representative for the Department of State. His real occupation was that of a junior case officer who would develop assets throughout Europe. His timing could not have been better since the Berlin Wall came down in 1989. A couple of years later the Soviet Union had collapsed.

The collapse of the Soviet Union meant turmoil for much of the decade that followed. Former KGB spies, businesspersons, politicians, and all sorts of individuals were settling into Western Europe. Asset development was ripe.

Michael's path took a different turn. Michael earned his non-official cover status since he scored the highest of his trainee class in nearly every category including creativity, close quarter combat, physical fitness and resistance to enhanced interrogation training, among many others.

"Michael, it's Paul. I'm heading to the office now."

"Paul, I'm in Turkey. I'm trying to recover a Mossad asset inside Syria. He apparently has information of a biological attack planned for the United States. Islamic State is behind it."

Paul's mind raced quickly. Though his efforts now focused on an emerging Russian threat, he was well aware of the developments in Iraq and Syria. Everyone in the world was aware of the terror group.

"How good is the source?"

"Mossad has run the source for quite some time. The source is reliable from what I can tell. We are working with them on this one."

"How can I help?" asked Paul.

"Well, an agent I'm working with here says she needs a dozen AT-4s as part of the extraction plan."

"You trust her?"

"I have to, Paul. No choice. But she is Mossad and assures me she needs them to support the operation."

"That's a lot of firepower. Where are they going?"

"If I had to guess, probably to one of the Kurdish groups fighting inside Syria."

"I'll need more than that, Mike."

"I know. Can you get them to me within forty-eight hours provided the operation is ready, and I deliver specifics?"

"Got to know where the weapons are going."

"You got it. Can I call tomorrow morning?"

"Yeah. I'll be in early, say eight?"

"Thanks, Paul. I will call you then."

Paul arrived at his office an hour later. Berlin traffic was horrific, and commonplace in many highly populated European cities. Two calls were in order. First, Paul would contact a colleague in Freiberg, Germany.

"Markus, it's Paul. I may need to move some equipment in the morning. Can you and your team be ready? Transportation will be to Euro Airport and we'll be using our usual aircraft. I will send the hangar information tomorrow around noon."

The Euro Airport Basel-Mulhouse-Freiberg, constructed soon after World War 2, was the ideal location. An international airport, serving the flourishing Alsace, North West Switzerland and Bade-Wurttemberg regions, it was prime real estate for moving cargo and passengers into and outside of Europe.

"What are we moving Paul?" asked the silver-haired veteran.

"A dozen AT-4s."

"Still plenty of those here, Paul."

"Thought so, thanks, Markus."

Paul soon hung up after exchanging pleasantries. The two veterans knew each other well, and despite Michael's urgency, Paul spent a few minutes talking to Markus about his family and plans for retirement.

Paul's next order of business was to call Jurgen, another colleague south of Freiberg in the beautiful town of Rickenbach, along the Swiss border.

"Jurgen, it's Paul."

"Hello Paul, how are you this evening?"

"Have to be short here, Jurgen. I need some cargo moved tomorrow evening, give or take a few hours. Can you have the aircraft fully fueled and ready? I hope to have more details in the morning so you can file your flight plan."

"Uh, sure. Duration of the flight, Paul?"

"Not sure, but the destination is likely in or near Turkey. It is fluid right now."

"I could fly the cargo directly to Larnaca on Cyprus. Might that work?"

"Too early to tell my friend. Could you refuel there and get into Turkey if needed?"

"Probably. It won't be easy, but I could make it happen."

"Let's just get the jet fueled and ready. I will be in touch sometime in the morning. Please be ready by noon."

Click. Paul ended the conversation. Jurgen always appreciated Paul's brevity. Jurgen profited handsomely from his relationship with Paul for nearly five years. While averaging two to three flights monthly, Jurgen's lucrative role as the pilot earned him a high standard of living. The occasional stop at remote parts of the world delivering cargo to nefarious individuals never really bothered him. The risk was always part of the business.

In the course of approximately fifteen minutes, Paul alerted his colleagues for a contingency that might never happen. Jurgen and Markus were informally aware of each other though neither man knew each other's specific role in Paul's operations. The less they knew, the less likely they were to jeopardize Paul's plans. CIA had actually implemented this policy from its inception after President Harry Truman signed the National Security Act of 1947.

Michael's request was clearly urgent and Paul learned a long time ago that operational parameters change instantly. Flexibility and decisiveness are required in the human intelligence (HUMINT) collection business. Paul's anticipation and preparation would pay off.

Paul glanced at his watch and observed it was approaching eight o'clock. Time to get home, he thought to himself. His date with Alexis was still on, and he would not let her down.

Iskenderun, Turkey – November 4, 9:20 PM

Shortly after leaving Michael, Elif instructed her two associates to go home. She would call them in the morning with instructions. However, before departing, Elif told them to pack and prepare to move the following day. They would be heading to the border in a day or two.

After Elif had entered her car, she called Raif.

"Raif, this is Elif. I need to speak with you this evening."

"Okay, what is this about" asked Raif perplexed.

"Our conversation last night. I have an update, and it's urgent."

"Shall I meet you at Eroglu?"

"No. I need to see you at your place. Will you be there in fifteen minutes?"

"Yes, Elif. I am here now. See you then."

Elif arrived ten minutes later. She already knew where he lived. Shortly after meeting him, standard protocol meant she had to do a thorough background check on her new asset. Though a petty criminal engaged in smuggling, his contacts in Syria made him invaluable. Until now, Elif never had a reason to visit his apartment though her associates routinely scoped the area to keep an eye on him.

Raif's apartment was bland. A drab brownish color covered his walls. Scarce decorative pictures hung on the walls, and Elif spotted few ornaments in the living room. The musty air in the apartment further reminded Elif that Raif did not spend much time here. This was odd she thought to herself.

Elif expected the apartment to be a bit more upscale. By all accounts, Raif was a successful smuggler satisfying eager buyers along the Syrian border. Several trips each month to the town of Nizip, in the Gaziantep province, should have afforded Raif a few luxuries. She began to wonder if he even lived there.

Her suspicions now aroused, she asked for some bottled water. Raif gladly obliged and moved toward the small refrigerator in the kitchen. He opened the door, and Elif noticed the near-empty refrigerator. Carefully questioning her asset, she asked why there was no food.

"I just returned from a trip, Elif."

Looking into the refrigerator, he sarcastically asked her if she wanted to go to the market with him. Somewhat satisfied, but more focused on discussing the operation, she laughed and said, "Let's just get to it."

The two sat down, and she told Raif the weapons would be available in a couple of days. She would personally deliver them near Nizip at a place of his choosing. From there, she and her associates would accompany him to the delivery.

"We have to be sure the weapons are going to the YPG," said Elif convincingly.

"That was fast. How did National Intelligence make such a quick decision?"

"I told them it was in our best interest for YPG to get more firepower."

"It is, but I expected it would take a few weeks."

"Frankly, me too Raif. However, the Islamic State is all over the headlines, and you see the refugees entering Turkey. Their migration across the border needs to end. The government is concerned we cannot handle many more of them."

"Why can't you just deliver them to me here? I can transport the weapons myself. A larger group may alert local police."

"Like I said, we have to be sure. It is my responsibility to get them to the border. I will also have a colleague from MIT."

Slightly frustrated, Raif agreed to meet her in Nizip.

"When will you depart for Nizip?" asked Raif.

"I'm not sure but let's be ready for the sixth, after dinner. I will call you when we are ready to go. Why don't you plan to get there tomorrow and settle in? Is there something you can do there to pass the time?"

"Yes. I'll find a place to stay."

Elif's next order of business was to tell Raif there would be another passenger that night. Puzzled by the request, he asked who it was.

Elif told him that he was the son of an influential member of Parliament who was working as a physician in Kobani with a private organization.

"Apparently, the doctor is stuck in the Islamic State held portion of the city. He has been sporadically communicating with his father through email. He believes Islamic State will soon find out his identity. He wants out and thinks he can cross the border more easily near Jarabulus."

An attempt to flee Kobani would surely result in a sniper's bullet from an Islamic State fighter perched atop one of the buildings. Raif thought the idea sounded reasonable.

"I've used the area before, the Turkish town of Karkamis sits right on the border. I could make that happen," said Raif confidently.

"Where will the AT-4s be delivered, Raif?"

"Near Jarabulus, actually, along the Euphrates. How will this doctor get across the border?" asked Raif.

"We're getting him out, Raif. You will drive us near the extraction point and wait for our return. You will not be crossing the border with us. It's too risky for you."

"We'll only need an hour or so. In addition, we will do it before delivering the weapons. Can I count on you, Raif?" asked Elif.

"Of course, Elif."

Elif had quickly developed a plan, though it still needing substantial preparation and refinement. The Mossad spy told Raif she would call tomorrow afternoon.

As Elif drove off, she could not help to think yet again how the apartment seemed out of place for Raif. Something did not feel right, she thought to herself.

Nevertheless, she needed to get home and update Tel Aviv as soon as possible. A good night's rest was also in order before returning to the safe house where Michael slept.

Erzin, Turkey – November 4, 10:45 PM

Passing the halfway point of his journey to Iskenderun, Kadir's cell phone chimed. The information he waited for had finally arrived. The message simply included an address where the Israeli spy was located. Dabria came through.

He turned to his passenger and handed her the phone.

"Confirm and pull it up please, Yaffa," said Kadir.

Confirmed. K, typed Yaffa.

She then entered the street address into her Apple MacBook Air laptop using the *Google Earth* feature. Who needs billion-dollar satellite programs she thought to herself. Modern technology, coupled with the advent of accessible commercial imagery, allowed anyone to enjoy the advantages of overhead collection. It was all free thanks to Google's army of software engineers in Menlo Park, California.

Yaffa proceeded to zoom in and print several overhead images of the property and roads nearby using her Bluetooth enabled portable printer. This would allow Yaffa to efficiently plan the entry into, and exit from the property, thereby improving Kadir's chances for success. Surprise is vital for contract killing, but only after meticulous planning.

The job of killing the Israeli spy was rushed. Kadir and Yaffa knew that, having only a short window of opportunity to plan. However, Kadir felt the agent would feel comfortable on his first day in Turkey. Without a 'portfolio' built, security might be negligible. Moreover, the chance of killing a Mossad agent was too much of an opportunity to let slip by. Kadir's attention focused on killing the man.

Yaffa examined the streets and alleys near the property. After careful review of the location, including a five-block surrounding radius, she determined the best entry to be the south side of the property, where vegetation and shrubberies offered good concealment. Kadir would then move north and make his way into the apartment through the front door from the eastern side of the structure.

"I think I've come up with something, Kadir."

"Good. We will be in Iskenderun in about twenty minutes. We'll find a place and run through it."

Kadir felt confident Yaffa's plan would work. She supported him for eighteen months and never disappointed the killer. As a former police officer in Ankara, Yaffa was meticulous, emotionless and calculating. These were qualities Kadir found necessary in a partner.

Flanked by the Mediterranean Sea to the west, the anticipation of killing the Jew became stronger as the two continued their journey along the southern route to Iskenderun.

**Mossad safe house, Iskenderun, Turkey –
November 5, 1:30 AM**

Awakened by the sound of his smart phone, Michael
viewed the message from Laura.

*Hi, Michael. Trip is going very well. Making good
contacts with several companies here. New York is cold!
Sorry, you had to leave. Looking forward to dinner
whenever you get back. XOXO. Laura*

Michael was excited to hear from her. She was
brilliant, beautiful, warm and compassionate and
everything he ever looked for in a woman. He wanted to be
with her. For only the second time in his life, he genuinely
felt in love.

From the moment, he saw her long black hair and
hazel eyes, he contemplated a less dangerous profession.
Twenty years of regular travel and dangerous missions had
left him longing for more. He needed a partner and did not
want to grow old alone. In Michael's mind, Laura was the
reason he needed to either retire or find a desk job in
Langley somewhere.

Michael replied.

*Great. Glad to hear it's going well. Have fun and hope
to be in touch tomorrow. Where would you like to eat?*

He then left his bed to get something to drink. His
thirst quenched after sipping on bottled water, he worked
his way back to the bedroom.

A cat's faint screech could be heard outside.

Positioned on the bed next to the pillow was his Ruger
LCP .380 automatic pistol equipped with a laser sight, the

perfect companion while traveling. The lightweight and highly reliable small weapon was always stored neatly inside a hidden compartment in his briefcase. The briefcase, developed by CIA's Science and Technology branch, was perfect for overseas travel and guaranteed the compartment undetectable from airport screeners.

Barefoot, Michael secured his pistol and carefully moved behind the door to the entrance of the bedroom.

The doorknob began turning slowly. Satisfied the lights were off, Kadir entered the apartment through the front door. With the lock successfully undone and Yaffa in the van nearby, he felt the operation was progressing as planned.

Just an hour before, Yaffa and Kadir had circled the complex and remained in the van until they were sure the target was alone and without support. The time for Kadir to strike was now.

As he pushed the door open slowly, Kadir observed the dark room the best he could. He noticed a sofa, a loveseat, and other interior furnishings common in one's residence. To his left he could see the open kitchen. The apartment smelled clean and fresh he thought, probably recently prepared for his target.

Kadir was able to determine a hallway leading from the end of the living room. There would be his victim as he gradually moved forward. Silence was now his best friend.

As he carefully progressed down the hallway, he saw an opening along the right side of the wall. Turning his head slowly around the door Kadir found the bathroom. Getting closer he thought.

A few feet further into his approach, he noticed another room to his left. The door was open. Peering his head around the corner once again, he only saw a bedroom. The bed appeared to be kept and orderly. A bit further down the hall would be the last room on the right. He had to be there, thought Kadir.

Moving ever so quietly, Kadir reached the final room. His heart began pumping faster, and his breathing quickened a bit in anticipation. The door leading to the room appeared cracked, approximately one-third of the way open. With his gun in the left hand, he leaned forward careful to not move the door further. He did not want to alert his target.

Michael, instantly recognizing that the intruder had entered the room, slammed the door violently against him. Michael was unsure who the individual was. If he could question the assailant, rather than kill him, he might figure out his motive.

Kadir, completely caught off guard, slammed into the wall. Michael instantly sprang from behind the door and powerfully struck Kadir in the forehead. Hearing a knock on the ground, Michael determined the intruder's weapon hit the floor.

As Kadir regained his footing, his left elbow inadvertently moved the light switch upwards. Both men would now see each other clearly.

Kadir observed Michael's pistol. Using both hands, Kadir lunged toward Michael and captured his left wrist.

Kadir's weight and thrusting motion turned Michael as his left arm hit the wall. Using a knuckle release technique, Kadir applied pressure with his thumbs in between Michael's center knuckles. Michael's .380 dropped to the floor moments later.

For the next couple of minutes, intense hand-to-hand combat ensued between the two men. Exchanging short thrusts, jabs, elbow strikes and body punches, neither man gained the upper hand. Michael and Kadir moved from the hallway to the living room as Kadir began retreating ever so slowly.

As Michael entered the living room, he quickly employed a round kick and swept Kadir's legs. Kadir fell to the ground. Lunging forward, Michael jumped onto Kadir and attempted to assume a ground strike position, used predominately by mixed martial arts fighters.

Before Michael settled atop, Kadir reached into his pocket and pulled out a long nylon cord. As Michael's momentum stalled, Kadir attempted to loop the cord around Michael's neck. However, Michael wedged his right hand under the cord preventing the makeshift noose from tightening.

Michael's breathing intensified as he furiously began punching Kadir in the head with his left hand while moving his right hand upward. This caused Kadir's hold to come undone.

Michael's last punch knocked Kadir to his side. As the men rolled, Michael took the cord and was now underneath Kadir in a semi rear naked fighting position. With Kadir's back on Michael's chest, Michael applied the noose onto Kadir.

Kadir, already severely bruised with mild concussion symptoms, fought Michael as long as he could. However, Michael's grip was too strong. After some time had passed, Kadir took his last breath. He now lay dead on the floor.

Michael got up, took some deep breaths and returned to the hallway. He gathered his .380 and quickly moved toward the front door. Sensing the killer's accomplice nearby, he exited the front door and saw Yaffa's van out of the corner of his right eye. He began to sprint toward the dark vehicle.

Yaffa was stunned. As she looked at the man from approximately fifty meters away, she knew Kadir failed. Without hesitation, she shifted her vehicle into reverse and quickly turned left onto the intersection.

Michael returned to the apartment. Having caught his breath and now compromised, he dialed Elif's cell number. Help would be on the way soon, she promised.

In the meantime, he would ponder the significance and timing of Laura's message.

Kenema, Sierra Leone – November 4, 4:00 PM

Manjo took a liking to Sheikh Cissi and his loyal deputies. Spending the last couple of days at the Mosque did him some good. He had the opportunity to read the Quran, converse with others, and simply escape the harsh realities of living in his desolate and poor village. He was making new friends and enjoyed his new experiences.

However, the anger and frustration of losing his father did not go away. He often wondered why the rich western nations could not fight the Ebola outbreak with the same determination and ferocity as killing Muslims throughout the Middle East and Africa. This perplexed the young man.

The Americans were spending billions of dollars hunting and killing Muslims in Iraq, Afghanistan, Yemen, and elsewhere. The French were in Mali doing the same against forces loyal to Ayman al-Zawahiri, Al Qaeda's leader since Bin Laden's demise.

America should do more to help his beloved country save lives, Manjo thought to himself. Sheikh Cissi was all too happy to reinforce these ideas in him.

In one of Sheikh Cissi's meeting rooms tucked away inside the Mosque, the two continued their dialogue.

"America picks and chooses the weak and suffering. They and her allies do not support Muslims. Look at how they are slaughtering Muslims around the world. Innocent children and mothers are being killed by drones. And they do not support us here while Ebola takes our families and neighbors," said the Sheikh in his deliberate and thoughtful tone. He continued.

"Join us Manjo. Leave the village and stay in Kenema with us. You are welcome here."

"I will Sheikh Cissi. Thank you," said Manjo with a joyful look on his face.

He and Sheikh Cissi's discussions made a lasting impression on the confused young man. There was a sense of community here not unlike his village to the north. Additionally, loyal followers of Sheikh Cissi shared a resentment toward the west, which he now developed.

Sheikh Cissi was pleased Manjo would remain. Another 'recruit' he thought to himself, if time and circumstances allowed it.

Mossad safe house, Iskenderun, Turkey –
November 5, 2:25 AM

Elif arrived after having quickly made her way from Arsuz to Iskenderun.

"What happened, Michael?"

"Someone tried to kill me, Elif. Who else knew I was here?"

"Just Nanook and Walid, myself and Tel Aviv, of course."

"How well do you trust Nanook and Walid?"

"Enough to know they were not behind this, Michael," said Elif passionately.

"Well, someone knew I was here. If not them, who?"

"The only place I can think of is Hatay. Maybe someone there recognized you?"

"No way, Elif. I've never been to Hatay or this country for that matter," said Michael.

"Let me check around Michael," said Elif as she began moving toward the dead killer.

Elif proceeded to stand over Kadir's lifeless body. She took a few pictures of his face.

Pulling up his long sleeved shirt, she noticed the tattoo of a black and green serpent on Kadir's left forearm. Then she lifted his shirt and checked for body markings on the stomach and chest. Nothing.

She instructed Michael to help her flip him over. Raising the shirt on his back, she found more tattoos. They were symbols of the Turkish underground, as Elif had seen them before. A contract killer, she thought to herself.

After a few more clicks from her smartphone, Elif had compiled a set of photos she hoped would identify the man. Soon, she would send them to her handlers in Tel Aviv for identification. First, however, she would call her associates.

"Nanook. Get to the safe house right away. Bring Walid."

"What is going on Elif? Are you, all right?"

"I am. Just get moving. I am leaving with our guest. You have your keys?"

"Yes."

"Good. Bring a cleaning kit and body bag. Dispose of the body right away. Check the hallway and living room for blood stains."

"Okay."

"I'll call in a few hours with an update."

Elif hung up and turned to Michael.

"We need to leave at once and go back to my place. Gather your stuff and let's go."

Michael appreciated Elif's confidence and orders. She was calculated. Here, Mossad was in charge, and he was along for the ride. She knew the lay of the land, the people, and was clearly prepared for some unforeseen tactical setbacks.

A few minutes later, Elif and Michael left. Heading toward Arsuz, the two proceeded to give each other an update of their earlier communications.

At approximately 3:15 AM, Nanook and Walid arrived. Dressed in gloves, and two bags full of cleaning supplies, they found Kadir's body lying in the living room. The coloration of his neck indicated he was strangulated.

Thirty-five minutes elapsed and the two men departed. Just before exiting the residence, they put on ski masks. This would ensure their anonymity just in case alerted neighbors awoke and witnessed their departure. Despite their van's proximity to the apartment and the poor lighting, they could not take any chances.

Using a carpet they brought with them, the two men moved the body inside the truck. Their next stop would be the Iskenderun Fish Harbor, a facility of three hundred various boats, and just a few miles away.

Turning left from Ataturk Boulevard onto Sahil Yolu drive, Walid parked the truck. Nanook exited the vehicle and moved toward one of the fishing boats in the marina. As Nanook began walking, Walid reversed the truck and drove off. Turning right back onto Ataturk Boulevard, Walid moved south to the rendezvous point.

In a few hours, Kadir's body would find itself at the bottom of the Mediterranean Sea.

Arsuz, Turkey - 5 November, 8:10 AM

Michael awoke. After sleeping for several hours, he was ready to get started. Sitting up on Elif's tan microfiber couch, he gathered his thoughts.

He noticed the beautiful room filled with plants and pictures of the Mediterranean. The local art decorated along the bright walls added a rather scenic touch and soft side. Nestled along one of the walls he saw a bookcase and wandered his way toward it. Elif's books would indicate her interests, he thought to himself.

Elif walked in.

"Interested in my collection, Michael?" asked Elif.

"Yes. What do you enjoy reading?"

"Ever heard of Nazim Hekmet? His poetry is inspirational and beautiful."

Michael smiled and said, "No. I have not had the pleasure."

"You will find him on the top shelf."

Unable to read Turkish, Michael moved toward Elif. The two needed to devise the plan to free Haris from Syria.

"I've made contact with a friend in Europe. He assures me he can get the missiles here within a couple of days. Where do you need them?"

"Can you get them here?"

"Let's find out," as Michael dialed Paul's number.

"Paul, good morning bud. Can you get the equipment to Iskenderun tomorrow night?"

"Not sure. Did you find out where the weapons are going?"

"Yes, to the YPG fighting Islamic State in Aleppo."

"Can I call you back in a few?" asked Paul.

"Yep. Standing by."

Paul called Jurgen right away. He asked the pilot if he could move the equipment to Iskenderun, Turkey. Wavering, Jurgen told him he could file a flight plan quickly and get to Larnaca. He could not guarantee Iskenderun.

"How much time do I have to get there?" asked Jurgen.

"Tomorrow night."

"That won't happen, Paul. The Turks require more time. I can get to Larnaca as early as this evening. Will that do?"

"I will call back shortly Jurgen." Click.

"Michael, I cannot get the equipment to Iskenderun by tomorrow night. But I can get it to Cyprus today in a place called Larnaca."

Michael muted his phone and turned to Elif.

"I can get the equipment to Cyprus tonight. But a delivery tomorrow won't happen."

"Where in Cyprus?" asked Elif.

"A place called Larnaca."

Elif turned to her phone. Pulling up Google maps, she entered the location. Seeing Larnaca along the south coast of Cyprus, she then calculated the nautical distance. One hundred and sixty-five nautical miles separated the city from Iskenderun. Larnaca also had a port. This could work she thought to herself.

Elif's mind raced with scenarios. After computing the distance, she determined the route could take approximately eight hours traveling at twenty knots. This was certainly achievable if calm seas prevailed. Elif then had to check the sea conditions.

Using a website specializing in sailing weather forecasts, she studied the projections for the next two days. After observing surface wind conditions, wave heights and directions, and surface pressures, Elif made the decision.

"Michael, we can make this happen. I will send a crew to Larnaca right away. They should be there before nightfall."

Trusting Elif's calculation implicitly, Michael turned his attention back toward Paul.

"Paul. Move the equipment as soon as possible. We will have someone meet your people in the port of Larnaca tonight. I'll send the details over later."

"Okay. Good luck Michael. Let us catch up when you have time. Stay safe my friend."

"Absolutely brother."

The plan was coming together. Michael would have his missiles in Larnaca tonight and Elif's associates would get them to Iskenderun tomorrow.

Elif offered Michael some coffee. Genuinely thankful for her hospitality and decisive decision making, he looked forward to her home brew.

"I need to take care of a few things, Michael."

"Where are you going?"

"Into Iskenderun. I need to prepare our transportation for tomorrow. Stay here and get comfortable. I'll be back soon."

Michael smiled and asked, "Isn't that what you told me last night?"

"Mossad owns this building. I promise. No surprises."

The down time would allow Michael to update Langley. His working plan and the developing situation with Haris were a top priority.

Before that, however, he would send Laura a short message.

He wanted to stay connected with her despite the newness of their relationship. Sending a short note while away would show he cared. He would make her feel special even if thousands of miles away.

Hi, Laura. Thanks for your message earlier. Are you back in Arlington or still in New York? Things here are hectic and I'm trying to sort out the mess. What kind of food would you like for dinner when I get back? Something Middle Eastern, perhaps Israeli, to remember the trip? Take care. Safe travels. Really looking forward to seeing you again. Mike

Turning his attention back to Langley, Michael would now update his superiors.

Freiberg, Germany – 5 November, 10:20 AM

Situated on the border of the majestic Black Forest Mountains, with the Schlossberg Hill to the west, residents of Freiberg, Germany went about their business. Hikers were ascending the Schlossberg, nearly one thousand five hundred feet in height, while tourists rode the nearly four-kilometer cable car from Gunterstahl to the Schauinsland Mountain.

Near the Historical Merchant's Hall, an iconic red building first constructed in the 14th century, Markus was finishing his morning cup of coffee and fresh brötchen. He adopted the cultural ritual known to all Germans as a young teenager while working as a tour guide.

Markus already spent the morning preparing his team at the warehouse. Approximately five kilometers south of Freiberg along Route 1, and just north of the town of Brand-Erbisdorf, the AT-4s were loaded and prepared for transport. All Markus and his team needed now were instructions.

"Markus, good morning, it's Paul."

"Good morning."

"We are a go for movement. Move to the airport and proceed to hangar seven. I will be there at one o'clock."

"Okay. Will you have time to stay for a while?" Always the social German, Markus invited his longtime associate despite the urgency in Paul's voice.

"Not this time, Markus. I am sorry. See you in a few hours."

"All right Paul. One it is at hangar seven."

Markus' short drive to Brand-Erbisdorf meant he and his team would be departing within the hour.

The AT-4 missiles, along with other Soviet era military equipment, had been located outside Freiberg since 1994. One of a dozen similar sites within Germany, these weapons caches were the product of an elaborate CIA operation implemented after 1993.

Spearheading the operation were Markus and his then young CIA colleague, Paul Hernandez.

Soon after the Soviet Union ceased its fifty-year existence, criminal enterprises began emerging from former held territories. One such place was Ukraine. There, Viktor Mogilevich began amassing a fortune sending weapons and equipment to war-torn Africa, among other places.

William Jefferson Clinton, the nation's 42nd President, authorized the clandestine program after seeing a sharp uptick of African warlords. Determined to reduce the transfer of Ukrainian stockpiles, he directed CIA to begin acquiring them directly from inside the new Republic.

Clinton's attention focused on one such warlord, Charles Ghankay, a ruthless guerrilla fighter trained by the Libyans, and founder of the National Patriotic Front of Liberia (NPFL).

Charles Ghankay and Viktor Mogilevich were business partners. Charles delivered millions of dollars of diamonds and currency in exchange for Viktor's armaments. The relationship endured throughout the First Liberian Civil War, which ended with the death of an estimated 600,000 people.

During the operation, Markus and Paul would periodically enter Ukraine and procure mostly small arms munitions and shoulder fired rockets, such as the AT-4. Posing as arms dealers with clients in South America, the two successfully purchased thousands of weapons and prevented their entry into war-torn Africa.

The operation would also ensure the United States had the ability to support rebel backed groups around the world without actually intervening, a preferred policy option chosen by the program's commander in chief. This method would later work well in places such as Afghanistan, where US-backed rebel groups would fight Al Qaeda and the Taliban.

Markus pulled in front of the truck carrying the AT-4s.

Looking down at his watch, he said, "Niklas. Grab a smoke. We move in ten."

Markus would enter the warehouse and review the cargo manifest one last time. He was ultimately responsible for the cargo's manifest and international shipping documents. Any setbacks or errors and Paul would have his head.

In the meantime, Paul and his driver were approaching the Berlin Tegel International Airport. In approximately twenty minutes, he would soon be airborne in his Gulfstream G650ER business jet. With a cruising speed of Mach .9, his trip to Freiberg would be short.

**Euro Airport Basel-Mulhouse-Freiberg, Germany –
November 5, 12:50 PM**

Markus and his team arrived at hangar seven a bit later
than anticipated. The cargo entrance was busy that day, and
the truck ahead of Markus was slow clearing customs.
Security was tight since earlier in the year, a manifest
seized by German Federal Intelligence, the
Bundesnachrichtendienst (BND), found containers of
illegal art destined for Charlotte, North Carolina.

The truck carrying Markus and his team drove into the
spotless hangar, leased by CIA through a subsidiary
shipping company. Driving slowly to their right, they
parked alongside the Jungheinrich forklift, with an operator
seated and ready for their arrival.

Niklas exited the driver's side and walked toward the
back where he released the rear hatch. His colleague, Alrik,
many years younger, jumped out the back, while the
forklift operator quickly moved behind the truck.

For the next several minutes, pallets and crates
containing the AT-4s were efficiently loaded into Jurgen's
plane, an Airbus A300-200F model purchased by CIA in
2011. The aircraft offered Paul maximum flexibility, heavy
payload potential, and a range of nearly eight thousand
kilometers. Today's shipment would be extremely light
when compared to the aircraft's capacity.

In the meantime, Paul and Markus stood off near the
rear entrance of the lower cargo bay. Markus needed
signatures, and Paul was all too happy to oblige. Even CIA

required documentation, and a dozen AT-4s needed accounting for to his superiors back in Langley.

"Okay Markus. Good work today. Know this was short notice. Enjoy the trip back home."

"We will Paul."

Markus rejoined his colleagues at the truck and off they drove. Paul entered the aircraft and met Jurgen in the cockpit.

"The cargo is onboard and secure, Jurgen."

"Thanks, Paul. I'm just flying to Larnaca, correct?"

"Yes. I will have someone contact you during the flight with instructions. Once on the ground, you will follow their lead to a designated location at the airport. Once the cargo is moved off the plane, you are finished."

"Spend some time in Cyprus. Get back here in a few days. Just let me know when you land."

"Will do, Paul. Larnaca is mild this time of year. I'll call soon."

A few minutes later, Paul and his driver left hangar seven. Now satisfied the operation was underway, he would return to his Gulfstream and fly back to Berlin. As he sat down and prepared to depart, Michael called.

"Paul. There will be a boat approaching the Larnaca port this evening around nine. The boat's name is the Gulet Sophia. On board will be two individuals working for my contact here. I am sending you their pictures in a few minutes. Can the cargo be ready by then?"

"Yes. The cargo should be in the air in a few minutes. I'll call Cyprus and set up the delivery."

"Excellent," said Michael.

"Anything else I can do, bud?"

"Not now. I will call when we have the equipment secured aboard the Sophia. Later, my friend."

Soon after Michael hung up, Paul would call his counterpart in Nicosia, Cyprus, home to the United States Embassy. Scanning his phone, he tapped on the name, Rick Killian, CIA's top spymaster in the Republic.

Paul vaguely knew him as Rick spent most of his time in North Africa and Italy. Their paths narrowly crossed on a few occasions, but the two men never worked closely with each other.

"Rick. Paul Hernandez, chief from Berlin. How are you?"

"Good Paul. It has been a few years. This probably isn't a social call, is it?"

"Nope. I am running an operation in support of a colleague. I have a plane landing in Larnaca tonight. I need to move its cargo to the port and loaded onto a ship named the Sophia Gulet. Can you get a crew to move it and secure delivery?"

"When will the plane land?"

"In about three and a half hours. Can I get you to notify the pilot to coordinate delivery?" asked Paul.

"Sure, Paul. I'll be glad to help. Larnaca is only about sixty miles away."

"I'll send his flight number and communications data to your office in about an hour. The contents are several large crates. You should have a small forklift available, if possible, at the airport."

"Okay. I can get a team down there in an hour if needed. We have enough time to get ready."

"Your team might have to help load the contents onto the ship. I'd like you to use agency personnel only, Rick."

Paul referred to using only CIA officers stationed at the Embassy. Local contractors, often employed by station chiefs, were not suitable for this mission. It was too sensitive, and Paul determined the contractors, regardless of their loyalties or lengths of service had no business knowing of the AT-4s.

"Will that be an issue, Rick?"

"No, Paul. I understand the request. I've got the people to do it."

"Thanks, Rick. I will send the data your people need very soon. I should be back in Berlin shortly."

Paul hung up. Confident his colleagues in Cyprus would secure delivery, all Paul needed to do was sit back and watch the operation unfold. By this evening, Michael would be on his own.

Nicosia, Cyprus – November 5, 2:40 PM

Inside the United States Embassy, located along the streets of Odos Metochiou and Ploutarchou, Rick Killian sat at his desk. Anticipating details from Berlin soon, he chose to eat lunch in the office. Today's feast was a chicken gyro sandwich with fries ordered from his favorite locale just blocks away. He could never get enough of the local cuisine despite approaching his third year as CIA's top intelligence officer.

Inside the Embassy's secure communication room, the message from Berlin finally arrived. With instructions for Killian's eyes only, the operator printed off the report and called Rick.

"Sir. We have a high priority message from Berlin. Your eyes only. The originator is Paul Hernandez."

"Thank you, Christine. I'll be right down."

As Rick made his way toward the communications room, he encountered Patrick O'Sullivan, one his deputies and soon to be a father. Pamela O'Sullivan learned of her pregnancy just three weeks ago.

"Pat. I need to see your team in my office in fifteen minutes. Are all your people on site?"

"Yes. Something come up?"

"Yeah. We are going to secure some cargo tonight and help transport to the port of Larnaca. I need aerial images and an advance team standing by. Berlin has asked us for support."

"Sure. I will get them ready. Is this going to be an all-night operation?"

"I don't think so, but we are waiting for a ship to arrive. Who knows what the Med looks like tonight?"

"Got it. See you in fifteen minutes."

Rick continued his descent to the communications room. Swiping his badge, he unlocked the door and entered the secure facility.

"Christine. Got something for me?"

"Here you go, boss."

Rick sat down. As he read the report from Paul's team in Berlin, he reminded himself why Paul Hernandez was a legend in the agency. Always meticulous, with potential contingencies addressed and prepared for, Paul's careful planning would ensure Rick's team would find few surprises or ask many questions.

A short while later, Rick and his team gathered. The group analyzed aerial imagery of the port, roads leading into the harbor, and other operational data. The advance team would arrive and split up in Larnaca.

The first team would arrive at the designated hangar by five pm and ensure its cargo remained secure. The second team would continue to the port and establish observation points directed at the slip where the Sophia would dock.

At seven o'clock, the rest of Patrick's team would arrive onsite and provide surveillance of the hangar, establish perimeter security, and load the plane's cargo onto their van. From there, they would transfer the cargo to the port and wait as standard movement protocol would be in place.

Rick recognized the team was a bit slim, and asked Patrick if they wanted to deploy their new drone, just recently shipped to Nicosia.

"I don't see why not. We can bring it with us. Lindey can fly it. She finished training last week. It will only enhance our view of the port. There should be no gap in coverage."

Rick turned toward Lindey and asked, "Do you feel comfortable flying that little thing?"

"I do. The technology is incredible. It practically flies itself and I can stay in one of the vehicles. Images are displayed in real time, and I'll pass any relevant information on our secure frequencies."

Patrick and the team were discussing the agency's newest micro drone, an enhanced version of the PD 100 Black Hornet 2.

The Black Hornet micro drone, first introduced by the Norwegian company, Prox Dynamics, had gained early success with some security forces. Early adopters included the British military.

The enhanced Black Hornet version was the product of a multi-year testing and development program. Langley scientists, cooperating with scientists at the Naval Research Lab (NRL) in Patuxent, Maryland, refined the micro drone for operational deployment.

The miniature flying robot provided superior tactical data. Handheld, and weighing in at less than twenty grams, the drone could provide thermal images and even included a microphone to capture sound when hovering.

Simple enough, thought Rick to himself. Pleased his team was prepared and had the intelligence they needed, he dismissed them. After Patrick's team left his office, Rick needed to get back to the communications room. From there, he would call the pilot of the A330 on a secure high-frequency channel. His flight number was XQ913.

"XQ913, this is NCC1701. Authenticate alpha omega."

"I authenticate papa hotel," said the pilot.

Rick thought the reference to papa hotel lacked subtlety. Nevertheless, he grinned softly and wasn't surprised it originated from Paul Hernandez.

Rick was satisfied that his communication with the pilot was secure, and asked where to meet him.

Neither man knew each other.

Jurgen simply replied, "Hangar eleven. On the northwest section of the airport, along Artemidos drive. My ETA is five-ten PM, over."

"Got it. NCC1701, out."

Rick sent Patrick the details. He would return to his office a few minutes later anticipating a smooth operation.

Kenema, Sierra Leone – November 5, 4:30 PM

Hello again, Manjo. How are your studies proceeding?" asked Sheikh Cissi.

"Very good, Sheikh Cissi. I'm beginning to wonder if I have another purpose."

"What is that, Manjo?"

"Farming is the only thing I know. It has been in my blood for generations. However, I believe I may have a duty to wage jihad."

Sheikh Cissi acted perplexed and simply asked Manjo why.

"A few reasons. First, the West and its allies are killing Muslims around the world. How much longer before they get here? Second, the United States could have prevented my father's death. They could have done more when Ebola struck this year. Finally, they are infidels. They do not believe in the prophet Muhammad."

"Jihad requires great sacrifice and commitment. Just days ago, you were not even practicing our faith, Manjo."

"I know. But I have learned."

"Learned what, Manjo?"

"That living a simple life as a farmer, while my brothers struggle, is no longer acceptable."

"But can you not serve the Prophet by providing food and helping others?"

"I could. However, I believe jihad is calling me. Should I purify myself of these thoughts?"

"What kind of jihad are you referring to Manjo?"

"The kind where I fight."

Sheikh Cissi thought for a moment. He quickly ascertained Manjo was serious but did not want to come across as too elated. He did not know him well enough, and the death of Manjo's father was still on his mind. Emotions clouded commitment, he thought to himself.

"Who do you want to fight?"

"The Americans."

"And how will you do that Manjo?"

"I don't know. Maybe you can teach me?"

"In due time, Manjo. For now, continue your studies. You have much to learn."

Sheikh Cissi returned to his office. A few minutes later one of the Mosque's caretakers entered, and Sheikh Cissi spoke.

"Foday. I just left Manjo. He wants to fight the Americans."

Chuckling ever so slightly, Foday asked, "Already? Foolish young boy."

"Maybe. But I have been asked to provide fresh recruits."

"How many?" Foday asked.

"A handful. They are not ready. However, I am afraid they won't be happy."

"When do they need them?"

"Right now, of course."

"They understand our situation here?"

"They don't care. At least that is what I read."

"We will just have to make them wait."

"Indeed. But for how long, Foday?"

"As long as it takes. They are not here in Kenema."

"For now, Foday. For now," said the Sheikh.

Turning his chair slightly to the right, he stared out the window. Sheikh Cissi had a tough decision to make. If he pushed too hard or too fast, the men would surely perish. If he moved too slowly, the dreams of a caliphate might disappear and his superiors would question his commitment.

The Sheikh turned back to Foday and spoke.

"Add Manjo to weapons training tomorrow. However, make sure he continues his reading. I am not certain he is committed. He is still angry."

"I understand. Will you join us in the morning?"

"No. I have other matters to tend to. Will your men be gone most of the day?"

"Yes. We will have them read in between training."

"Okay, Foday. Let's meet here again tomorrow afternoon."

Foday left the Sheikh's office. Walking down the hall, he turned right and began walking up the stairs leading to the second floor. Manjo would be in the third room on the left.

The room where Manjo stayed the last few days was drab as just two bunk beds and some old drawers filled the room. On the ceiling was an old wobbly black fan slowly turning its three plastic blades. Often alone the past few days, Manjo relished the visit.

"Manjo. I want you to join some of us in the morning. We are leaving town. Pack your Quran and drink plenty of water tonight."

"Where are we going Foday?"

"Leaving for a village west of here. We leave after morning prayers."

"What are we doing there?"

"You will find out in the morning. I suggest you get plenty of sleep."

"Okay Foday. I will be ready."

Soon after Foday left his room, Manjo looked up toward the ceiling. His mind raced with anticipation and questions. What would tomorrow be like, he pondered. Would Sheikh Cissi test his determination to wage jihad? Was Sheikh Cissi upset with him? Would he get a chance to prove his resolve?

A couple of hours later, Manjo would eat his dinner, finish his chores and return to his new home. Manjo became anxious, and it took a considerable amount of time for the young man to fall asleep.

**Larnaca International Airport, Larnaca, Cyprus –
November 5, 5:15 PM**

Flight XQ913 arrived as scheduled and Jurgen's
Airbus 330 slowly pulled into the hangar. Waiting for him
were two associates responsible for handling his aircraft
while Jurgen was in town. As the aircraft came to a stop,
Jurgen and his co-pilot, Lukas, lowered the rear ramp and
worked their way toward the back of the aircraft.

Upon exiting, two individuals dressed in khakis,
collared shirts and blazers greeted them. While in flight,
Paul's updates kept Jurgen abreast of the situation. There
were no surprises.

"You must be Jurgen?" asked one of the men.

"I am. Are you are from Nicosia?" asked the German.

"Yes."

"May I see your identification?"

Removing the identification badge from his rear
pocket, the black haired man proved he was from the
Embassy.

"Can't be too careful, huh," asked Jurgen in a sarcastic
sort of way.

Clearly displeased, and with his dinner date canceled
earlier, the man simply replied, "Nope."

"Well, you guys enjoy. My work here is done. Time
for a drink."

As Jurgen walked off, a forklift operator began to grab
hold of the pallets and moved them to the awaiting van.
Before exiting the hangar, he overheard two men discuss

the movement to the marina. The AT-4s were loaded in less than ten minutes.

Patrick noticed their van exiting the hangar. As soon as the van departed the last gate at Larnaca, they would quickly move behind it and become the trail vehicle.

Larnaca Marina was less than ten kilometers away. The duration of the trip would only take sixteen minutes.

Moving north along route B4 and flanked by the Larnaca Salt Lake to the west and the Mediterranean to the east, Patrick's team was ahead of schedule. The short drive was magnificent as a cool breeze flowed off the Mediterranean waters.

Larnaca was breathtaking. Patrick had not enjoyed the pleasures of its warm and inviting people since arriving on Cyprus. This was a good place to bring his wife for the weekend, he thought to himself.

As Patrick and his team were five minutes from the Marina, it was time to execute the next stage of the operation. First, they would move the van and secure it near the slip designated earlier in the afternoon by Rick. Second, his team would park at designated locations around the Marina to begin the tedious task of observation.

Hours of persistent surveillance is normal for CIA intelligence officers. Though technology, aerial reconnaissance, and other capabilities are widely available, operations in crowded civilian areas restricted their use.

Cyprus was also an ally and a peaceful country. Aerial intelligence gathering systems were not available to his team nor were they deployed there. For this operation,

Patrick and his team had to do reconnaissance the old-fashioned way. They had to 'watch' the Marina from their vehicles and trust their instincts while they waited.

The Sophia was approaching.

Ankara, Turkey – November 5, 5:20 PM

It was time for Dabria to deliver the bad news. She was unable to kill the visitor and target on Nasir's kill list. Yazza already reported Kadir's failure and Dabria could no longer keep Nasir waiting. A second phone call to the leader in Rukob, Yemen was in order.

"Nasir. It's Dabria. The man got away."

"I thought you were going to take care of this, Dabria?" asked Al Qaeda's leader from his remote hideout.

"I planned to. He must be a professional. Who is he Nasir? I used my best man."

Nasir was clearly disappointed with Dabria. He did not have much time, as this was Dabria's second call in as many days. He could not allow the Americans to triangulate his location. Reports from international news agencies over the years suggested that America could target cell phones using satellites.

Low earth orbit satellites (LEOs) were now commonplace, ever since the Soviet Union first deployed Sputnik 1 in October 1957. Dozens of countries around the world now employed the satellites found at distances ranging from one hundred miles to just over one thousand miles above the earth's surface. With their ability to make one revolution around the earth in ninety minutes, they provided intelligence agencies with enormous data.

LEOs permitted intelligence agencies to conduct numerous types of reconnaissance missions. Most common was the imagery exploitation of manmade structures and natural terrain features. They also acted as gateways for the transmission of sensitive data to analysts and consumers around the globe.

"Then you will do it, Dabria. Only you. You must not fail. He has caused my organization significant damage. I want him dead. We still have the addresses, Dabria. Do not contact me until you finish the job. Am I clear?"

"You are."

Nasir hung up. Recognizing Nasir's intensity and tone, she knew the time had come. Dabria's past was now catching up with the talented intelligence officer.

While on assignment in Yemen in 2012, the Al Qaeda network discovered her identity. Her capture occurred while meeting with a source in Yemen's capital of Sana'a. The source turned out to be an Al Qaeda sympathizer who was attempting to join the organization.

Dabria's incarceration was in Al Hudaydah, a city of four hundred thousand residents located near the capital. During her captivity, she would suffer from enhanced interrogation techniques, commonly used in the region.

Her captors used a variety of these techniques including waterboarding, sleep deprivation, and white noise. However, Nasir, then a deputy commander of Al Qaeda, made sure his men did not beat the young woman. If he could somehow turn her, he would have an asset to exploit in the future.

Without marks on her body, her supervisors in Yemen might think she was simply unable to communicate due to the remoteness of her location. The ploy worked.

Dabria began talking after the fourth day of her captivity. Her abductors learned she was single but had an extended family in Istanbul, along with others in the eastern part of Turkey. They told Dabria her family was within reach and would be targeted if she failed to cooperate in the future.

Nasir eventually told her that she could return to MIT, and would provide her with some information about the group's finances. The amount of damage to the organization would be minimal, but it would allow Dabria to provide her supervisors valuable tactical intelligence. Nasir recognized Dabria's professional ambitions at MIT and used this information while recruiting her.

Nasir's inquiry in September was unusual as he rarely contacted the MIT rising star. The queries and requests for information he did make, however, focused mostly on Turkish intelligence efforts in the region, and MIT's cooperation with the United States.

Immediately after Nasir's phone went silent, Dabria began preparing for her task. Already aware of Kadir's failure, she called her operations center.

"Tadio, any news of our visitor at Hatay yesterday?"

"Yes. He was captured on video surveillance in Iskenderun yesterday afternoon."

"Was he alone or with company?" asked Dabria.

"He entered an apartment with a woman. She is under investigation as a possible Mossad officer, according to the file."

"Do you know if he is still in the apartment?"

"No, the camera feed stopped working last night."

"Okay. I have been feeling very tired the last few days and am going to take a couple of days off. Keep me informed of any developments."

"Yes, ma'am, I will."

Unbeknownst to Dabria and her counterintelligence unit, Elif had already disabled the surveillance camera the night before. The camera would not be operational for several days.

Dabria soon packed some clothes, her firearm, and a few other items. The seven hour journey to the coastal city of Iskenderun had begun as she wondered what her fate would be. Would her encounter with the stranger be any different than Kadir's? The compromised MIT officer would soon find out.

**Vogue Exclusive Club, Larnaca, Cyprus –
November 5, 8:45 PM**

Jurgen sat at the bar inside the Vogue, one of the
hottest dance clubs in Larnaca. Since his arrival, Jurgen
began drinking heavily. For the past several months,
Jurgen's excessive drinking began to catch up with him.
Tonight, he could not control himself.

Approaching Jurgen was a beautiful woman with long
auburn hair. Her white skirt and indigo blue blouse left
little room for imagination.

"Hi. I am Sonia. Have I seen you here before?" she
asked smiling.

"Well, hello Sonia, I'm Jurgen."

The woman and her colleague sat behind Jurgen at one
of the tables just an hour earlier. He never noticed them.

Flattered by the woman's advances, Jurgen told her he
was a pilot and had recently flown in some cargo from
Berlin.

"What did you deliver, Jurgen?" asked Sonia, while
gently touching his left knee.

"No idea. I just fly the stuff, and they move it to the
marina. I do not know anything else nor do I really care.
They had an SUV."

"What? Are you a smuggler or something?" she said
jokingly.

"Ha. No. But something like that Sonia."

"Sounds interesting," she said as she moved closer to
Jurgen.

At this point, she determined Jurgen was unable to control his desire to boast. She sized him up quickly and recognized the man was intoxicated and unaware of her true intention. As far as Jurgen was concerned, Sonia was just a local girl at the hottest club looking for some fun.

"Want to tell me more, maybe at my place later?" asked Sonia.

Jurgen was enticed by Sonia's advance and asked if he could dance with her as the night was still young. Though quite drunk at this point, his good fortune would need to wait.

"Maybe after a few dances, Sonia. Come on. Dance with me."

"Okay, but let me use the little girls' room. I'll be right back."

Turning back to the bar, Jurgen motioned for the bartender. "This is going to be a great night. I'll have another Zivania."

Sonia entered the bathroom. Once inside her stall, she pulled the cell phone from her purse and texted her colleague inside the Vogue. It would be too loud for him to hear the incoming call, anyways.

We may have something. This guy says he brought unknown cargo to the airport this afternoon. It was moved to the Marina. We are looking for a black SUV.

Sonia and her colleague, Mory, were regular patrons at the Vogue. In fact, they had noticed Jurgen several times there over the past year. They had never approached the sociable German, until now.

Club Vogue was a known hot spot to one of Larnaca's most notorious crime rings, led by Spiro Kostopoulos. Among Spiro's illegal activities, drug trafficking was the most lucrative to his family's business. Members of the criminal organization routinely used the club to entertain their associates and colleagues. The group viciously eliminated any competitors in Larnaca upon learning of their activities.

Larnaca was a major distribution gateway for illegal drugs shipped from Turkey. Spiro's gang would use the port of Larnaca to receive these drug shipments and distribute to their dealers throughout Cyprus.

Mory read the text from Sonia and quickly replied.

Got it. Entertain him through the night. Find out what you can. Let me know where you go, and I will have someone pick you up in the morning.

Mory motioned to one of the men near the exit of the club and whispered in his ear. Moments later, Mory was gone.

Arsuz, Turkey – November 5, 7:00 PM

Michael and Elif were sitting on the couch, as they did the night before. For the past hour, they spent time getting to know each other, as Elif spoke about her childhood with a gleam in her eyes.

"I remember growing up in Tel Aviv. It is so beautiful. I recall the summers, and swimming in the Mediterranean, snow cones, festivals and all the people along the Jaffa boardwalk. I will return there soon, I hope."

Tel Aviv, Israel's second-largest city, and the Middle East's third-largest economy, was a thriving community of artists, clubs, bars and a burgeoning gay population. A more secular scene in Israel, tourists flocked to the city for their annual vacations.

Elif continued talking of Tel Aviv.

"My teachers taught me so many things there. Before Mossad recruited me, I thought about being a writer."

"What kind of writing?" Michael asked.

"Children's books. The idea of inspiring children was a passion of mine. It still is. I lost my parents when I was a little girl."

Sensing the deep wound in her voice, Michael sought to get her attention back to her writing.

"I'm sorry Elif. That must have been hard for you. Have you written any stories?"

"Not yet, but someday. Maybe when I have my own children. I love their innocence."

"Why not at least start? I can see the passion in your eyes."

"Too busy. My career is very important to me and my job right now is with Mossad. There will be time in the future."

Elif then opened her laptop, and the two waited. A few minutes later, the first message from Haris arrived. Michael sat upward next to Elif but recognized she was in charge. It was her source, and she knew what Michael needed.

Ayse. Can you get me out?

Yes, Haris. Can you make your way to Jarabulus, along the border?

I know it. Yes, I can be there tomorrow before midnight. How will we find each other?

Do you have a cell phone?

I will once I leave.

Not now?

No. I do not travel with one.

How will you get one?

Leave that to me.

Before Elif would provide further information on the extraction, she needed intelligence for Michael. This was a joint operation, and the consequences of a bio-weapon in America would be catastrophic.

Do you have more information on Shirazi's intentions?

Overheard him talking about the Kenema Mosque in Sierra Leone. Shirazi directed someone there to transport Ebola into the United States.

Where and how? That seems farfetched Haris.

I do not know much more Ayse. Shirazi was confident it would work. Someone is to be infected. We need to finish up quickly. I only have another minute.

Okay. Once you start moving. Call cell 90 326 215 6007.

Will you send me coordinates on the way?

Yes. Do you have access to GPS?

There was a thirty-second pause. Haris returned.

Yes. My life is in your hands Ayse. Once they notice I am gone, they will come after me.

I understand. I will get you out Haris.

See you in Jarabulus. Until tomorrow Ayse.

Yes. See you there.

Elif turned to Michael.

"Now all we need are the weapons."

"Yes, I'll feel better when your guys pick them up in Larnaca."

"How about some dinner? Let us get out of here, and I will show you Arsuz. There is a gorgeous cafe along the water not far from here. Walid will let me know when he has secured the missiles and is underway to Iskenderun."

"I would like that. Let me shower and change into some fresh clothes."

Elif and Michael arrived at the Nazbalik Evi Restaurant. The lovely seafood restaurant located along Cumhuriyet Boulevard was the perfect spot for Michael to relax and learn more about the ancient coastal town.

Arsuz, with previous names including Khabev and Rhosus, dated its history back to Roman annexation in 64

B.C. Some records indicate the town existed hundreds of years earlier in the Seleucid Empire. The Arsuz shoreline was also full of ancient ruins from the Roman and Hellenistic periods.

Michael and Elif enjoyed their meze, also known in the region as a mix of small appetizers. Michael enjoyed the hummus and baba ghanoush the best. For their main meal, they had lightly seasoned fish grilled to perfection. Washing the food down with Raki, Michael became content.

"There is a children's shelter near here that I occasionally visit," said Elif as she and Michael awaited their coffee.

"What do you do there?"

"Most of the time I read to them. Sometimes I help the girls brush their hair and just talk to them."

Elif, though a trained killer and intelligence officer for Mossad, was a compassionate woman who had tremendous empathy for the kids there. She should, he thought to himself; as she grew up without the love and support of a mother and father.

Elif clearly loved the young homeless children in Arsuz. Michael began wondering if she became too close to them.

"How often do you see them?" Michael asked.

"Oh, I guess about once a week, unless I'm out of town. It was part of my cover here. They grow on you."

"I imagine they do," said Michael.

"How about you Michael? Any children?"

"No. I am not married, but I met someone back home that may change that. We've only met recently, but I really like her."

"Tell me about her."

"Well, she is an investment banker. She travels to New York City often, likes to read and is a history buff. She is also outgoing, very intelligent, and the most beautiful woman I've ever seen."

Elif knew Michael was in love. He probably would not admit it, but his eyes told her the story.

Michael realized the conversation had become personal. Nothing wrong with that as two professional spies were getting to know each other, he thought to himself. However, he remained focused on the AT-4s.

"Any news from Larnaca?"

"No. I imagine they are still an hour or two out."

"Shall we go back to your apartment soon?"

"That's probably a good idea. Who knows what will await us on the border."

A short while later Elif and Michael returned to the apartment. Elif told Michael she would wait in her bedroom for news. After Elif had excused herself, Michael sat on the couch as another update to Langley was in order. After that, he would take care of personal business.

Thirty minutes later, Michael checked his cell phone.

Surprise me. Laura

Laura's short message for Michael was expected. His response would be short as well.

Michael remembered her vivid description of a trip to Paris on their first date and he decided on a French venue.

French. Maybe dinner will bring back memories for you. I may be unavailable the next couple of days but will be in touch as soon as I can. Michael

While he was anxiously waiting for news from Larnaca, Laura replied.

Maybe dinner will make memories for BOTH OF US. Stay safe. Laura

After Michael had read the message, Elif entered the living room with a serious look on her face.

"What's the news from Larnaca?"

Ceyhan, Turkey - November 5, 10:30 PM

Dabria's approach to Iskenderun was ahead of schedule. In an hour, she would arrive in the city and meet a contact from the local police there. He was trusted and would be unaware of her true intentions. Time to call the young man, she thought to herself.

"Mert. It's Dabria. I should be there before midnight."

"Okay. I'll leave for the cafe now and wait for you."

"Did you get the information I asked for?"

"Yes. I have the address."

"Thank you. Does anyone else know?" asked Dabria.

"I did it myself as you instructed. You know I still want to join."

"I know, Mert. There should be an opening in a few months. Nice work. See you soon."

Dabria encountered Mert six months earlier at an intelligence conference in Adana. The purpose of the gathering, including national police officers and Turkish intelligence, was to improve intelligence sharing. While there, Dabria found Mert attractive, young and ambitious. She would exploit these traits in order to have an asset in the future. A true intelligence professional can never have enough trusted assets.

It worked. After spending several long nights in the company of each other's arms, Mert's infatuation with Dabria became evident. He was hers and she could do with him what she wanted, within reason of course. If it meant violating investigative procedures, Mert was all too willing to do it. Moreover, supporting MIT would be favorable to his career and no Iskenderun police supervisor would scold him, he thought.

Tonight, was no exception. She would soon be in Iskenderun, have a place to sleep, and the intelligence she required.

All was proceeding according to plan, thought Dabria.

She then decided to make a short stop into Ceyhan as it wouldn't take her more than thirty minutes. Mert would wait and Dabria's late arrival would only increase the young man's anticipation of her.

Ceyhan, mostly known as a transportation hub for Russian, Middle Eastern, and Central Asian oil and natural gas, was also famous for its Adana Kebab. Dabria was hungry and needed nourishment. A short rest from the long journey was in order.

There are many variations of the Adana Kebab. Dabria would savor the taste of the Porsiyon, her favorite Kebab served on flatbread with red peppers, parsley, and roasted tomatoes. Hot hummus would complement her meal.

Dabria pondered the task ahead of her as she sat down for the late-night meal. She would soon have the address where Nasir's target would be, at least according to Mert. From there, she would need time to recon the location, and determine the best time to strike. Unfortunately, she thought to herself, there would be no backup.

Nasir's instructions were clear. Dabria had to kill the man by herself. She had no authorization from MIT, and she was still fearful of Nasir's reach. A failure now would surely mean death for members of her family. There would be too many questions if she attempted to alert them.

After Dabria paid her server in cash, the journey to kill Nasir's target would continue.

Larnaca Marina, Larnaca, Cyprus - November 5, 10:15 PM

Patrick and his team remained vigilant while waiting for the boat to arrive. He directed communications checks every fifteen minutes, standard for a surveillance mission of this type. Team members inside vehicles at three different locations shared stories with each other to pass the time.

Lindey, sitting behind Patrick, had the micro drone ready if any unusual activity occurred. She was not flying it due to a limited battery life. Once deployed, the micro drone could remain airborne for only twenty-five minutes. Patrick had no idea when the boat would arrive, only a window as briefed by his boss.

"We have movement near team three. Looks like two vehicles entering the marina from the north gate," said one of Patrick's men on the group's shared frequency.

"What are they driving, Dan?"

"Looks like Mercedes four-door sedans to me. I can't tell for sure due to lighting."

The vehicles could just be a group of people getting ready for a trip, thought Patrick to himself. In Cyprus, evening departures from a marina were common. Tonight, however, he would not take any chances.

"Okay. Keep an eye out."

Slowly turning left, the two sedans made their way into the marina. As they approached the first paved road, one vehicle turned right and headed south while the second vehicle turned left and drove north. The vehicles were moving slowly.

"One vehicle just headed south. The other turned north," reported Dan.

Since Patrick and his team expected the boat's arrival to be in the northernmost section of the marina, he turned to Lindey.

"Time to use our new toy, Lindey. Get eyes on the southern vehicle."

Lindey quickly opened her window. In seconds, the micro drone began its short flight to the southern end of the marina.

"Will. The second vehicle should be approaching your location in a few seconds. Let me know when you see it."

Patrick knew something was odd, but could not be sure at this point. Two vehicles just entered the marina after ten pm. However, rather than driving to one of the parking lots together, they split up and went in two different directions.

Maybe one group was making their way to the Yacht club to get some supplies, Patrick considered to himself. On the other hand, maybe one of the vehicles was simply dropping off a passenger to use the restroom. Too early to tell. The situation would have to unfold.

Situated along the northern slip, the van carrying the AT-4s was waiting. Inside were Patrick, Lindey, and Miles, the newest member of Patrick's team.

"I see it," said the driver. "There, just up ahead."

"Okay. Circle back slowly, Zevket."

Zevket and Mory parked the vehicle at the far most paved lot, approximately fifty yards from the SUV.

"Kaan. The SUV is here. Turn around and meet us on the north side of the marina. Pull behind us but turn off your lights as you approach."

Mory carefully rolled down his window for a better view. He could not tell if the vehicle was running. However, he could see the driver. Maybe his information was good after all.

"Our vehicle just turned around. Moving north," said Lindey.

At the same time, Patrick heard from Dan.

"The vehicle just parked in the northern lot. He's just sitting there now."

"Copy. Keep eyes on him."

A few seconds later Dan updated his boss.

"The second vehicle is making the turn into the northern lot. Just pulled up behind him."

Patrick turned to his driver. "Not sure I like this Miles," said Patrick calmly.

After the second vehicle pulled up behind Mory and Zevket, its driver and passenger exited the vehicle. They walked up to Mory and awaited instructions.

Mory turned to Kaan. "Go take a look. Find out who is in the truck and what they are doing?"

"Two men just exited the rear vehicle, Patrick. Getting closer to see if I can pick up their audio."

Lindey moved the micro drone in closer. Hovering around twenty feet above the second vehicle, Lindey turned on the acoustic monitoring device, even though it would begin to decrease the battery's life rapidly.

Overhearing the chatter, she turned to Patrick.

"Two of them are coming for a visit. Think they're police or security?"

Immediately after hearing the news, Patrick noticed the Sophia approaching from a distance. The timing could not have been worse.

"Could be, Lindey. No one should be aware of us. The Sophia is pulling up now."

As the two men slowly approached Patrick and his team, Lindey observed the two men reaching for their waist. Both pulled out Sig Sauer .9 mm pistols and placed the weapons behind their hip. They were now twenty meters away.

Still unsure of exactly what was transpiring, Patrick decided to remain cool. He still had time to adjust, as it would take another twenty seconds for the men to reach the SUV.

"Will, you and Jeff get out of your vehicle and move quickly north along the eastern dock. Let me know when you have eyes on the two sedans."

Turning to Lindey, Patrick said, "Let's find out who they are and what they want."

As the two men made their way to within ten meters of Patrick's SUV, they raised their pistols and pointed them at each of the driver's doors. The men were no longer cautious and now considered a direct threat.

Lindey, after moving the micro drone closer, also noticed the men had gun silencers attached to the end of their pistols. The possibility that they were law enforcement diminished.

"Stay inside, Lindey."

Patrick exited the vehicle and turned to the approaching individuals. He would stop behind the SUV.

"Can I help you?" asked Patrick.

"What are you doing here?" asked Kaan as he directed his pistol at Patrick's head.

"Just waiting for friends. They are pulling into the marina now. Is there a problem?"

"What's inside the SUV?"

"Nothing. Why do you ask?"

Patrick also heard from Will. He and Jeff were just south, about 15 meters from the lot and had eyes on their boss. Meanwhile, Dan and his partner, George, had their sights on the two men.

"Then you wouldn't mind if my friend checks inside?" asked Kaan.

"I would. Are you police?"

Slightly chuckling and amused by the question, Kaan told him no.

"Then why would you look into my SUV?"

"I'm holding the gun. I will ask the questions. Do you understand me?"

Meanwhile, satisfied Kaan had the situation under control, Mory began walking toward the group.

"Third man approaching, Patrick. He's carrying a weapon."

It was time for Patrick to act. The Sophia had arrived, and his window for delivery was tight.

"Look, nothing bad has to happen right now. I will tell you what. You turn around and leave. If not, you and your friend are going to get hurt."

Patrick recognized he might unnerve the man, but he knew the situation dictated a strong response. The delivery of the AT-4s had to begin immediately after the Sophia docked. There was little time to de-escalate the situation.

Kaan understandably felt challenged. A killer with a short-fused temperament, Kaan's ego was vulnerable. Having served multiple sentences in prison over the years, Patrick's lack of respect unhinged Kaan. The killer quickly walked forward and fired two shots. As Patrick noticed the aggressive move, he attempted to quickly reach into his jacket and secure his firearm. It was too late.

Patrick immediately fell to the ground. The second bullet entering above the left lung would prove to be fatal.

Immediately after seeing their boss hit the ground, Dan and George fired a single shot from their rifle. Both men in their sights would die instantly.

Seeing his colleagues fall to the ground, Mory quickly dashed back to his vehicle. Once inside Zevket pushed the accelerator to the floor and turned the car around.

Firing several shots into the vehicle's rear window, Will and Jeff began chasing Mory's vehicle around the corner. They were unable to hit the driver or passenger as the vehicle separated itself from the CIA officers in hot pursuit. In a few seconds, Mory and Zevket would exit the marina and escape.

At the SUV, Miles and Lindey attempted to help Patrick. The two recognized Patrick's lungs were filling up with blood. Patrick was dying. Turning to Lindey, Patrick uttered his last words.

"Get the AT-4s on the boat now. Then get out of here."

Fighting for every breath, he finally said, "Tell my wife I."

He could not finish the sentence, but Lindey knew what he meant.

Patrick took his last breath. His beautiful young wife would never see him alive again, and their child would grow up without him.

Spooked by the gunfire near the parking area of the marina, Walid and Nanook grew concerned. Something has gone awry, the men thought to themselves. Would they get their AT-4s as Elif had instructed?

A few minutes later, Lindey arrived at the Sophia.

"You are from Iskenderun?"

"Yes."

"We have to expect the police soon. I need you men to move over there and begin moving the crates. My guys will help you."

Walid and Nanook, aided by the rest of Patrick's team, proceeded to move the crates onto the Sophia in about ten minutes. Lindey and Dan would move Patrick's body into the van.

Shortly after Lindey and the rest of the team departed the Larnaca Marina and turned south, police lights became visible. Two Turkish police cars zoomed past the caravan and turned into the marina.

The Sophia, her crew, and the AT-4s were already underway, slipping into the shadows of the Mediterranean Sea.

Nizip, Turkey - November 5, 10:35 PM

Raif had arrived in Nizip earlier in the afternoon and was anxious to meet Sami. Sami was a business partner and contact within the region. They would at the Olympiyat Internet Cafe located along Mustafa Koymen Boulevard, in the heart of the city.

Located across from the flourishing cafe was the Nizip stadium, home to the city's professional soccer team. In a city just twenty miles from the Syrian border, it was one of the few communities in Nizip brimming with life. Syria's civil war and its battle with Islamic State had not yet reached the inner sanctum of Nizip.

Raif was also nervous. On his previous visits to Nizip, he always drove alone when distributing products to his customers. Tonight, he would have to explain to Sami that he would have guests joining him. If he dared to arrive at the delivery point with unexpected visitors, his customers would surely be displeased.

Raif had been selling to the Islamic State for five months now. Before that, he mostly sold medicines, cigarettes, water and clothing to displaced Syrians along the border.

Soon after meeting Sami, his new friend told him he could make more money selling to the Islamic State. They had more cash and his profits would increase significantly if he sold cell phones, radios, global positioning satellite devices, video games, and various other electronics. Sami was an Islamic State sympathizer and scout in Nizip.

Sami's extremist views did not resonate with Raif. Raif was simply a smuggler and entrepreneur who saw the opportunity to earn more money. Simple greed, not ideology, motivated the Turk.

While waiting for Sami, Raif pondered how he would explain the presence of Elif and her colleague. His customers would surely think they were spies attempting to gather information on the group's activities in the area.

No matter what story Raif concocted, he did not see a scenario where Islamic State buyers would either be spooked and leave, or worse; kill him and his guests. The risk of losing business with the Islamic State was too great. His relationship with Elif would likely end at the delivery.

"Hello, Raif," said Sami as he joined him at the cafe.

"Hey Sami, how are you tonight, my friend?"

"Good. So, you have AT-4s coming tomorrow?"

"Yes. But there is a slight problem."

"A problem? My friends do not like problems, Raif."

"I know, but the only way I could get the weapons was if I agreed to have my contact deliver them with me. And there may be two others."

"Who is your contact?"

"An MIT intelligence officer. She has no idea the weapons are going to Islamic State. She thinks they are going to the YPG."

"How can you be so sure, Raif."

"I can't. But how would she know?"

"You asked her for the weapons?" said a stunned Sami.

125

"Yes, you asked if I could get the AT-4s, and I did."

"And who are the others?" asked Sami.

"One is a colleague of hers, probably MIT, and the other is a doctor fleeing Kobani. She mentioned they were getting the doctor out before we deliver the weapons. They might keep the doctor on the Turkish side of the border. I don't know anything about that right now."

"Our buyers will not like it, Raif, even if it's just your MIT contact at the delivery."

"They don't have to know Sami, do they?"

"I cannot lie to them Raif. They would kill me if they found out."

"But how would they know, Sami?"

"When I arrange the delivery Raif, there will be questions. Right now, you cannot even tell me how many individuals will be with you. They probably will not be buying from us again. I cannot have three people show up when they expect one."

"What do you suggest, Sami?"

Sami sat back in his seat and began to think. Neither he nor his Islamic State customers liked complications. Tomorrow's delivery just became complicated, Sami thought to himself. Moreover, he just notified them of the AT-4s earlier in the day.

"Leave it to me, Raif. I will make sure you remain safe."

Of course, Sami was not being very honest with him. Sami knew other smugglers in the region. Nizip and the surrounding areas were full of men like Raif. Tomorrow, however, he had to deliver the weapons as promised. Raif and his companion(s) would have to die.

Sami's plan was simple enough. He would inform his customers that Raif had acquired weapons through a contact from MIT. Unaware of this development, he would recommend they kill him and anyone else after securing the AT-4s. They would be happy to kill them, Sami thought to himself. Better yet, they might try to kidnap them for cash, information or propaganda.

The more Sami thought to himself, the more he felt the plan would work.

"Sami, I don't want to get hurt over this. The only way I could make this work was to agree they accompanied me," pleaded Raif.

"It's okay. Do not worry, Raif."

Sami pulled out a small piece of paper and handed it to Raif.

"Here are the coordinates. The delivery will be just northeast of Jarabulus on the Euphrates. I want you to be there at two-thirty am. I'll let them know you won't be alone."

"All right, Sami. I trust you."

"There is nothing to worry about, Raif. They will be pleased once they see the AT-4s."

Arsuz, Turkey – November 5, 10:55 PM

Elif entered the living room where Michael sat.

"There was a problem at the marina. Apparently, there were visitors and shots were fired," said Elif.

"Your guys okay? Did they secure the weapons?"

"Yes. Your colleagues quickly moved the weapons before departing. As Walid and Nanook were leaving the port, they saw local police arriving."

"Any more intel, Elif?"

"No. Can your colleagues in Cyprus can give us an update?"

"I'll call a friend and see what he knows. Is there a chance our timeline has been compromised?"

"No. They will contact me in an hour with an update. If anything changes, I'll let you know."

Michael was uneasy. As he opened his laptop to contact Langley with an update, he could not help to think what went wrong. Michael did not believe in coincidences, though he conceded random occurrences were possible.

Michael spent the next several minutes updating Doug and the rest of his team in Langley by using an online message application on his laptop. He provided them with details on the pending weapons transfer using Elif's contact. He also reported what Haris said about the Kenema Mosque, which was not much at all. Finally, Michael requested intelligence on the site in case he needed to get there quickly.

After he had sent the secure message, Michael picked up the phone and called Paul in Berlin.

"Paul, did you hear about Larnaca?"

"Yes, just got the intel. It appears we lost one of our own."

"What the hell happened?" asked Michael.

"Our team in Cyprus couldn't tell me much. It appears a local gang affiliated with a transnational organized crime group caught wind of the shipment. They're looking into it as we speak."

"How the hell did they find out?"

"Too early to tell, Mike. Cyprus said they knew where to be and what to look for. My pilot might have screwed up."

Michael figured his pilot would know nothing of the cargo's contents. He continued pressing Paul.

"Can you confirm that before tomorrow night? We are moving the cargo to the border and do not want any more surprises. Just text me as I might not be able to answer."

"I'll try. Cyprus will want answers too. I'll be in touch, Michael."

The unfolding of events in Larnaca disturbed Paul. This was personal. His operation cost the life of a young CIA officer and new father. A phone call to Jurgen would come quickly.

Michael returned to the sofa and closed his eyes. His last thought was of Laura in her white dress and long black hair as he slowly drifted to sleep.

Kenema, Sierra Leone – November 6, 8:50 AM

The short trip to a nearby village west of Kenema was rough and full of bumps and twisting turns. Potholes along the dusty dirt road forced a slower rate of travel as Manjo's body swayed from side to side in the rear of Foday's jeep. Accompanying them were two other vehicles with members of the Kenema Mosque.

Sitting next to Manjo was a young man who arrived at the Mosque two months earlier. He was a slim, younger man probably in his early-twenties. They barely spoke before this morning, and the trip did little to change that.

As the caravan made its way around the final bend, Foday instructed his driver to pull next to the first shelter nearest the patch of trees. Three other similar structures were within fifty meters. Manjo did not see any inhabitants or signs of recent activity.

Foday instructed Manjo and the young man to get out and move inside the shelter. He ordered the others to do the same. Manjo could feel the intensity echoing from Foday's voice. Whatever he was about to do was serious, he thought to himself.

"This morning we are going to conduct weapons training on the AK-47. Following that, we will work on hand-to-hand combat. Studies will continue during periods of rest," said Foday.

The AK-47, also known by its Soviet designation as Avtomat Kalashnikova, is a gas-operated assault rifle. Select Soviet army units first received the weapon in 1948.

Most users and analysts refer to the rifle simply as Kalashnikov.

The AK-47 remains the world's most popular and sought-after rifle. Used by insurgents, regular military forces, and drug trafficking organizations (DTOs) in nearly every region of the world, the rifle has proven its reliability and durability for decades. Countless variants of the rifle exist, but the design remains the same.

"You will need to drink plenty of water today. It will be hot, and I do not need any of you passing out," said Foday.

Foday departed the shelter and an older man in his early 50s greeted Manjo and his fellow trainees. He handed each of them an AK-47 and instructed them how to load and fire.

The Kalashnikov is a remarkably simple weapon to use. It only requires the operator to load a magazine, pull back and release the charging handle and fire. Located on the right side of the barrel is a large safety lever which prevents the charging handle from being pulled to the rear.

A standard magazine is loaded with thirty rounds of ammunition, though variants include a forty round magazine and even a seventy-five-round drum. When the AK-47 fires in automatic mode, mayhem and death soon follow.

After approximately twenty minutes of instruction, the gray-bearded trainer took Manjo and the others outside. They moved along a dirt trail for a few minutes and arrived at the open field, nestled between large trees.

Manjo's enthusiasm was evident. He began smiling as he quickly determined he would fire the world's most popular weapon. He enjoyed himself and the morning's brisk temperature only made him more excited. Manjo was on an adventure.

As Manjo approached the makeshift firing line, a second man appeared and handed him a magazine filled with ten rounds. He did not utter a word. Soon after each of the remaining three trainees received their magazine, orders came to fire at the targets in front of them. They would fire only in semi-automatic mode.

Manjo thought it was odd his instructor did not focus on breathing techniques before arriving at the field. Nevertheless, he judged the target's distance at thirty yards. Slowly placing his left knee onto the sand, he assumed his firing position.

After firing his ten rounds, he noticed seven inside the target, a silhouette of an upper torso and head. Not bad, he thought to himself wondering how the others performed. The best of the others only hit their target twice.

For the next fifteen minutes, Manjo continued firing at the target, improving with each turn. On his final attempt, he hit the target with all ten rounds he was issued. Foday stood at a distance staring at the transformed young farmer.

Impressed by the young man's ability to shoot, the gray-bearded man instructed his assistant to extend Manjo's target to eighty yards. He would surely falter at that range, as most do, he thought to himself.

Manjo took aim at the target and fired off ten rounds. Five shots pierced through the paper silhouette. Foday had seen enough.

"Break time. Go back to where you started, drink some water and begin your studies. Wait for my return."

An hour passed while Manjo continued reading from his pamphlet.

America is an evil nation that turns a blind eye to the suffering of our people in Sierra Leone. Death will find its way to the wicked oppressors. Ebola kills our citizens while America drops its bombs on the faithful. Where are you, my young Lions of Sierra Leone?

The passage would continue to express further anti-American rhetoric. Manjo's anger over the loss of his father only fueled his burning desire to read on. However, Foday returned.

Foday adjusted the afternoon training schedule. The four trainees would now engage in hand-to-hand combat drills before moving back to the range.

Manjo learned many skills in the ninety-minute training session. They included takedowns, strikes, and choking techniques. Foday knew the group needed further training, but it was a start. He was more concerned with studying Manjo's strength, willingness to learn, and physical fitness. He thought training in the afternoon heat would be a good test.

"Manjo. You go to the hut over there," said Foday pointing to the furthest shelter.

The three other young men would separate between the remaining two shelters.

A few minutes later, Foday joined Manjo.

"Manjo. Are you sure you want to wage jihad?"

"I am. The past several days has changed my thinking. I'm no longer destined to be a poor farmer."

"You understand that jihad means killing others?"

"I do."

"Have you ever killed a man, Manjo?"

"No."

"It's not easy. Especially the first time."

Foday stared into the young man's eyes. Ten seconds later he coldly asked, "think you can do it?"

Manjo slowly nodded. He was now committed and his conversion to violent extremism was nearly finished.

Berlin, Germany – November 6, 9:00 AM

"Jurgen, it's Paul."

Jurgen was groggy and slightly hungover from his visit to Club Vogue the night before.

"Yes, Paul? Why are you calling me?"

"You sound tired. Have company last night?"

"Yes, I got lucky."

"Good. I need you and the plane back here this afternoon. I have another shipment to get out. I will meet you at the airport. Be ready to fly by three o'clock."

"Where am I going now?"

Jurgen was disappointed. He hoped to remain in Larnaca for a few days as Paul indicated in Freiberg.

"I'll let you know this afternoon," said Paul.

Paul's gut and intuition told him Jurgen had somehow compromised the operation. Rick Killian's team was solid. His officers did not even know the contents of the cargo.

The odds Rick maliciously jeopardized the mission were inconceivable. Rick, like his station chief counterparts, was above reproach.

The other scenario Paul played out in his mind focused on Jurgen. He did not know where the cargo went. Could he have overheard members of Rick's team, he thought to himself? Maybe.

Paul picked up the phone and called Markus. They would have much work to do this afternoon.

Department of State, Washington D.C. – November 6, 9:25 AM

Leslie Parson assembled her analytical team. Leslie became team chief for the West Africa branch just two short months ago. Earlier in the morning, her boss, Joe Trevone, called her regarding a short notice request from CIA, an unusual occurrence. Leslie and her analysts had the morning to prepare first draft materials for review. She would give the CIA what they could.

Leslie, a young woman at only twenty-eight years of age, was a rising star in the Intelligence Community (IC). The Bureau of Intelligence and Research (INR) selected her as a junior intelligence analyst after she completed her Master's degree in International Affairs from Georgetown University. Her thesis on water shortages in the region won accolades from professors on campus to intelligence analysts around the Washington, D.C. beltway.

Hesitant to join INR after one of her professors said it was the stepchild of the intelligence community, Leslie took the risk and never looked back. The opportunity to begin her career in the Africa directorate was too good to pass up. Performing intelligence analysis for the State Department provided her the prospect of supporting policy making while the agency promoted American values and democracy around the world.

It was a perfect match for the brilliant analyst whose progressive political views were widely known to her colleagues.

She spent considerable time in Liberia as a young child. The daughter of missionary parents from Albany, New York, Leslie traveled throughout many parts of the West African region. The majestic beauty and ruggedness of the countryside captivated the young woman. She made numerous friends throughout the region and still communicated regularly with many of them.

At fourteen, her father told her she would move back to the United States with her grandparents near Albany. That was the plan at least. Though devout Christians, Leslie's parents promised themselves they would allow their daughter the opportunity to live a normal high school life back in America. She refused.

Leslie spoke Hausa, one of the most common languages found in West Africa and by persons of Fulani ancestry. She also subscribed to numerous news outlets, followed bloggers, and politicians within the region on social media. Twitter is the preferred open source media of any credible intelligence analyst whose work focuses on social and political trends. Leslie was no different and acutely tuned into the region. Utilizing more open source data than derived from classified sources, Leslie's analytical rigor was unmatched.

At the onset of the Ebola outbreak in early 2014, President Barrack Hussein Obama, the nation's 44th President, requested her by name for a briefing after her analysis appeared in a President's Daily Brief (PDB). Three days later, she sat in the White House Situation room with the President, his chief of staff, national security advisor, and members of the National Security Council.

Her insight into the region and ability to articulate the conditions on the ground left the audience with few questions. She would accurately forecast Ebola's outbreak in the region and regularly brief advisors and medical teams traveling to the area. Leslie was the most sought after analyst in the intelligence community for West African issues, despite her youth.

"Okay. CIA has submitted several requests for information (RFI). First, they would like to know what we know about the Kenema Mosque. Everything we have is what they want. Profiles, members, imagery, financials, they want it all," said Leslie.

The requirement was a bit vague like so many other requests from policy makers or other intelligence agencies.

"That narrows it down for us, huh?" said Jeremy.

"Second, they want to know if there are any links between the Kenema Mosque and transportation companies. Langley is concerned that when more Ebola infections occur, more people will attempt to flee the region. Lastly, they also want to know if we have heard any chatter on biological weapons moving into or out of the region."

"There are no bio weapons in West Africa," said Jordan, as if the group did not already know that.

Jordan was the newest member of Leslie's team. She was selected by Human Resources, but never Leslie's first choice.

"The request came from DO, so my suspicion is that they are running an operation in the area and need whatever we have. Jeremy, I want you to run query searches on all reports with the keywords Kenema Mosque. Carl, begin a link diagram analysis of the Mosque's leader, staff, maintenance, then further down. Run all known associates, friends, family, etc, etc. Maybe we'll pick up something before noon."

Leslie assumed searching for the words 'Kenema Mosque' would yield a productive outcome from the classified database. There were very few clandestine reports coming in from the region. Therefore, she expected the results would be manageable for analysis in the short time she had available.

Tactical intelligence collection and support to military operations mostly focused on Iraq, Syria, Yemen, and Somalia. Strategic collection efforts included Russia, China, and North Korea. West Africa was not a priority given the immense challenges confronting President Obama and his national security team. That is until December 2013, when Ebola struck a young child in Guinea.

The President was decisive from the beginning of the Ebola outbreak, despite media attacks from conservative outlets. A cautious and thoughtful man, he received periodic updates and briefings on the situation in West Africa. When the President and his team anticipated the situation spiraling out of control, he issued instructions for the Department of Defense (DOD) to deploy medical teams and supplies to the region.

Leslie instructed the team to work until twelve. They would then reassemble to discuss what they learned. Leslie returned to her office and immediately called Joe. The urgency of the request still bothered her.

"Joe. I have the team working on some things now. But can I ask why the rush?"

"Come on up to my office, Leslie. I was just about to go find you."

Leslie entered Joe's office. He was a middle-aged man who had served with INR for over twenty-five years. He served as the Deputy Director of the Africa Directorate, and never promoted again. It did not trouble the man. He always felt more comfortable inside INR's analytical offices, and senior executive service (SES) never really excited him. A higher pension and rank were not worth the years of headaches, inability to implement change, and time spent traveling to unproductive conferences. Joe was where he belonged.

"Leslie, what I'm about to tell you stays with us, got it?"

"Yes, of course."

"Langley's real concern is that Islamic State HQ has directed someone at the Kenema Mosque to transport an individual with Ebola to the United States. Larry and I think it is insane. Langley concurs. The probability of even trying is less than ten percent while the probability of success is near zero percent."

"If everyone is so sure the hypothesis is nuts, then why task my team?"

"Langley wants another look. And you're the best in this part of the world, Leslie."

Leslie sat back in her chair and looked into Joe's eyes. The idea did not seem as far-fetched to Leslie. Groupthink in the intelligence community regularly leads to failure. She thought back to the 9/11 failure where most terrorism and Al Qaeda analysts couldn't imagine a scenario that involved planes flying into the world trade center towers and the Pentagon. This had the same feeling, she thought to herself.

She was unaware of any active terror groups near Kenema looking to strike the United States. Sure, it had its share of gangs and criminal organizations, but Islamic State and AL Qaeda were not active there.

"Why is that crazy, Joe?"

"Leslie, who is going to infect themselves with Ebola and attempt to enter the United States? And even if they do, there is no chance for an outbreak here."

"Just because it hasn't been tried doesn't mean it's crazy. Look at 9/11. The hypothesis is intriguing."

"Leslie, let's forget about a possible outbreak here for now and stick to the likely exit points. Langley wants locations to potentially target for collection if necessary. You can get back to the outbreak tomorrow."

"Okay. We'll have some data for CIA in a couple of hours."

As Leslie began the short walk back to her office, the crazy notion of an Ebola-infected terrorist attempting to enter the United States was a reasonable course of action for Islamic State. If successful, the deep psychological impact to America would result in a collapsing stock market, the potential for hundreds, or maybe thousands of infections, and widespread general panic. If the plot failed, Islamic State would lose nothing.

As she sat in the plush leather chair, her mind became fixated on a scenario that would be unimaginable. *What if the terrorist rode the subway rail system in a major metropolitan city? What if that person spent an entire day coughing or sneezing in crowded metro cars?* The deadly virus could then transmit from commuter to commuter. Infected individuals, mistaking their symptoms for the common cold or flu, would then infect countless others during their daily commutes. The number of infections could theoretically be in the thousands.

Leslie looked at the map of Sierra Leone. Daunting she thought to herself. There were hundreds of methods and locations to escape from Sierra Leone. The individual could fly, walk, drive, or travel by boat.

Leslie began to *red team*, a technique taught to intelligence analysts. The method is simple in theory. The analyst will look at problems or courses of action through the eyes of his or her adversary. Unfortunately, analysts rarely practice the technique, often because they do not understand their enemy or learn to think like them. Sun Tzu would be disappointed.

In order for Leslie to think critically, she had to clear her mind. First, she would direct Jordan to create a PowerPoint slide with a map of Sierra Leone. Jordan would then highlight the airports and airfields within the country, and finally, all marinas along the east coast. Secondly, she directed Jordan to contact the National Center for Medical Intelligence (NCMI) and request a conference call for 10:30 AM. Leslie knew one of the analysts there. She met her in Washington, D.C. during a symposium over the summer, and the two remained lovers ever since.

National Reconnaissance Office, Chantilly, Virginia – November 6, 9:35 AM

Reginald Carter assumed his official duties as the Director, Mission Operations Directorate (MOD) at the National Reconnaissance Office (NRO), the first African American to accomplish the honor. It was long overdue. He previously served as the interim Director for five months, after his boss retired unexpectedly after a routine colon cancer screening.

The National Reconnaissance Office, formed in 1961, is one of the seventeen intelligence agencies in the United States. Its directive is to design, build and operate the nation's spy satellites. Without the brilliant engineers and scientists at NRO, strategic intelligence collection would come to a standstill.

NRO built satellites for several government agencies, including National Security Agency (NSA), National Geospatial-Intelligence Agency (NGA) and the Defense Intelligence Agency (DIA). These satellites provided signals intelligence (SIGINT), geospatial imagery intelligence (GEO-INT) and Measurement and Signature Intelligence (MASINT).

His administrative assistant was on the line.

"Sir, I have a Doug Weatherbee on the line for you. He says it is urgent. He would like to go secure."

"Patch him through to the STU, Naomi."

Reginald referred to the Secure Telephone Unit on his desk. The STU is a secure telephone line found in most offices within intelligence agencies. When a key on the phone is turned, conversations become encrypted and secure. It allows users to communicate without fear of monitoring.

"Reginald, it's Doug. I need some imagery. I don't have the time for a high priority request."

"What does CIA need now?" asked Reginald.

He grew tired of CIA's short-term wishes years ago.

"I'd like some images of the Kenema Mosque. I'll send the exact grid coordinates with the request to your collection management office."

"What NIIRS resolution are you looking for?"

"How about seven or better."

NIIRS stood for the National Imagery Interpretability Rating Scale. Satellite images were rated on quality. The higher the imagery rating on a scale of one to nine, the clearer the image becomes. Modern satellites have the ability to "zoom in" and capture NIIRS nine ratings. A rating of nine allows an image that shows the number of screws on the side of a missile.

"I don't think that will be a problem. I will talk to one of my collection managers. Will 1:00 PM work, Doug?"

"Yes sir, it will."

Fort Detrick, Maryland - November 6, 10:30 AM

Ten-thirty am was quickly approaching, Kerry thought to herself. Leslie would be calling any moment.

The telephone rang precisely at ten-thirty am. Leslie was always punctual, regardless of the occasion.

"Hi, Kerry. Do you have some time to spin me up on early Ebola symptoms and dormant periods?"

"Sure. How much time do you have?"

"About ten minutes. I've got a hot request and work to do."

Kerry, a strong-willed former nurse, joined the National Center for Medical Intelligence (NCMI) in 2011. She spent time in western Africa after high school while serving in the Peace Corps. That was the primary reason for her assignment to the West African analysis team.

The NCMI is a component of the Defense Intelligence Agency. Its mission is to perform predictive analysis of health issues that could affect US military and civilian populations. It works closely with the Centers for Disease Control (CDC) in Atlanta, Georgia.

"Okay, Leslie. I'll try to spin you up on what we know."

Kerry first started with the symptoms, which included fever, headache, muscle pain, weakness, fatigue, and vomiting.

"Symptoms are known to appear as early as two days based on our research. But they average eight to ten days."

"Those are the signs of the common cold or flu," said Leslie.

"True, but also of malaria and typhoid seen in regions stricken by the disease," said Kerry.

"Then how can medical professionals accurately diagnose the disease to determine if it is, in fact, Ebola?"

"That's the challenging part. There are several diagnostic tests available including virus isolation, polymerase chain reaction (PCR) and antigen capture enzyme-linked immunosorbent assay. Sometimes it takes three days after symptoms start for the disease to be diagnosed from a blood sample."

"Okay Kerry, so even patients suspected of contracting the disease are isolated until tests confirm or deny the presence of Ebola, right?"

"Yes."

Leslie pressed her further.

"What if a person with Ebola rode the blue line from the Springfield metro station to the Pentagon? Could there still be infections by simply coughing or sneezing?"

Leslie referred to one of the metro lines found in Washington, D.C. that moved tens of thousands of passengers daily.

"Yes, of course. Imagine the number of people who ride the metro each day who have a cold, cough, headache, or other issues impacting their immune system."

Kerry, already wondering why Leslie called rather than speaking at their townhouse, asked why?

"I will talk to you about it later," said Leslie.

"What time do you think you'll be home?"

"It's probably going to be late, babe. Can you make me a plate?"

"Of course, I'll wait up."

Leslie wished Kerry a great day and hung up. She immediately began to think about the problem further. She would ignore Joe's instructions and formulate scenarios.

Leslie would not do what so many of her predecessors did before 9/11. No hypothesis, no matter how unlikely, would go unexamined.

New York, New York – November 6, 11:30 AM

Climbing out of his black Chevrolet Suburban, Peter Marsico and three other men made their intimidating presence known. Heavily armed with snub-nosed shotguns and MP5 machine guns, the Hercules team wore combat helmets and body armor. This morning's last stop would be at the New York Stock Exchange, along the Broad Street entrance.

Many tourists stopped talking and gazed at the team while others simply froze, clearly startled by their presence. A few local vendors, though familiar with the team's presence over the years, still looked awestruck. The crowd looked on with immense pride, clearly satisfied with Police Commissioner Raymond Kelly's decision to create the team and others like it after 9/11.

A few yards from the team stood Jason, a member of the intelligence division at the New York City police department. His job this morning, was to observe the crowd adjacent to the Hercules team.

Jason looked for suspicious individuals who might try videotaping the team or write notes about their equipment and weapons. He also looked for alarmed individuals who may have been scouting the area. He noticed nothing out of the ordinary except a few individuals taking pictures.

As soon as the team exited their SUV, the radio call came in.

"Team Delta, proceed to New York City Finance Department building, 66 John Street. Shots fired. Possible hostage situation on the third floor."

The team quickly entered the Chevrolet Suburban and sped off. Within minutes, they arrived at the building finding two other New York City patrol cars parked at the building's front entrance.

"What do we know?" asked Peter.

"Not much. Dispatch called and said there was an individual on the third floor. A couple of shots were overheard. Inside one of the offices is a man holding a female hostage. SWAT is on the way."

"How far?"

"Maybe fifteen minutes. But in this traffic, might be longer."

"I'm moving my team in. Inform dispatch. Secure the people coming out."

Working his way through the two dozen citizens scrambling through the door, Peter and his team moved in. Security guards were calmly instructing the building's employees to exit quickly with their hands up.

"You know which office the hostage is in?" asked Peter to the first security guard he met.

"Third floor, office 306."

"What do we know about her captor?"

"He's carrying some sort of pistol. I'm not sure what kind."

Peter's team quickly climbed the stairs and arrived on the third floor. Office 306 would be to the right.

As Peter and his team slowly moved down the hallway, they could hear shouting. There were a few frightened employees still in their locked offices. However, the panic-stricken third floor was mostly quiet as some employees chose to remain in place and sheltered.

Peter carefully approached office 306. Inside he could hear a woman clearly in distress.

"Shut up, this is the last fricking time. Shut up!" yelled the deranged man.

"Hey, buddy. This is Peter Marsico of the New York City police department. What's the problem?"

The gunman, rattled by his presence, turned toward the door.

"Don't come in here man. I've got a gun."

Peter could tell the man was frantic.

"Stay away, or I'm going to shoot her," yelled the gunman.

"Why would you do that, man?" he asked while peering into the office.

Peter observed the gunman standing behind the woman with his weapon pointed at the door.

"I'm going to kill her man. I mean it. Don't come in here."

Peter concluded the man was under the influence of alcohol or some kind of illegal narcotic. He was not convinced the gunman was serious. Rationally talking to the man and calming him down was not going to happen in this situation, thought Peter to himself. Aware a hostage negotiation team would be arriving soon, Peter turned to his group.

"I'm going in. I don't think we can wait for the negotiators," whispered Peter to his team.

Peter entered the room with his pistol in hand, pointing toward the floor along his right hip.

"I told you not to come in here man," yelled the gunman as he erratically pointed the weapon at Peter.

"I just want to talk. No one is going to hurt you."

The gunman fired at Peter hitting his body armor above the left chest. Peter instantly drew his weapon and aimed at the gunman. The single shot hit the man's head and pushed his body into the window. Three seconds later, he lay dead on the floor.

Frantically screaming, the woman rushed to Peter.

"Ma'am, go outside. Some officers will help you."

Peter walked up to the gunman and saw his unresponsive body on the floor. He figured he killed the man but checked his pulse to be sure.

A few minutes later, New York City police units swarmed the finance department building. Ambulances and other public safety representatives found their way as well. As Peter and his team descended to the first floor, they knew what would await them that afternoon.

This was Peter's first deadly shooting on the New York City police force since he graduated from the police academy six years ago. With the reputation of a brash former Navy Seal, he knew there would be scrutiny.

Peter understood there would be an investigation. His superiors would question his decision to enter the room. Hostage negotiators were on their way, which would only add to the complexity of the investigation. Trusting the process, and having a spotless record, Peter felt his actions were justifiable and correct given the tactical situation.

He and the rest of his Hercules team were now on their way back to the Counterterrorism Bureau headquarters. His Commander, a salty old Brooklyn cop and member of the unit since its inception in 2002, waited patiently.

Errol Flynn Marina, Port Antonio, Jamaica – November 4, 10:45 AM

Dayo Bundu arrived at the Errol Flynn Marina. Its tropical beauty and breathtaking views of the nearby lush hills and the enchanting Blue Mountains mesmerized the young man. He observed the clear blue waters of the lagoon and even caught a glimpse of the cruise ship filled with excited tourists. Having just arrived the evening before at the Sangster International Airport in Montego, he was eager to perform his task.

Dayo would scout the Marina and observe for any law enforcement personnel. Port Antonio had the reputation as a safe community with low crime rates. He assumed he would encounter a minimal twenty-four-hour security force and the occasional harbor patrol.

Located near the south end of the West Harbor and adjacent to the launching ramp, Dayo spotted a possible helicopter landing area. He thought three or four helicopters could land there if needed. A few minutes later, a helicopter descended into the area that confirmed his calculation.

Dayo was feeling hungry, and he made his way to the crew bar. While casually strolling, he noticed a swimming pool and shower facilities. He even spotted a small building used to clean laundry. The marina had everything his visitors might require, if needed.

He took some notes while sipping local rum punch. The Sheikh ordered him to stay away from alcohol and other such vices, but how would anyone know, he thought to himself. Dayo was unclear how long his trip in the city would be, so he took every opportunity to enjoy himself.

After finishing Ackee and salt fish, a Jamaican national dish, Dayo made his way to the shipyard and fueling jetty. After speaking with one of the marina's employees there, he learned the marina's security team conducted twenty-four-hour patrols of the shipyard. The added security was reasonable and no threat to his visitors.

Dayo returned to the Trident Hotel in Port Antonio. Situated on the flawless, pristine waters of the Caribbean, the upscale hotel offered all the amenities Dayo needed while he waited. He had known Sheikh Cissi for fifteen years, and the Sheikh's trust in Dayo was evident by the plush location he found himself. He checked his watch and realized it was time to call him soon.

Using the phone located in one of the conference rooms, he placed the international call to Kenema. Aware of the electronic eavesdropping techniques used by the National Security Agency and other western countries, Dayo's call was short and informal. He and the Sheikh had rehearsed it well.

"Sahr. Hello. I arrived yesterday evening. The passports are in order, and things here look great. I visited the Mosque this morning. They are anxious to begin the student exchanges."

"Oh, that's excellent Dayo. How was the flight from Cuba?"

"It was safe, and the people here are so inviting."

"Very good, Dayo. Call me in a few days with an update."

The two proceeded to make pleasantries for another minute or so and quickly hung up.

Sheikh Cissi, listening attentively for the words safe and inviting, believed his quickly devised scheme was on track for stage one. Stage two belonged to his trusted captain and crew.

Raqqa would be pleased he thought. They had to be, considering the amount of the deposit to his Mosque's Bank in Freetown. The transfer, a sum equivalent to three hundred thousand US dollars, routed through several international financial institutions, paid for the operation. Sheikh Cissi had no intention of disappointing Raqqa, despite being located thousands of miles away. The Islamic State had a deep reach.

Kenema, Sierra Leone - Nov 6, 3:45 PM

Manjo and his group returned to the firing range. Next up was the Chinese type 54 pistol, also known as the "black star."

The type 54 pistol, first copied from the Soviet Tokarev TT-33 in 1951, is still in use in some Chinese military forces, specifically the People's Liberation Army (PLA). Consumers of the effective, but sometimes unreliable pistol, are still in Mozambique, Angola, and Sudan, among others. It is still the choice of many criminal organizations found in western Africa.

Manjo was nervous. He had difficulty controlling his breathing. The discussion with Foday was still fresh on his mind. Nevertheless, he had to focus on his target.

After Manjo and the other trainees had received their magazines, they received instructions to load their pistols. They could begin engaging their targets when ready.

Manjo raised his left hand and fired. The bullet hit its intended target.

Death came quickly to the young man standing to the left of Manjo. The single shot to his head entered above his right temple and into his brain.

"Stop firing. Stop firing. Stop firing," yelled the old gray-bearded man.

The two men to Manjo's right were clearly distressed. Dazed and confused, they looked at each other hoping one would reassure the other that all was okay. They had absolutely no idea of what just transpired or why Manjo shot Julius. Nor did they have time to react.

Manjo stood over the lifeless body. Blood was oozing from the man's right head. Manjo thought it would be bloodier. The act of killing a man had not yet set in. He stared across the field and into the bright blue skies. Remorse and guilt consumed him, though no outward signs were evident.

Foday began barking instructions.

"Musa and Tejan, Manjo was ordered to kill Julius. We caught him stealing from the Mosque a few days ago. Sheikh Cissi will not tolerate such criminal behavior. He was a disgrace to our Mosque. Manjo killed him as he was instructed."

He turned to Manjo who still gazed into the tree line.

"Manjo, you will be joining our brothers in Iraq and Syria soon. You are now ready."

Manjo rotated to Foday and looked into the man's eyes. He shared Foday's optimism.

"Musa and Tejan, take Julius to the trees up ahead. Dig the ditch at least four feet into the ground. Come find me after it's done."

Foday turned back to Manjo.

"Manjo, walk with me."

Manjo did as he was directed.

"How do you feel, Manjo?"

"It was a little harder than I thought."

"It's much harder to kill a man up close. It is more personal. It is intimate. Not many young men could do what you just did," said Foday.

"So, am I leaving soon?"

"Yes, you and I will both be leaving," said Foday as he put his arm around Manjo.

Foday and Manjo soon returned to the shelters. Foday instructed Manjo to resume his studies and that someone would pick him up before the drive back to Kenema.

About an hour after Musa and Tejan began shoveling the soft dirt from the ground, their ditch reached four feet in depth as Foday instructed. Tejan returned to the shelters and found Foday. He proudly professed the ditch was ready.

"Very good, Tejan. Soon you will be following in Manjo's footsteps. I'll be there shortly."

A few minutes later, Foday and one of his associates arrived at the ditch. Foday inspected the hole and was pleased.

As he stood back up at the front of the ditch, he reached behind his back, pulled out his "black star" pistol and shot both of the young men. Foday had killed before, and they died quickly. At least he was merciful.

Sheikh Cissi ordered the killings to ensure the young trainees could never speak again, if questioned. The new recruits had not yet earned his trust and were expendable.

"Bury them, Victor. I will drive Manjo back to the Mosque. Check in with me when you get there."

Manjo and Foday drove east back toward Kenema. Their unlikely journey together was already underway.

Euro Airport Basel-Mulhouse-Freiberg, Germany – November 6, 2:15 PM

Jurgen and his co-pilot parked the Airbus A330 aircraft into hangar seven. Paul and Markus were waiting for him. He smiled in their direction but sensed something was wrong. Paul did not appear pleased as Jurgen and Lukas exited the plane.

"Lukas, Markus and I need to speak with Jurgen in private. There has been a delay in the transport until tomorrow. Go home and wait for instructions. Good work yesterday."

Lukas could feel the tension in the air and quickly left the hangar. He had only been Jurgen's co-pilot for nine months but sensed his growing dependence on alcohol during previous operations. He wondered if Paul had made the connection as well.

Paul motioned Jurgen to walk with him to the vehicle near the rear of the hangar.

"Our delivery at the marina was nearly compromised last night. One of our officers in Cyprus is dead. What the hell happened?"

Jurgen acted puzzled by Paul's request and proceeded to give an accounting of his activities after arrival in Larnaca. Paul, a clandestine veteran, and expert at body language, knew right away Jurgen made an error in judgment.

"After I landed I checked into my hotel and went to a club." Jurgen felt he was in trouble and became jittery as his breathing intensified. One of Markus' associates joined them and stood behind Jurgen.

"Did you speak to anyone at the club about the operation?"

"No, Paul. I have never discussed an operation with anyone. Not even my wife."

"Then you won't mind taking a polygraph, Jurgen?"

Jurgen became more uncomfortable. He was not a trained operative, only a contract pilot, who delivered cargo to destinations arranged by his employers.

"Why the hell would I need to do that, Paul?"

"Do I need to remind you we lost an agent? This is non-negotiable Jurgen."

Jurgen was surrounded by Paul, Markus and an associate. He felt cornered and trapped. There was no way to get out of this, he thought to himself. He determined honesty might be the appropriate choice.

"Paul, I might have said something to a girl there. All I said was that some cargo was going to the marina. I drank a bit too much. That is all I said. She was just some girl looking for a good time. I would not know anything else, Paul. You know that," said Jurgen frantically.

"We never talk about our business, Jurgen. I thought I made that clear years ago. Never."

"I'm sorry Paul. I will stop drinking. I know I have a problem. It starts now. I promise."

"Would you remember the girl if you saw her again?"

"I think so," said Jurgen immediately.

Paul's eyes turned to Markus as he barely nodded his head to the longtime friend and trusted associate.

Markus struck Jurgen in the back of his head with his pistol. Jurgen fell to the ground and blood swelled his head from the impact. Jurgen was now unconscious.

Paul and his two associates placed Jurgen in the back of their tinted black sedan and began the trip to the farmlands at Brand-Erbisdorf.

Waiting for Markus at the entrance of the barn, a middle-aged man opened its old wooden doors.

During the trip, Paul received updates from Rick and his team in Cyprus. Several images of individuals flashed across his secure iPad. Rick's team had spent all night and the morning looking at criminal gangs in and around Larnaca. Narrowing their search to ,known organized syndicates and their associates, rather than street gangs or petty criminals, would increase Paul's chances of identifying the woman. Rick had concluded the individuals at the marina were professionals.

A short time after their arrival, Jurgen awoke and was clearly startled. Tied to a chair in the center of the barn, he began pleading his case to Paul, who sat directly in front of him.

Paul proceeded to show Jurgen pictures of individuals from Larnaca. Included were known girlfriends and wives of the Spiro Kostopoulos syndicate. Jurgen looked at nearly twenty photographs and none appeared like Sonia.

"I don't see her, Paul."

"Look again, Jurgen. I have a dead CIA officer in Cyprus. The woman you spoke to is responsible."

"She's not there," he began whimpering. "I'm sorry, Paul. Please."

Paul sat up. Even if Jurgen identified a woman, the intelligence would be worthless since he was admittedly intoxicated at the time he met her. Rick would want to know how he obtained the intelligence. Paul was not going to send Rick and his team on a wild goose chase. Their time would be more valuable working with the Cyprus authorities and Larnaca police.

Paul was a fiercely loyal man and gifted leader and experienced a momentary ethical crisis. Though no stranger to killing rogue contractors or foreign spies, he never took a liking to killing. To kill someone meant the individual deserved it. He was unsure if Jurgen had reached this threshold.

Jurgen and Paul reached the termination phase of their relationship. Though most clandestine officers end relationships with their assets due to retirement, job transfers, and other routine life circumstances, rarely did termination mean death.

The problem confronting Paul was clear. A man succumbing to alcohol and incapable of keeping secrets became a liability. Paul's risk of exposure due to a loose tongue was too great of a risk to his operations. Jurgen had to die.

Paul turned to Markus.

"Do it now."

Without hesitation, Markus drew his firearm and fired a single shot into Jurgen's head. Jurgen's head jerked back and then slouched forward in the chair.

"Take me back to the hangar, Markus."

Paul and Markus drove back to the airport while one of the men in the barn began the task of disposing Jurgen's body. No one would ever find Jurgen again, including his wife.

As Paul's plane reached cruising altitude over Germany, he had two things on his mind. First, the problem in Larnaca would be in Rick's hands to solve. He was confident they would identify their agent's killers. Secondly, he needed to convince Michael his operation was not in jeopardy, at least as far as he could tell.

Port of Iskenderun, Turkey – November 6, 2:45 PM

Michael and Elif arrived at the designated pier and waited for Walid and Nanook. They were to arrive at 3:00 PM, per their previous update. The pair already prepped their truck for delivery.

The long journey to and from Larnaca took its toll on the two men. Both men were experienced seafaring captains and familiar with the Mediterranean. Rotating behind the console every three to four hours, eased the burden.

Once the Sophia came to rest, its crew, along with Michael and Elif, began to unload the cargo into their truck. Walid and Nanook had already packed the AT-4 weapons into new containers they brought with them. The transfer to the Range Rover took ten minutes. Elif chose the vehicle to remove any suspicions from Turkish security or police forces as they approached the border.

Elif and Michael soon approached Highway 91 and moved north. The beautiful three-hour trip began with breathtaking sights of the Mediterranean to the east. Flanked to their west were the ancient Nur Mountains, also known as the Mountains of Holy Light. Nanook and Walid traveled close behind and would provide support during the extraction of Haris and subsequent delivery of the AT-4s.

Michael and Elif passed the time by vividly sharing memories of their families, childhood, and training. A mutual trust already developed between the two professional spies and they felt at ease in each other's presence. Of course, operational specifics outside of securing Haris and delivering the AT-4s, were off limits.

As the two approached Nizip, Elif called Raif.

"Raif, we are about five miles from Nizip. We will be at your location in twenty minutes."

"Very good, Elif, I have some food and drink for us."

"Is everything ready for the evening?"

"Yes."

Michael found Nizip warm and inviting. The streets were crowded with residents and lined with shopkeepers and coffee houses. However, he did observe some makeshift camps to the west of the city, probably being used to house refugees fleeing the nightmare in Syria.

The house on the northeastern edge of Nizip was small and surrounded by trees and brushes. It offered a small opening leading from the driveway that ended alongside the house. There, Walid and Nanook parked the truck carrying the AT-4s. Each man would take turns remaining in the vehicle, while the other napped. Elif led Michael to the front door where Raif stood waiting for them.

The three sat down where Raif would brief them on the plan to deliver the AT-4s.

"How many buyers will be there, Raif?"

"My contact said there would be himself and two other vehicles. I assume around five or six men."

"Will they be carrying weapons, Raif?" asked Elif. Michael sat back and listened. This was her operation, and he was along for the ride.

"Yes, they usually carry weapons."

"What kind of weapons? Small arms, rifles?"

"Both."

"Are you sure your contact will be there?"

"Yes."

"Who is your contact?"

"A colleague I work with when selling at the border. He can be trusted."

"Is he YPG?" asked Elif. After all, she was placing some trust in the smuggler.

"No. But like me, he has family fighting in Syria."

"How long have you worked with him?"

"About two years now. It will be fine, Elif."

Michael was not so sure. He knew Raif had provided her information for a year, but this would be the first time she would be on the border. Michael was not as concerned for Elif's safety, rather the reliability and loyalty of the contact. Michael knew she was capable of defending herself.

"Do they know you will not be alone?"

"Yes. I told them I would have a few friends."

"Where is the precise location, Raif?"

Raif moved the map closer to Elif and Michael. Raif pointed his finger to a tiny patch of land at the end of the trail that ran directly toward the Turkish and Syrian border. To the east of the dirt road, and just a couple of hundred feet further, was the mighty Euphrates River.

"We will park as close to the trees as we can. Then we will walk to the banks of the river and wait for their arrival," said Raif.

"How will they get across the border? That looks like barbed wire to me."

"This is an older map, and only some of the wire is still there. YPG controls the area on the Syrian side. It is one of many crossing points they use to get into and out of Turkey."

"What about Turkish border patrols? I know they have them, and assume they patrol the area."

"They do, Elif, but I pay the border chief in Karkamis each time I make a delivery. They have an outpost near the border. We will simply drive by, conduct our business and return the way we came in. I am leaving now to make the payment."

Elif finished and was satisfied with the details Raif provided. She had a few more questions but could wait until Raif's return. She and Michael would use the time during Raif's absence to finalize plans for Haris' escape.

Elif sent a message to Tel Aviv. It included a quick update on the extraction plan for Haris and their plan to deliver the weapons. Elif included the exact grid coordinates so 'eyes' could track their movement and observe the area.

Mossad, like many intelligence agencies, enjoyed the luxuries of overhead collection, particularly satellites flying in low earth orbit. Israeli drones were not available to support Elif due to their location along the border. The risk of detection was too great.

Supporting Elif and Michael would be the Tec Star spy satellite, an Israeli built synthetic aperture radar with real-time video feed, among other collection capabilities. Launched from India, the Tec Star was capable of real-time intelligence support to Israeli intelligence, military commanders, and policy makers concerned with ongoing developments in the Middle East.

Michael was impressed and thankful that Elif was a deliberate and thoughtful planner. Elif was clearly a seasoned and decisive operative, he thought to himself. Michael still had some reservations with Raif and his contact, however, Elif trusted the man and so he went along. He had no choice.

"I like the area south of Karanfilkoy," said Elif.

"It's open and in no man's land. There will probably be a few Islamic State snipers in the area," said Michael.

"True. However, my intelligence says they do not have night vision capability. Either way, it is going to be tricky for all of us. We will have Nanook and Walid in support. They will each have a sniper rifle fitted with night optics."

The Israeli Galil sniper rifle was a superb weapon and used by Israeli Defense Forces (IDF). It could fire twenty rounds and included a bipod for support. The stealthy characteristics of the weapon also included a flash hider and threads for silencers. Walid and Nanook would have the full complement of available items. Elif acquired the weapons after Mossad began supplying some of its agents and their contractors in the region for just such an occasion.

"It looks like there are some old buildings on the south side of town," said Michael.

"Yes, Michael. Imagery shows the buildings are uninhabited."

"It's practically a ghost town. That's good and bad for us."

"True. But good, I think," said Elif as she smiled at her American partner.

"We'll have to send Walid and Nanook in early. I would say ninety minutes to be safe. That should give them time to find good observation points."

"Agree. I will give Haris the grid coordinate for this destroyed farmhouse on the Syrian side. We will quickly cross the border and link up with Haris there. It's only a few hundred feet, and we should be back within minutes."

Michael was not keen on crossing the border with only Walid and Nanook in support. However, the barren wasteland along the border offered easy access into Syria. Not many people were trying to get into Syria, he thought to himself.

Innocent civilians fleeing the brutal civil war and Islamic State militants inside Syria, were aware of designated locations along the border to seek refuge. One of them was along the border between Karkamis and Jarabulus. Karanfilkoy was a good spot and away from Turkish attention.

"Where will Nanook and Walid be after we get him out?" asked Michael figuring Elif had already thought of it.

"I'm going to have them follow us. They will remain behind and provide support while we deliver the AT-4s. They may be YPG, but we can't be too careful."

"I thought you told Raif it would only be the three of us?"

"I did. I will tell him later," said Elif without concern.

"That might spook him."

"Yes. It might. However, he needs to sell the AT-4s. He will fall in line with it."

"If not, Elif?"

"Then we get Haris out. Moreover, you will get the intelligence you need. Raif will continue to be an asset, regardless."

Michael realized Elif had examined all angles of the operation. She was correct that Haris was the primary objective, while Raif's delivery to YPG was secondary. Mossad continued to live up to its reputation as one of the finest intelligence organizations in the world.

Barma, Sierra Leone – November 5 – 10:25 PM

Approximately nine miles north of Barma, Sierra Leone, the newly constructed emergency field hospital remained busy. The hospital sat on a small two-acre site nestled in between foliage. Built just two months ago with seventy-five beds, the hospital, and its remaining staff were overwhelmed. Nearly thirty percent of the doctors and nurses there became victims of the Ebola outbreak.

Mud surrounded the hospital while sludge occupied several locations through the camp. Some plank boards along the ground were evident, which eased the mud's relocation between housing tents, isolation shelters and staff quarters.

The morgue was located on the eastern side of the hospital. There were two deaths this evening, and another ambulance was on the way, presumably filled with Ebola patients. This place was the epitome of hell.

Fallubah, a loyal follower of Sheikh Cissi hid in the nearby trees. The last two hours were unpleasant for the subdued young man as he sat nearby the tent, which housed the lab. While waiting for his opportunity, he had to listen to the groans and cries of the infected. The sounds of the sick and dying began to affect him.

Security at the hospital site was nonexistent. There was no need for it, as Medicins Sans Frontieres never imagined someone trying to sneak onto the deadly site. Nor did they have the funds to pay anyone, if they could even find willing volunteers.

Fallubah noticed the lights of an approaching vehicle in the distance. Moments later he heard one of the doctors instruct the individuals inside the lab to join him. They were already dressed in their suits since they had to be ready for victims at any moment. Other staff members were already retired in their tents for the night. Fallubah found his opportunity.

He entered the tent through an opening in one of the corners nearest a pole. It was just large enough for him to slip through the narrow gap. As he stood up, he quickly scanned the tent for where the blood specimens were. It did not take him long to figure out which ones were contaminated with the Ebola virus.

Handwritten on many of the tubes included the words *positive with Ebola.* Also documented, were their arrival and date of death for those who perished.

Fallubah reached into his backpack and pulled out the contents he needed for transport. Included was a foam vial holder with nine slots, one plastic container, a hard case, and two ice bags. Reaching into the case, he placed the vial holder on the table.

Carefully removing each plastic tube with blood from Ebola victims, Fallubah began filling his vial holder. There were only six vials in the lab visible to him, more than enough he thought. It took him less than one minute.

His next step was to place the foam vial holder into the plastic container. Foam layered the top of the container to ensure the vials could not move during transport. Fallubah then moved the container into a hard case also layered with foam. The lightweight, watertight case had two powerful hinges and a padlock hasp, which added an extra layer of protection. Fallubah, satisfied the vials were secure, placed the plastic case into his backpack.

Fallubah would exit the tent the same way he entered. He carefully moved through the trees and arrived at his vehicle approximately fifteen minutes later. Sheikh Cissi will soon be pleased, he thought to himself.

Ar-Raqqa, Syria – November 6, 7:45 PM

Haris returned to his room and made his final preparations. Today would be his last day as a member of the Islamic State. He planned his escape in every detail from the moment he departed the Mosque to the drive north along the border. The only specifics he lacked were the linkup point with Ayse and the exact time of the rendezvous.

He would make his way along Highway 4 directly to Jarabulus, blend in with the civilians there, and wait for the extraction. The trip would take approximately three hours as he anticipated several Islamic State roadblocks near Jarabulus and Ain Issa.

Haris exited the Mosque and quickly found a cab, a preferred method of transport for Shirazi and other top commanders. The use of taxis allowed Islamic State to move freely within the city and avoid detection from overhead drones.

"Haris entered a cab and is moving west. Should I follow him?" asked the man.

"Yes. Let me know where he goes."

Ahmed Al-Diri, the man responsible for Shirazi's protection in Ar-Raqqa, instructed that Haris would be followed. Haris was a trusted confidant and one of Shirazi's top personal bodyguards, but Al-Diri had strict instructions from the Caliph. Ahmed's spies would follow all members of Shirazi's protection team, whenever they departed his location.

Haris was aware of the procedure as Shirazi adopted the rule months ago, after a failed assassination attempt from a rival Islamic State cleric near Mosul.

He arrived at the apartment building and quickly made his way to the drab studio. His small, lightweight rucksack, already packed earlier in the day, sat on the kitchen counter. Inside were his GPS-enabled cell phone, night vision goggles, two pistols, a map, flashlight, radio, and several bottles of water. He needed nothing else. Haris was either going to die tonight or cross the border and escape Shirazi's inevitable collapse.

"He's back in his apartment complex," said the man ordered to follow him.

"Wait a few minutes and see if he comes out," said Al-Diri.

Shirazi and Haris would soon depart the Mosque at 9:20 PM to move to another location. Al-Diri knew it was odd for Haris to leave so close to their departure. Shirazi moved through Ar-Raqqa every twenty-four hours in at least a dozen different locations which were chosen randomly.

Haris grabbed his pack and quickly moved to the bathroom in the back of the apartment. He opened the window, slid through it, and ventured out to the alley. Turning to his left, he quickly walked to the intersection to the nearest road and turned right. There he would make his way four blocks to where he parked his car a day earlier.

Within minutes, Haris was on Highway 4 traveling north.

"He is still in there."

"Go inside. Now. Find him. I want to speak with him."

The man did not hesitate and did as he was instructed. He quickly entered the apartment building and knocked on the door. His knocks became louder as Haris did not respond. Finally, the man plowed his boot onto the door handle and broke it open.

Nothing. Haris was not inside. The man then moved into the hallway and checked the bathroom. The window was open. He was gone.

Haris was running for his life.

"He's not here. The window to his bathroom is open. He must have left."

Al-Diri was furious. Recognizing the gravity of the situation, he immediately made his way into the Sheikh's corner suite and delivered the news. Unsure of Haris' motivation, his first consideration was to the Caliph.

"Caliph, Haris has left. He went to his apartment and fled through his bathroom window."

Shirazi sat calmly but perplexed by Al-Diri's update.

"Are you sure? He has been with us for many years. I find the idea preposterous."

"I am. I want to get you out now. I will find Haris, Caliph."

Shirazi turned away from Al-Diri for a moment and contemplated the many reasons why he might flee. This troubled the ruthless leader.

"Where will he go?" asked Shirazi.

"I doubt he would move south into Iraq. We control all the lands to the border. Assad controls most of the territory to our west, and I am sure he will not try to slip through regime forces. Since we control all lands east of Raqqa, my first guess would be northwest toward Turkey. His best chance of escape would be with the Kurds. It is only one hundred and sixty kilometers to the Turkish border. If I were fleeing, that's how I would do it."

"Bring him back alive, if possible. Alert all our commanders, nonetheless. Start with Hassan in Kobani. I will be ready momentarily."

Al-Diri notified the two men standing outside the suite that Shirazi would leave in five minutes.

Traveling at approximately ninety kilometers an hour, Haris soon made his way to Ain Issa. Ain Issa was a devastated small town along Highway 4 that Islamic State routed months earlier. Many of the residents were already dead or escaped the initial onslaught. Numerous buildings were empty and war-torn from artillery fires. Glancing at his GPS, he noticed he was approximately two kilometers from the city's entrance along Highway 4. Time for a look, he thought to himself.

Haris stepped onto the desert and looked through his night vision goggles, acquired years ago from a dead Iraqi officer near Fallujah. Peering down Highway 4, he saw no activity or signs of a checkpoint. He would enter Ain Issa with ease. As he began slowly driving into the town, he placed the banner of Islamic State onto his dashboard.

Winding his way through the narrow roads of Ain Issa, Haris observed the checkpoint directly in front of him. At the northern edge of town, a barricade consisting of loose barbed wire and two vehicles on each side of the road were visible.

"As-Salam-u-Alaikum," said Haris as his vehicle came to rest at the barricade. He noticed a four-foot gap between the wire and front bumper of the Islamic State pickup truck to his left.

"As-Salam-u-Alaikum. Who are you and where are you going?" asked the teenager.

"I'm Haris. I have a message for Hassan Akbar in Kobani. The Caliph has sent me."

"You have your papers?"

"Yes."

Haris handed the teenager his documentation proving Islamic State membership.

"Hold on. I will return in a few minutes."

Haris observed the boy walk to the vehicle on his left. Inside sat another young man but clearly older. Probably the leader of the security detail, Haris thought to himself. Haris remained calmly in the vehicle while the two talked.

The vehicle's passenger, along with the teenager, now walked back to Haris. Haris did not like the development.

"I was not told of any movement tonight," said the man.

"You weren't supposed to. I come from Raqqa. I need to speak with Hassan Akbar, commander in Kobani."

The young man, clearly unamused by his lack of awareness, pressed Haris further.

"My orders come from Hussein, my commander here in Ain Issa. You will have to wait until I get permission to let you out."

"I don't have time to wait. I need to see Akbar within the hour. My orders come from the Caliph himself. Do you and your commander want to be responsible for causing a delay in the Caliph's instructions? I am growing impatient. Let me through."

The brash young man thought for a moment. He was a recruit determined to prove himself to his commander and comrades. He grew tired of the security detail and craved an opportunity to fight in Aleppo. He would have none of it.

"I'm going to check with my commander. It will only be ten minutes at most. I cannot allow anyone to pass. You understand, don't you, Haris?" he said with a bit of sarcasm while looking at his paperwork.

Staring into the man's eyes and showing his displeasure, Haris simply said, "Make it quick."

Two minutes later Haris noticed one of the men in the vehicle along the right side of the barricade talking into his radio. His eyes were immediately focused on Haris as he turned to his associate sitting on the driver's side. The two men then slowly exited their vehicle.

Haris immediately felt uneasy and convinced something was wrong. Unsure of their intention, his nerves were flaring as he depressed the pedal on the floor. He drove directly toward the opening on the left side of the barricade. While making his escape, he collided with the right front engine compartment of the Islamic State vehicle.

He began speeding north along Highway 4 and noticed a vehicle behind him as he raced from Ain Issa. After a few minutes, Haris realized he would not lose the Toyota pickup truck to his rear. The driver and passenger sprayed bullets at Haris' Jeep but few hit their target. He also spotted a second vehicle coming into view.

Haris could no longer allow the pursuing vehicles to continue chasing him. An errant bullet would eventually hit a rear tire, he thought to himself. He had to fight.

Reaching for his AK-47 rattling on the passenger's seat, he grabbed hold of the weapon and placed the stock through the left window. Haris turned the steering wheel to the left and slammed on the brakes. Coming to a rest in the middle of the road, he waited for the approaching vehicles.

Looking through his sights, he calculated roughly five seconds before a good shot presented itself. He would aim at the driver hoping to cause the vehicle to swerve and crash.

Haris squeezed the trigger. The bullets sprayed through the driver's front windshield. The driver's chest shattered open, and he immediately lost control of the vehicle as it flipped onto the desert. The second man broke his neck and died instantly upon hitting the dirt.

In the distance, the second vehicle began to slow down. As the vehicle and its passengers were approaching Haris' position, a third vehicle came into view in the distance. The Islamic State fighters in Ain Issa were determined to catch Haris.

Haris recognized the situation changed drastically, and decided to turn the tables on his pursuers. He straightened his Jeep and sped toward the two vehicles who watched in bewilderment. As he closed the distance between the vehicles and himself, he quickly veered off the highway, slammed on his brakes and took aim at one of the vehicles.

Haris fired several bursts which killed the driver and wounded the passenger. The passenger exited through the door and raced behind his truck. He returned fire and sprayed bullets toward the front of Haris' jeep.

It finally arrived as Michael instructed. Unbeknownst to Haris, circling overhead was the MQ-9 Reaper drone equipped with the latest next generation precision guided munitions. A remotely piloted vehicle with operators as far away as Las Vegas, Nevada, the MQ-9 was capable of flying up to forty-two hours. Tonight, the drone would only fly a maximum of fourteen hours due to the full payload of munitions it was carrying.

Earlier, Michael had convinced Doug to push US Central Command for the support. He thought military drone pilots were vastly superior to those at CIA. Michael used them whenever he could. Wrestling two Reaper drones from United States Central Command (CENTCOM) was not easy, but Doug convinced them after discussing the potential intelligence windfall from Mossad's source.

The drone fired a single AGM 114 Hellfire II missile into the rear vehicle. The explosion killed each occupant instantly and body parts would hit the ground in moments. Haris was stunned by what just transpired, grabbed his pack, and leaped out of his jeep. He immediately began running into the desert.

He wondered if the next air strike would be directed at him. Haris was convinced that American military intelligence assessed the group of vehicles as Islamic State fighters traveling north toward Kobani. Haris moved approximately thirty meters away from the vehicle. He figured he should at least try to evade the drone, though its thermal Infrared (IR) capability would make it highly unlikely.

Haris heard his phone ringing while lying on the cold desert sand. It was Elif.

"Haris, it's Elif. Get back in your vehicle and keep moving. We will cover you until you are safely across the border. The American drones are above and will follow you."

"But how did you know where I was?" asked Haris.

"After you called, our assets picked you up. Never mind. Get moving Haris. We're watching the rendezvous point."

Haris immediately stood up and sprinted back to his vehicle. It would probably take Islamic State assets in Ain Issa a while to figure out what happened. In less than an hour, he would reach his designated location. Haris jumped into his jeep and continued north. Jarabulus would be more difficult, he thought to himself.

Kobani, Syria – November 6, 8:37 PM

Hassan Akbar and his deputy commanders were meeting at the old war-torn school building on the far southern side of Kobani. Kobani had become a barren wasteland where Islamic State fought from abandoned buildings and burnt out shops. The smell of rotting corpses filled the streets after brutal fighting the last few days.

His headquarters, filled with dust, a few rations of food, cases of water, and batteries for his radios, remained mostly barren with few Islamic State fighters.

Akbar, like many Islamic State fighters, communicated using short-range radios on the battlefield. He also used couriers, depending on the situation. Though easily intercepted, they provided a cheap method of communication. Specific tactical orders were rarely issued, but their commanders used the radios in cases of imminent danger or inspiring words of wisdom.

Usama Bin Laden famously thanked his loyal fighters at the Battle of Tora Bora in 2001, using short-range radios. Before slipping through the eastern passes leading into Pakistan, it appeared he and his fellow Al Qaeda fighters lost the battle. Al Qaeda quickly became overwhelmed while fighting Afghan Mujahedeen, the CIA special activities division, countless military aircraft, and United States Special Operations Forces.

Akbar's encrypted cell phone rang. He and other regional commanders used them in Syria and Iraq, along with senior members of the Military and Intelligence councils.

"Hassan. It is Ahmed. One of the Caliph's bodyguards has gone missing. I think he may be heading north."

"So, what, Ahmed. Why is this my concern?"

"The Caliph wants him captured quickly but kept alive. They go back many years from their days in Iraq."

"Ahmed, again, why is this my problem? You know what I'm dealing with here."

Hassan Akbar exercised great control on the phone. He despised Ahmed and felt he did not belong in Shirazi's inner circle. He was devious, temperamental, and showed little concern for the Caliphate. An ex-Iraqi senior intelligence officer for Saddam Hussein, Ahmed was driven by greed rather than by ideology.

Shirazi paid Ahmed well and their relationship dated back to Shirazi's imprisonment in Iraq in 2001. There, Ahmed showed Shirazi restraint from brutal interrogation typically performed by Iraqi intelligence. When Shirazi needed ex-regime soldiers and intelligence officers to expand the Islamic State, Ahmed was near the top of the list.

President Saddam Hussein did not have much on Shirazi then, and Ahmed figured he could be a reliable source for the regime in the future. He did not foresee President Bush and General Tommy Franks' expertise to crush Hussein's Republic Guards and remaining military forces in a matter of weeks in 2003.

In addition to Ahmed's status as ex-Iraqi intelligence, Hassan also disliked the man's lack of combat experience. While he and his fellow Islamic State loyalists fought the

Kurds, Syrian regime forces and western allies, Ahmed sat in Raqqa doing nothing. The Caliphate was expanding without Ahmed spilling his blood.

"The Caliph and I are concerned with his disappearance. The amount of information he holds on our operations here are significant. We cannot let him be questioned by Syrian forces, Turks or the United States."

"Why don't you send some of your men, Ahmed?"

"I can't spare them, Hassan. We are stretched thin since the Caliph is moving more frequently."

More gibberish from the Iraqi, Hassan thought to himself. Nevertheless, Shirazi's orders were clear and he had to obey.

"Who is he?" asked Hassan indicating his desire to get back to the business of capturing Kobani.

Ahmed revealed his name.

"Haris? Really? I never thought he would leave. Tell the Caliph I'll get the word out."

"Call me first, Hassan, if you have any news."

Unimpressed by Ahmed's arrogance and disrespect by issuing him the instruction, Hassan simply hung up the phone. Ahmed did not deserve a response nor was he worried about what he might think. Shirazi had always sided with his military commanders in the past.

Hassan sat back a moment and thought about what might happen if Haris tried to make his way toward Kobani. Worse yet, what if he slipped through? There were no good outcomes here, he thought to himself.

First, Shirazi would blame Hassan for his escape if the former bodyguard slipped through his lines. Secondly, Ahmed would probably get credit from the Caliph if his forces captured Haris. Therefore, there was nothing in it for him or his men. Third, by sending troops to set up additional security checkpoints around his area of operations, it left his fighters more thinly stretched than they already were.

Hassan issued orders to his deputy commander. There would be additional security patrols along the roads leading into and out of Islamic State positions around Kobani. His deputy would also send a dozen men to help patrol Jarabulus, one of Akbar's strong points in the region.

Creech Air Force Base, Nevada - November 6, 8:58 PM

Lieutenant Colonel (Lt Col) William Johnston sat at his console. One of the most experienced drone pilots in the United States Air Force, he had the good fortune and added pressure of flying one of the drones in support of CIA over Syria. He did not know who the man on the ground was, or why CIA wanted him alive, but he had a good imagination.

His only job tonight was to observe and report movement along Haris' route and engage any targets authorized by his Commander, Colonel Travis O'Malley, a stubborn and hard-headed Irishman from Long Island, New York. O'Malley, piloting the second drone, would be in constant contact with Michael Brennan using a secure satellite link. He would only refer to Michael as his call sign, *Ghost Rider*.

"I see some movement south of Kobani. Looks like four pickup trucks traveling southwest at approximately sixty kilometers an hour," said Johnston, a graduate from the United States Air Force Academy, located in Colorado Springs, Colorado.

"Copy. Keep eyes on them, Billy. Too bad we are flying protection detail tonight. These are good targets for Central Command."

"Wilco."

Johnston updated his boss again a few minutes later.

"They are moving away from Kobani. Now ten kilometers and still moving southwest."

"Do you see anything else?"

"Negative. I see nothing else moving in the area."

"Zoom out and check for additional moving target indicators (MTIs)."

"Still nothing."

"Copy. Stay with the pickups."

"Ghost Rider, we have four pickups moving toward Jarabulus. We see nothing else."

Michael simply replied, "Roger."

Haris was in trouble. Akbar's fighters only had to travel forty kilometers until they reached Jarabulus. He had no idea just how critical the brash and experienced Air Force Academy graduate would be in the coming hour.

Karanfilkoy, Turkey – November 6, 9:30 PM

Michael and Elif slowly approached the south side of Karanfilkoy. Walid and Nanook were already at their observation points. A barren desert lay in between the city and the Syrian border.

"What is the distance from you to the border?" asked Michael.

"Just under two hundred meters," said Nanook.

Michael observed the terrain, using his scope, and noticed two trails leading toward the border. He determined it made more sense to redeploy Nanook and Walid closer. The open area from Jarabulus to the linkup point was approximately one thousand yards, and he wanted to cover Haris' escape from the town if he came under fire.

He turned to Elif and offered the suggestion, respecting her authority over the two men. Elif agreed, and Walid and Nanook began their approach to the border.

Both men would slowly move along the trail and settled atop dunes located mere yards from the frontier. They could see Jarabulus clearly from their vantage points, checked in with Elif, and indicated they were in position. Michael was satisfied.

A few moments later, Elif's cell phone rang. It was Haris.

"I am approaching Jarabulus now. Another fifteen minutes or so," said Haris.

"Okay. We are ready, Haris. You may be speaking to my boss as he has direct contact with the drones flying above. Just make your way to the linkup point regardless of what happens. We are waiting for you."

"See you soon, Ayse."

Michael would have to wait a little while longer before Haris made his way to the extraction point. The man's intelligence had better be good, he thought to himself.

Kenema, Sierra Leone – November 6, 9:55 PM

Sheikh Cissi sat in his office. Foday soon joined him while carrying a large backpack. He wore jeans, sneakers and a casual red t-shirt with a Coca-Cola logo on the front.

"Are you ready, Foday?" asked Sheikh Cissi.

"Yes. We are leaving shortly and will make our way to Sulima. Fallubah assures me he will be off the coast by midnight. Manjo and I will arrive shortly before eleven o'clock. That will give us time to get to the beach and wait for the boat."

Sulima, a tiny coastal town in southeastern Sierra Leone, was the ideal location for Manjo and Foday to begin their voyage across the Atlantic. Located at the entrance to the Moa River, Sulima's pristine beaches would offer Foday and Manjo ideal spots to join Fallubah. Freetown, the largest city and port in Sierra Leone, did not afford Foday the secrecy he and Manjo required, due to local police and maritime surveillance forces.

"I pray for a safe and successful journey, my old friend. May Allah watch over you," said Cissi.

Foday stood up and offered his Sheikh a final tribute for entrusting him with the undertaking. This was his honor, and he would not disappoint Cissi or their Caliph.

A few minutes later, Foday and Manjo departed Kenema and headed south to Sulima. Manjo would never see his home again.

The forty-five-kilometer trip to Sulima took the two men nearly an hour, as they had to travel slowly over the muddy dirt road.

Foday finished issuing instructions to his driver who then turned the vehicle around and began to drive back to the Mosque. This would be the last time Foday communicated with Sheikh Cissi until the mission was over. The Caliph would eventually learn of its success or failure soon enough.

Foday and Manjo turned south along the beach and walked for approximately two hundred meters. There were no souls in sight; only the sounds of the crashing waves hitting the beach.

Manjo carried the lightweight and inflatable two-person rubber dinghy with them. Once the two men arrived at their chosen departure point, Manjo inflated the dinghy. Their next move was to simply sit and wait. Thirty minutes went by until they observed the boat in the distance.

Using his flashlight, Foday signaled three bursts of light toward the boat. Nothing.

A few moments later, he tried again. A flashlight aboard the boat did the same. Time to move.

Manjo and Foday grabbed their backpacks and slowly walked into the frigid Atlantic Ocean. Manjo worked his way into the dinghy as the waters began rising past their waistlines. He was not an experienced swimmer, and so Foday would have the burden of swimming out past the waves as Manjo worked the aluminum oars.

Foday no longer had to contend with the rolling three-foot waves as they were now approximately sixty yards away from the beach. He quickly joined Manjo, and both men began rowing toward the boat awaiting them.

They reached the anchored vessel within fifteen minutes. Foday and Manjo kept rowing until they reached the boat's stern side and stepped onto the fifty-foot yacht using the ladder on the swim platform.

"Fallubah. Nice to see you," said Foday with a large grin emanating from his face.

"Welcome aboard the Black River, Foday," said Fallubah.

The Black River, a modern monohull carbon fiber boat was capable of averaging fifteen to twenty-five knots in good sailing conditions. Fallubah secured the anchor, entered the captain's cockpit and fired up the engines. The three men were on their way to Jamaica, nearly four thousand nautical miles away.

Foday turned toward his native Sierra Leone and gazed into its mystical beauty one last time.

Jarabulus, Syria – November 6, 10:23 PM

Haris was now about three kilometers from Jarabulus. Islamic State took the small town sitting along the border before the campaign to capture Kobani. It was an ideal location to move men and supplies across the Euphrates. Due to its historical insignificance, the Kurds concentrated on Kobani to the west and Aleppo to the southeast.

Haris knew the actual number of Islamic State fighters in the town to be less than twenty. Jarabulus, already sparsely populated before their arrival due to Syria's civil war, was even less so now. For all practical purposes, the city was a barren wasteland filled with empty buildings and lifeless residents who could not escape.

Haris stopped just short of the city's entrance on Highway 4 like before. He noticed an Islamic State checkpoint as expected. He then reached into his bag and pulled out the radio. Scanning the known frequencies of Islamic State, he quickly identified what channel the local fighters were using.

He heard chatter regarding the movement of some vehicles to block the entrances into the city. However, it appeared they reinforced the southern checkpoint and even had reconnaissance patrols in the area.

Haris wasted no time and drove off the road and into the desert. He turned off his lights and slowly drove across the sand toward the southwestern part of Jarabulus. The city was just a few kilometers away as the moon's light radiated in the distance above the town. He wondered if it would be smarter to make the remainder of the trip on foot.

It would take more time but he was ahead of schedule, and the vehicle would be easier to detect.

Haris exited the vehicle, grabbed his rifle and looked at his map and the surrounding terrain one last time. The extraction point with Ayse was now approximately two and a half kilometers to his northwest. He verified the GPS coordinates on his cell phone and began walking. Haris only carried his automatic rifle, map, cell phone and radio as he moved toward the border.

Haris was close.

Two hundred yards into his hurried pace, Haris heard a sound coming from the other side of a nearby dune. It sounded like an engine. He froze instantly to hear more. Suddenly, an Islamic State fighter appeared at the top of the dune looking right at Haris.

Haris immediately drew his AK-47 and fired at the man striking him in the abdomen. A few seconds later, he heard two men shouting over the radio. The chase was on.

Haris began sprinting as fast as he could in the loose desert sand. Within seconds, he heard the explosion.

"Engage the target. Take him out, Billy," said Colonel O'Malley.

"With pleasure."

A few seconds later, Lieutenant Colonel Johnston acquired his target and fired another AGM 114 Hellfire II missile.

"Target destroyed," said Lieutenant Colonel Johnston.

"Roger. Zoom out and look for any additional movement."

"Cannot see anything right now. Turning north toward Jarabulus."

"Copy. That should keep the others pinned down in the city."

Colonel O'Malley continued to keep Haris within his sights. He zoomed out to get a better view of Haris' surroundings. He saw no signs of activity within fifty meters of his current location.

Haris continued to move northwest. He glanced down at his phone and realized he was within two kilometers. Only two long kilometers over open terrain, he thought to himself.

"Ghost Rider. One vehicle destroyed near your asset. We see no other threats as of now."

"Roger. We heard it." Michael did not engage in further communications. It was unnecessary as his military drone operators were involved in the fight and he had little to offer anyways.

"You guys see anything yet?" asked Michael.

Walid and Nanook turned their scopes toward the direction of the explosion but saw nothing. There were too many dunes between them and the blast area.

A few moments later, Nanook reported seeing some smoke or dust, but he could not be sure which. Michael saw it as well and turned to Elif.

"I think I'm going to move forward to the linkup point. Haris will not be here for some time, and I would like to move closer. I don't see anything up ahead."

"I will join you, Michael," said Elif.

Michael and Elif slowly crawled over the border, cautious of any Islamic State snipers that might be in the area. A few minutes later, they reached their objective.

"Nanook and Walid. Can you see us?" asked Elif.

Both men saw them clearly. They continued scanning the open area southwest of Karanfilkoy, but only observed a few old buildings and farmhouses. The two trusted contractors saw no signs of enemy movement.

Haris continued to march closer to the extraction point. Just to his north, he saw an empty bombed out shed. As he approached the structure, he heard a radio. The volume was low, and he was unable to recognize the chatter.

He attempted to bypass the location by moving west. The detour would add time to his journey, but he could not risk further confrontation. He came across a hill forty-five meters later.

Haris began traversing the hill and decided to assume a low crawl position to deliberately work his way over the crest. Haris reached the top of the hill when he felt the bullets fly by and spraying into the sand around him. Islamic State had found him and notified their headquarters in Jarabulus.

Haris quickly sprung to his feet and raced down the hill. He sprinted for approximately thirty meters until he found some concealment in the nearby brush.

"Engaging targets," said Colonel O'Malley.

The Colonel did not see the two Islamic State fighters tucked behind the shed from his viewing angle.

Nevertheless, they were now visible and moving toward Haris. O'Malley fired a single Hellfire missile at the men.

The missile struck the desert floor just a meter from the lead pursuer and killed him instantly. The blast knocked the second man to the ground. Clearly injured, he was not an immediate threat to CIA's asset.

"Ghost Rider, one individual down. The second appears to be injured. Your asset is just sitting there."

"Roger. Any movement in the vicinity?"

"Just the wounded individual on the ground."

Michael turned to Elif and told her the news.

Colonel O'Malley zoomed back out and continued to observe his target. One lucky bastard he thought to himself.

"Billy. Anything on your monitor?" asked O'Malley.

"I see one truck on the western edge of Jarabulus sitting on the road with two individuals inside."

"Copy. Keep eyes on them."

Elif called Haris on his cell.

"Get moving, Haris. No threats around you now."

"Okay, Ayse."

Haris pressed on. He carefully scanned the desert in front of him and he continued moving north. There could be Islamic State fighters anywhere, he thought to himself. Despite having support from Elif, he grew more cautious with each step. Haris was getting closer to the border.

"Movement, approximately seven hundred meters. Look to your eleven o'clock, Elif," said Walid.

Elif turned and saw Haris. He was moving slowly and methodically toward her position.

"Two men, five hundred meters and moving southwest," said Nanook.

"Keep them in your sights," said Elif.

The radios were now bursting with chatter around Jarabulus. One of their own was attempting to flee. The Caliph expected him captured or killed immediately. Now racing toward Jarabulus was Hassan Akbar with five of his veteran soldiers accompanying him. Hassan pushed up his arrival near the city where he had another matter to resolve.

"A second vehicle just pulled up alongside our friends at the western entrance into Jarabulus."

"Any movement?" asked O'Malley.

"They just took off. Heading west. Zooming out."

"Roger."

"The trucks just dropped off four individuals about one kilometer along the trail. Truck is now heading back toward Jarabulus."

"Looks like they are getting eyes on the road. What do you think, Billy?"

"Agree. They probably think they have the asset identified somewhere near his current location. Since he has to move north, he will have to cross the road. They will get eyes on him then."

O'Malley zoomed out to get a better picture. Up ahead, he could see the trail and the group of men. Two remained, while the other two split up along both sides of the road. They began walking east.

"Ghost Rider, your asset is going to have to cross a road in approximately two hundred meters. You might want to let him know. Two individuals are located approximately three hundred meters to his northwest along the road. Two people are walking east."

"Roger. We saw the trucks and see the individuals now," said Michael.

Elif instructed Walid to keep his sights on the two men at the end of the road. She then asked Nanook for an update regarding the two men he spotted earlier.

"They are still moving southwest. I don't think they can see him," said Nanook.

She dialed Haris yet again.

"Haris, up ahead you will encounter a road. There are two men patrolling it while two others remain to your west. Keep the line open."

Haris was being hunted, he thought to himself. He sensed his chances were slipping away.

Michael now believed the situation became untenable. He had to act quickly if Haris had any chance to survive.

"Elif, I am going to make my way to the dune up ahead. I can cover Haris' crossing. When I get in place, have Nanook take out the two men standing along the road."

Elif agreed.

"Viper 6, I am moving south toward the road. There's a patch of brush about 40 meters from there," said Michael quietly.

"Copy Ghost Rider, I see you now."

Elif waited for Michael to get into position. Michael and Haris would only be two hundred meters apart. A few minutes later, she ordered Nanook to fire.

The first man hit the ground moments later. As the second man turned to look, Nanook hit him in the back. The two other Islamic State fighters patrolling the road were two hundred meters away and unaware of their comrades' demise.

"Both trucks making a U-turn. Now heading west toward the asset," said Johnston.

O'Malley had a decision to make. He looked into his monitor and could see the asset and his CIA contact nestled near opposite sides of the road. Two trucks filled with Islamic State militants were approaching their position.

"Billy, engage the trucks right away."

Anticipating the order, Johnston already had his sights on the lead truck. Firing another Hellfire missile, the truck broke apart and came to a stop seconds later.

The driver of the rear truck swerved, narrowly missing the destroyed vehicle in front of him, and slammed on his brakes. Both men quickly exited and scattered into the desert. Moments later a second explosion rocked the vehicle setting it ablaze.

Chaos had ensued west of Jarabulus.

Haris observed the explosions from his position along the road. He rose to his feet and sprinted across the paved road. One of the two patrolling terrorists noticed him in the confusion.

The men raced toward Haris, spraying a volley of bullets in his direction.

Michael took aim and fired his weapon. The first man died instantly as the second individual darted into the desert. Michael lost him due to his vantage point.

"Haris, one of my men is located twenty-five meters ahead. He will guide you back to me," said Elif.

"Haris. Over here," said Michael.

Haris raced to join Michael near the brush. For the first time in several hours, Haris found a friend.

"There is another shooter near us, about forty meters to the west. Follow me."

Michael and Haris moved east as he did not want to lead the remaining gunman toward Elif.

"Walid, where are the two individuals?" asked Elif.

"They froze after the explosions. They are just lying on the sand."

"If they move, eliminate them."

Michael stopped to look through his scope as he and Haris made their way around a nearby dune. He saw no signs of remaining Islamic State fighters. Michael and Haris continued moving toward Elif.

A few minutes later, he and Haris arrived at Elif's location. Michael instructed her to take Haris back to their vehicle and would cover their movement.

Unbeknownst to the group, approximately three hundred and fifty meters to their east, there stood a torn down farmhouse. The nearby shed was occupied by a lone Islamic State sniper. Walid and Nanook scanned the facility several times during the evening, but saw no signs of movement.

The lone sniper popped his head above the concrete and quickly acquired his target. He had been there all along and received instructions from Jarabulus to fire at the traitor when possible. The sharpshooter looked for the man with boots west of his position and patiently found him.

The bullet punctured Haris' neck and he fell to the ground. Just mere yards stood between him and the border. The sound of the sniper's rifle gave away his position. Walid and Nanook turned their scopes toward the shed.

Both men saw the shooter lower his head behind the barrier. Neither had a shot from their position.

Michael sprinted toward Elif and Haris. Haris was bleeding out.

"What more can you tell us of Kenema?" asked Michael as he figured Haris would be dead shortly.

Haris, barely able to speak, simply uttered, "The Sheikh at Kenema Mosque knows the plan."

The former Islamic State bodyguard and Mossad asset turned toward Elif and uttered his last words, "Almost made it."

Michael and Elif dashed back to Karanfilkoy. Michael immediately asked Nanook if he saw signs of the sniper. Nanook did not see him and said he thought he was still at his location. Michael asked him where he was hiding.

"Viper six. I have a sniper approximately four hundred meters east of my location. He's behind a shed near an abandoned farmhouse. Requesting you take out the target. We are moving away from the area, over."

"Copy, Ghost Rider. Good luck," said O'Malley.

"Thanks for the support. Ghost Rider, out."

"Billy, I have one more target for you."

A few seconds later, Lieutenant Colonel Johnston would have his last kill for the evening. Haris would be avenged.

"Time to go home, Billy." O'Malley and Johnston turned their drones north and began the flight back to eastern Turkey to an undisclosed airfield.

Michael and Elif drove back into Karanfilkoy. The two would rest and prepare for their delivery at two-thirty. They pondered if the events in Jarabulus would spook Raif's buyers.

Karanfilkoy, Turkey – November 7, 12:08 AM

Michael had some time to spare before the AT-4 delivery. He reached into his pack, pulled out his cell phone and sent Laura a message.

Hi, Laura. What an eventful day so far and I am not even finished. Am thinking about you and hope you are doing well. Have you returned to D.C. yet? I keep thinking about our first date. Wish I was there with you now. I am lucky to have met you. Getting excited over the prospect of eating French cuisine soon. Michael

Elif turned and smiled at Michael.

"Are you writing her?"

"Is it that obvious?"

"Yes," said Elif laughing.

"I've never felt this way before. I guess I was always too busy traveling and working for the agency."

"I understand. I had someone once."

"Who?" Michael asked.

"He was Mossad. He died in Jordan two years ago. I miss him."

"I'm sorry, Elif."

"Me too," said Elif as she stared out the window.

"Mind if I take a quick nap?" asked Michael.

"No. I'll wake you when Raif gives us the go ahead."

Michael drifted asleep within minutes as he had the uncanny ability to nap at a moment's notice.

Ziyarete, Syria - November 7, 12:35 AM

Hassan Akbar arrived in the border town of Ziyarete after returning from Jarabulus. Haris was dead, and he personally notified the Caliph. Hassan avoided calling Al-Diri and enjoyed keeping him out of the loop.

He then turned to one of his associates in Ziyarete.

"Where are the weapons being delivered?" asked Akbar.

"At our usual site along the Euphrates northeast of Jarabulus. The delivery is scheduled for two-thirty," said the Islamic State combatant.

"It's my understanding there will be a Turkish intelligence officer and two others with the driver?"

"Yes. Our friend in Nizip confirmed again this evening."

"Who are the two individuals accompanying MIT?" asked Akbar.

"Allegedly, it's her superior and a doctor fleeing from Kobani."

"Makes sense. They think we are YPG and this is our first supply of weapons from Turkey. They need the doctor for information. We need him for ransom. How many men will you have?"

"I am taking six."

"No. You are taking twelve."

Hassan Akbar and his five trusted deputies would join them.

He ordered two vehicles to depart Jarabulus and drive along the roads and trails west of the city since he was wary of the drone strikes conducted earlier. No reports of damaged vehicles came across the radios.

Ninety minutes later, satisfied the drones were no longer operating in the skies above, the first of three vehicles moved southwest toward Jarabulus. Akbar decided to split the group and drive along separate routes just to be sure. They would reach the delivery site in less than fifteen minutes.

Akbar's group arrived. Flanked by the Euphrates River to his right, the three vehicles waited. Sitting in the rear vehicle were Akbar and his driver. Three of his passengers joined the group of men ahead while one man flanked the rear of the vehicle.

Slowly driving under the Jarablus Bridge, actually located inside Turkey and along the border, Raif, Michael, and Elif now entered Syria. Raif grew more nervous as he approached the group of men. Michael and Elif sensed the man's anxiety, and slowly moved their weapons onto their laps.

Elif stopped the vehicle approximately thirty yards from the collection of men and vehicles directly in front of them. She kept the engine running as dust spilled off the riverbank.

Two men moved forward and flanked their vehicle. Raif exited the passenger side and walked to the lone man awaiting him. Raif's twenty meter walk seemed like an eternity.

"Raif, nice to see you again. You have weapons for us?"

"Yes, Houmam. In the back. The woman wants to speak with you. She thinks you are YPG," whispered Raif.

"First, you will show me the weapons."

Raif led Houmam back to the truck. Houmam stared into the eyes of Elif as he walked by. The disdain and resentment emanating from his eyes indicated he was not YPG.

Nevertheless, she remained in place. Nanook and Walid remained thirty-five meters behind her in the tree line.

Houmam looked into the back of the truck and saw the containers filled with AT-4s.

"There are a dozen here, Raif?"

"Yes, I saw them pack the weapons earlier."

"Who is the man in the back seat?"

"I do not know him. She brought him to observe the transfer."

Houmam walked back toward the front of the truck and looked into Elif's eyes.

"Why does MIT want to help us now? You have never supported our efforts against Islamic State."

"We believe it's time. How much longer before Islamic State penetrates Turkey?" she asked.

Houmam did not immediately respond. Rather, he casually nodded his head.

"I will be right back. Raif, come walk with me to my vehicle. You will need payment."

The two men stopped in front of the lead vehicle. Houmam turned to Raif.

"What did I tell you the first time we met?"

"Always come alone, Houmam."

"That is right. So why break my rule?"

"It was the only way to secure the weapons. I had no choice. She insisted."

"How do I know she is not here collecting information on us?"

"She is convinced you are YPG, Houmam."

"How do you know that, Raif? Enough talk."

Houmam drew his pistol and fired a single round into Raif's head. Immediately upon drawing his weapon, Elif ordered Nanook and Walid to engage the two men opposite their truck. They had no chance to discharge their rounds at Elif or Michael.

Elif placed the vehicle in reverse and slammed her foot onto the accelerator pedal. The loose sand of the shorelines caused a delay. Houmam and the other Islamic State members began spraying bullets at Elif.

Michael sat forward from the rear seat and returned fire as Elif finally got the truck to begin moving rearward. Elif was operating on instincts as she ducked below the front windshield.

Soon after Elif and Michael moved, their progress stalled. Several of the Islamic State bullets found their way inside the truck's tires. The soft sand prevented the truck's rims from barely turning.

Nanook and Walid fired off several more rounds each killing four additional fighters before dashing forward.

"Out. Get out," yelled Michael.

Michael and Elif worked their way to the back of the truck. Meanwhile, Akbar and the remainder of his men advanced forward. An intense gun battle followed for the next three minutes.

Nanook, working his way along the Euphrates took out two more combatants. Walid remained pinned down approximately ten meters from Michael as he had open terrain to traverse.

A lull in the battle ensued. Akbar and his men were issuing verbal commands in an attempt to flank them. Walid took the opportunity to join Elif. As he approached the vehicle, an enemy's sights found him. Three rounds fired from a set of scrublands twenty meters away entered his body.

"Nanook, make your way to the vehicle," shouted Michael.

Michael leaned to the left edge of the truck and sprayed bullets along the riverbank to cover Nanook's advance.

"They are going to come from our right through the vegetation. They cannot move along the shoreline, there is too much open space. Elif, you cover the area just in case one or two try."

Michael wished he had his drones back.

"How many are left?" asked Nanook.

"Maybe six or seven, I think," said Michael.

Elif's cell phone rang. It was Tel Aviv.

"There are two men sitting behind one of the trucks ahead of you. Five others are at your three o'clock, approximately fifty meters," said the operator.

"Michael, two up ahead and five moving around our position. They are approximately fifty meters away," said Elif.

Mossad's decision to provide overhead support to Elif's delivery proved invaluable. The Tec Star low earth orbit satellite passed the thermal imagery directly to Mossad's intelligence operations center. Michael now had additional 'eyes' from the Israeli Tec Star satellite flying three hundred kilometers above.

"We can't sit here. We do not know what other type of weapons they may have. Nanook, keep your sights on that clearing ahead. They will have to cross it or come directly at us. I'm going to flank them from their left."

Off Michael ran. Heading into the foliage, he began working his way around the advancing Islamic State fighters. Several minutes later, he waited and began scouting the terrain in front of him.

One by one, he picked off the first two men. Akbar and the two others immediately dispersed around the surrounding vegetation. They enjoyed limited concealment except Akbar who found a nearby tree with thick surrounding brush. Michael could no longer see him.

Akbar barked out orders.

"Attack the vehicle. Move now."

The two fighters pinned behind the second vehicle rushed forward. Moving side by side, they sprayed Elif's position with bullets. Nanook rolled onto his stomach and fired from the ground. The first man fell to the dirt. Elif finished the second one moments later.

Michael decided to flank the lone fighter hiding behind the tree. He had the advantage of an infrared scope, so he took his time. He found a clearing as he carefully moved forward. The lone remaining Islamic State fighter was now approximately twenty-five meters ahead of Michael.

Michael took a deep breath, exhaled, and gently squeezed the trigger. He hit Akbar directly in the side of head shattering his skull.

Hassan Akbar's jihad was over.

Michael slowly moved back toward the vehicle ensuring he did not spook Elif or Nanook. He called out to them.

"Elif, the five men here are dead. How are you and Nanook?"

"Clear here, Michael. Come on in."

"These guys were not YPG." said Michael.

"Probably Islamic State. Raif had me fooled."

"You're bleeding Elif."

A stray bullet hit Elif in the arm during the firefight. The excitement and adrenaline kept her from even realizing the wound.

"It's not that bad. I'll make a tourniquet."

Michael turned to Nanook.

"Let's take one of the trucks, load the AT-4s in the back, and get the hell out of here. More of these bastards could be on the way."

"We are bringing Walid back, Michael," said Elif.

"Of course, I understand."

Fifteen minutes later the group drove back under the Jerablus Bridge and into Turkey as bodies lay scattered along the Euphrates. The trip to Arsuz would include long periods of silence and reflection for both Elif and Michael.

Arsuz, Turkey – November 7, 1:48 PM

Michael awoke from his deep sleep. He was unsure if Elif was in her bedroom, but he decided to let her rest in case she was.

It was time to update Langley. Michael reached for his secure cell phone and called Doug.

"Doug, we lost the source along the border last night. Before he died, he said the Sheikh at Kenema was involved in the Ebola plot."

"What did he say?"

"That was it. Just that he knew of the plan."

"No other specifics?" asked Doug.

"No."

"So, we don't know yet if the individual has left Sierra Leone?"

"No. We cannot be sure of anything at this point."

"How the hell would he or she get out?" asked Doug though he had analysts looking into several scenarios.

"I doubt they will try using commercial aircraft. Security is probably tight due to the outbreak. My guess is he will travel by boat and either enter the country via Brazil or somewhere in the Caribbean."

"Well, security is definitely tight at all airports. My analysts tell me there is a probability of less than ten percent the individual would get onto a plane," said Doug.

"Let's work on the theory Islamic State is moving the individual by boat. If that is correct, then we have time to gather Intel. I need to get to Kenema as soon as possible."

"Agreed, Michael. How soon can you travel?"

"I can be ready tonight. Think our friends at Mossad would allow Elif to join me?"

"Thought your update earlier said her source was supplying YPG and they turned out to be Islamic State. You sure you need her?" asked Doug a bit sarcastically.

"Yes. She is a superb collector and operative. Her source had her fooled. It has happened to all of us, Doug. Do you recall what transpired in Yemen? The extra support from Tel Aviv might come in handy."

Doug sighed and paused a moment. He agreed the added collection effort from Mossad might help his already stretched resources. In addition, many at the intelligence directorate dismissed the plot's viability.

"Let me call now and gauge their reaction. They might want her looking into the dead contact. Let me get back to you later."

Doug called forty-five minutes later.

"Michael. Mossad is open to the idea. They have agreed to let Elif join you in Kenema."

Doug paused for a moment and continued.

"Understand something, Michael. Most of us around here think the idea remains preposterous. That someone could arrive in New York, and infect people with Ebola just does not fly with most analysts. And even if a few individuals were infected, we have the medical facilities and resources to save them."

"What if they are wrong, Doug. What if the individual rides a subway for a day, or even longer, and simply coughs and sneezes around people. Hundreds of people could be infected, and there would be panic, not to mention the possible loss of life."

"Yes, Michael. That could happen, and analysts are looking at several hypotheses. Stay focused on Kenema and get the Intel we need. If this is even true, they may still be in the early planning stages and not even off the ground yet. Mossad will transport you both to Kenema. Check your file later for what we have on the Mosque there. Let me know when you have something."

Doug hung up. Michael wondered if Elif was aware of the development.

A short while later Elif exited her bedroom.

"Guess we are going to Kenema," said Elif.

"When?"

"This evening. They are sending a plane to Hatay and then we will fly directly to Sierra Leone."

"Good. Let us grab a bite to eat. I'm starving," said Michael.

State Department, Bureau of Intelligence and Research, Washington, D.C. - November 7, 2:30 PM

Leslie and her colleagues convened for the second time in the bland conference room. Surrounding them were whiteboards and sharpies. They were in the middle of red teaming, a process whereby an intelligence analyst thinks like an adversary and develops several courses of action.

"Carl, your turn," said Leslie.

"One way I would introduce Ebola into New York City is through the blood supply. I would task an individual with getting into a blood bank and simply infect the blood inside. Maybe a place like the Red Cross. I am sure their security is lax."

"Okay. How would you do it?" asked Jeremy.

"I would simply trade out good blood bags with Ebola-infected bags."

"But how would you get infected bags through security and into the country?" asked Leslie.

"I would infect the individual just prior to their departure. They could then remove some of their blood once they arrive."

"That would mean the individual has learned to use a syringe properly, and store blood. And how would you infect the person without infecting those around him?"

"A blood transfusion."

"You really think Islamic State has the resources and know-how to do this?"

"Probably not. But it's a possibility, though unlikely." said Carl.

"Jeremy, what have you come up with?" asked Leslie.

"I would dispatch the individual aboard a commercial airliner. Let him infect a few people on the plane and hope some of those infect others. Then those would infect more and so on. If only one of those passengers die, Islamic State could achieve significant propaganda value from it."

"Then what would the individual do once they land?"

"Mingle within the population before he could no longer walk or move around. He could also acquire explosives and blow himself up in a crowded restaurant or cafe in the city."

Jordan chimed in.

"Would a terrorist actually do this? If I were committed, I would prefer a quicker death. A slow painful death does not fit the narrative."

"True. It does not fit the profile. Maybe the individual is unaware he or she has Ebola? Maybe he or she is told it's something else?" said Jeremy.

"Maybe. However, I agree with Jordan. Even someone committed to the jihad is unlikely to go through the horrific pain and suffering. I would prefer a quicker death," said Leslie.

Jordan had her first productive idea for the group in quite some time. Leslie turned to her.

"Okay, Jordan. Your thoughts?"

"I would identify a blood bank in or near a city hospital. Infect the blood, similar to what Carl suggested, and then blow myself up in a crowded area near the blood bank. When injured people are transported to the hospital, some of the infected blood would be transferred to them."

Leslie thought the idea was possible but a little farfetched. In her mind, severely injured people from the blast would likely remain in the hospital for days and weeks. Therefore, the staff could identify the virus and keep it contained within the facility. However, Jordan's manner of thinking pleased Leslie.

"Let me tell you all what I think. What if the individual arrives in the city and simply rides on the subway for several days sneezing and coughing at nearby passengers? In a few days, infected passengers would probably think they simply have the onset of a cold or the flu. It would take days before the infection caused them to visit their doctor or go to the hospital. Then, as the pain becomes unbearable, our target conducts a suicide attack somewhere in the city."

The group nodded in agreement. They all decided Leslie's scenario was possible but so were the previous courses of action. Jeremy then raised a question.

"How would this guy get into the city? Think he would travel by commercial airliner or another way?"

"My guess right now is via commercial aircraft. It is quicker, has potential secondary effects, and there are no bans on flights from the region as of now. It is my understanding that airport security officers look for passengers exhibiting signs of the disease. However, if the target exhibits no symptoms, he or she would be free to travel. I could see a scenario where the individual enters via a cargo ship or some other vessel, but I would go with the aircraft at this point."

Jeremy turned to Leslie and spoke.

"I agree. The commercial airliner seems the most plausible at this point."

"Okay, I want each of you to keep evaluating your working hypothesis. Work out the holes and let us get back at it in the morning. I also want each of you to identify all major airports and airlines in the region with known flights into the United States. There are probably several handfuls of flights each week that connect into South America or Europe. Carefully look at all possible routes," said Leslie.

Leslie returned to her office and picked up the phone.

"Joe, we have a working theory on how it might be done. We believe commercial aircraft is the most viable option from the intelligence we have. We are not ruling out other transportation means, but an airliner is the most likely course of action."

"Okay, anything showing up on your queries? Any information in the database on biological weapons or Ebola?"

"Nothing out of the ordinary. I see no chatter on the subject other than reports of the outbreak and what some NGOs are doing there."

"This is obviously not enough to go higher with, Leslie."

"I agree, Joe. Was CIA satisfied with our initial report?"

"Appears so. No one believes the scenario could happen, except you at this point. I hope you are wrong on this one."

"Me too, Joe. Nevertheless, we cannot stop working on the hypothesis, no matter how unlikely. Think other agencies will share their Intel with us if they pick up something?"

"I would like to think so, but you know how that goes sometimes."

"Yes, I do."

"All right, Leslie. Keep at it. This remains your priority for the near future. Be prepared to brief higher headquarters or another agency as soon as tomorrow. Standard briefing."

"Will do."

Leslie hung up the phone and stared at the picture over her desk. It was a shot of ground zero where the World Trade Center buildings collapsed from unforeseen intelligence estimates. She dared not dismiss this theory, despite its perceived madness and low probability for success.

Hatay, Turkey – November 7, 7:30 PM

Michael and Elif arrived at the Hatay airport.

"Nanook, I want you to make the arrangements for Walid," said Elif.

"Of course, Elif. He was my friend. I will miss him."

"Where will he be buried?"

"I will bury him outside Arsuz overlooking the Mediterranean. He loved it there. There is a cemetery near the ocean."

"He was a good man, Nanook, and one of the best I ever served with. I am not sure how long I will be gone. After you give Walid a proper burial, I want you to start looking for a new man."

"I have someone in mind."

"Someone I know?"

"No. Have a good flight, Elif. Let me know when you return, and I will pick you up."

Michael turned to Nanook and thanked him for his support the night before. He offered Nanook one final condolence for Walid and began climbing the stair ramp. Elif was now closely behind him.

The single bullet entered Elif's lower dorsal cavity, and she fell forward onto Michael. Michael immediately recognizing the fatal shot and scanned the surrounding area for a shooter.

"Nanook, did you see where it came from?" yelled Michael.

"No, Michael. The only place I can think of is the hangar ahead of us to our left. It must have come from there."

The pilot raced from his cockpit and quickly made his way to Michael and Elif.

"Elif, are you okay?" asked the pilot.

She was barely able to speak as she turned to the pilot.

"Get this man to Kenema. The mission must proceed as planned."

"We have to get you to a hospital now," said the pilot.

"No, he must get to Kenema as soon as possible."

"Nanook, get her out of here. I am going after the shooter. Pilot, keep the plane running. I will be back shortly," said Michael.

Michael pulled out his weapon and fired several shots into the open hangar. He fired several more rounds as Elif and Nanook entered the vehicle. He spotted the shooter peering their head from around the corner of the hangar's entrance.

"Nanook, drive toward the hangar before you leave. Fire into the opening and keep the shooter pinned inside."

Michael followed behind the car as Nanook fired into the opening. As Nanook came within ten meters, Michael motioned he was going inside.

"Get out of here," Michael yelled.

Michael immediately began to fire in the direction of the shooter. As he approached the entrance, he saw no one behind the walls. He then peered his head around the corner and observed an individual running toward the back of the shelter behind a shipping container.

Michael reloaded. He fired several rounds toward the shooter as one bullet narrowly missed the individual's head and smashed into the wall.

The container was small. It was only four feet wide and nearly four feet in height.

Michael decided to slowly walk toward the container and fire one round every few seconds to keep the shooter's head down.

The shooter drew their pistol and stood up as Michael got closer. The person managed to fire a single round that narrowly missed Michael.

Michael did not hesitate. The shooter fell backward as he fired three rounds into her chest.

"Who the hell are you?" asked Michael.

"Dabria Uzun, MIT."

Dabria knew she was dying but decided to communicate with her killer anyway.

"Why the hell did you shoot at my friend? She could be dead within minutes."

"I was aiming for you. Nasir wants you dead."

"Nasir from AQAP? How the hell do you know him?"

Dabria was unable to speak and died.

Michael checked Dabria for a cell phone and found it in the back pocket of her jeans.

He only noticed a few calls, but all were to Yemen as evident by the numeric sequences. He did not have time to look further as local police would probably be on their way soon.

Michael rejoined the pilot at the stair ramp a few minutes later.

"Let's get the hell out of here. Turkish police could be arriving within minutes. How long before we get to Sierra Leone?"

"We should be in Kenema in about seven hours, Mr. Brennan."

"Okay. I wonder how Elif is doing? Get us airborne."

Barma, Sierra Leone – November 8, 10:20 AM

Lucee finished her tenth long day in a row. She was due for a break and her co-workers at Medicins Sans Frontieres agreed. They urged her to go to Kenema and relax for a few days. She had earned it.

The previous five days were the worst since she began working with MSF. All told, she helped bring over twenty-seven bodies to Barma and other field hospitals near Kenema. The death toll was mounting, and there seemed to be no end in sight.

"Go to Kenema, Lucee. Relax for a few days and escape this horror," said her supervisor, a strong-willed German doctor in charge of the facility.

"I know I need it. All these people? The countless others. They need me."

"They need you, but I also need you. I want you healthy and well rested. Please go to the city, Lucee. Take a long bath, read a book, or simply catch up on your sleep. Be a woman for a while and escape this dreadfulness. We will still be here when you get back."

"Are you sure?"

"Yes."

Lucee drove off a few minutes later. There were several groups of fleeing civilians lined along the road. For many, leaving the countryside for sanctuary inside Kenema seemed the only hope. There were doctors in Kenema and plenty of water provided by non-government organizations.

Lucee spotted a young girl holding a boy's hand as she was nearing Kenema. The girl, probably ten or eleven years of age, had no shoes and worn-out clothing. The young boy was dressed the same.

"Where are you going?" asked Lucee.

"To the city, with my brother."

"Where are your parents?"

"They died."

"How long ago? How did they die?"

"Ebola killed our family last month. Our village did not want us anymore."

"How are you feeling?"

"We are fine."

Lucee was impressed with the resiliency and courage of the young girl. The young boy did not speak. He was wary of Lucee and tightly gripped his sister's hand.

"I want you both to get in the back. I will take you to Kenema."

Lucee arrived in Kenema approximately twenty minutes later. There was a protest underway by groups of individuals convinced the Ebola virus was a hoax to steal blood. Lucee was aware that many villagers surrounding Kenema believed this government conspiracy during her attempts to pick up suspected victims. The open borders between Sierra Leone, Guinea, and Liberia compounded the spread of Ebola.

"Hello. My name is Lucee."

"Hello. How may I help you?" said the young woman at the shelter.

"I found these two walking along the road. Their parents are dead. Do you have room for them?"

"No. However, I will find them a place. How did their parents die?"

"Ebola. However, they show no symptoms and their parents died last month."

"You are sure they do not have Ebola?"

"They are not showing symptoms. If they were, I would not have brought them here. I work for MSF."

"You will need to fill out some paperwork. Please be as precise as you can regarding their family."

Lucee finished and said goodbye to the children. A short while later she checked herself into the Capitol Hotel, an upscale venue in eastern Kenema. The hotel mostly catered to western business people and relief workers flying into the region.

Lucee was an affluent woman whose father served in the government. Idealistic and determined, she left a safe and promising career as an artist to work for MSF. She needed to speak to a girlfriend.

"Leslie. Hello from my beautiful country."

"Hi, Lucee. How are you today? I haven't heard from you in quite some time."

"It's horrible here. Protesters are in the streets convinced the government is trying to steal their blood. The losses in Barma are now one hundred and ninety-seven. Similar numbers are everywhere I go. We cannot contain the outbreak."

"I am sorry this is happening, Lucee. I wish I could be of some help."

"I know. How are things in Washington?"

"Better here. You sound tired."

"I am, but more sad than anything else. I just picked up some children and had to bring them to a shelter here. They lost their parents and I'm not sure how much more I can take of this."

"Be strong, Lucee. They need you there. You are where you belong. I am praying for your safety."

"Thank you, Leslie. I am going to sleep now and will call again soon. I fear the numbers will be higher."

"Take care."

Lucee drifted to sleep dreaming of a country free from the killer disease.

Langley, VA – November 8, 1:30 PM

"Zach, it's Doug Weatherbee. How are you, bud?"

"Doing well my friend. How are things at HQ?"

"The usual. Headaches, budget constraints, and politics. Same old bureaucratic nightmare."

"No better here but different circumstances. We are getting reports from all over the region that Ebola is spreading. I'm not sure this thing is going to be contained anytime soon. Did your office get the intel for the off-site your people requested?"

"I did. Thank you. Feeling here is the same. That is why I am calling. One of my people landed in Kenema early this morning. They are looking into a report that Islamic State is attempting to use Ebola as part of an attack."

"Islamic State? They do not operate in Sierra Leone. You have reports of cells operating here?"

"No. I have not heard that. But we have a source who said they were looking at transporting an infected person."

"Into the United States?"

"Yes."

"How would they do that? Security at airports are tight, and they are looking for passengers with symptoms. Travelers are now required to fill out forms before flying."

"Another reason for the call. Can your people look at potential scenarios where an individual might get out? What I am looking for is specifically how the person would do it. What is the most likely course of action? You know

Sierra Leone better than any of our analysts in the Directorate of Intelligence (DI)."

"Doug, there would be dozens of ways. The borders with Liberia and Guinea are wide open as security is nonexistent. There is nothing to stop someone from leaving the country. The only real maritime security forces are in Freetown. Unless the individual is showing symptoms, they could fly out of the country from several different airports with international flights."

"Zach, work on the assumption the individual shows no signs of the disease. Give me your best estimate. Can you narrow it down to three courses of action?"

"When do you need it? You know we have a slim staff here."

"How about tomorrow? I will call again in the afternoon. Sound reasonable?"

"Sure, Doug. We'll see what we come up with."

Doug hung up the phone and began the long walk to DI.

"Chris. Got a minute?"

"Doug, what brings DO in my office this afternoon?"

"Have your analysts come up with anything in reference to the Ebola scenario I posed to you the other day?"

"Yes. They do not think it is credible, Doug. There are too many factors limiting its success. Not to mention the unlikely ability of the virus to spread in the United States."

Doug did not subscribe to the theory either, but he pressed for the reasons why the analysts arrived at their conclusion.

"Why is it not credible?"

"First, we spoke with NCMI. They believe our immune systems are much stronger than people who live in Sierra Leone. Second, if an infection were to occur, we have the medical facilities available to treat the patient. An outbreak is a near improbability as far as NCMI is concerned. Third, what terrorist is going to infect himself, and only hope he infects a few people? The probability of mass casualties is again very low."

"What if the individual infects himself after arriving in the United States?"

"Doug, how the hell is someone going to transport the virus into the United States undetected?"

"Don't know. That's why I'm asking you?"

"Doug, I've got analysts working around the clock looking at Russia, China, Yemen, Middle East, rogue cyber criminals, etc., etc. We are not going to examine this further. You may want to use your resources elsewhere."

"What about the psychological impact if just a few individuals are infected? The amount of propaganda Islamic State would generate is enormous."

"Then the country will be scared for a few days and turn their attention to the NFL playoffs soon after. Mass casualties are not possible, Doug."

Doug partially agree with him, despite Chris' arrogance.

"Weren't you on the Bin Laden desk before 9/11? Did anyone back then think it was possible to hijack four aircraft and attack the Twin Towers? Did you forecast the Pentagon strike? No need to answer that one, Chris."

Doug worked his way back to the office.

"Anne, please get me a secure line to Michael."

"Will do, sir. Give me a few minutes."

y thing relevant was the imagery of the Mosque and h
ture."

"I know. It's all we had. His name was not found in
ny of the database queries we ran."

"Probably because he has not been targeted."

"Yeah. Sierra Leone has never been a high priority f
lection."

"What does Freetown know?" asked Michael.

"I spoke with them earlier. They are going to give m
nething tomorrow."

"Okay. I plan to scout the Mosque tonight and see
at security measures I can find. Can you get Freetown
k into any cell phones he may be using? He may not
n be here right now."

"I'll pass it on. Mike, DI continues to believe the plc
udicrous. They are no longer looking at it as a viable
eat. I am getting some pressure to either confirm this c
ve on. I need you to get to Cissi in a day or two. Not
e if the Director has the stomach for more guessing.
's been asking why you are not in Libya."

"Any analysts you know taking this seriously?"

"I think one is. Apparently, INR has an analyst still
king at scenarios. She seems fiery and taking the threa
iously. I hear she is very good."

"Okay. I will push forward with the recon tonight an
ke a play for Cissi tomorrow. Any word back yet on t
-site?"

Capitol Hotel, Kenema, Sierra Leone - November 8, 2:10 PM

Michael reached for his cell phone after finally waking up from a deep sleep. There were two messages. He read Aaron's first.

Michael, Elif did not make it. She died this morning. Thought you should know. I pray for a successful conclusion to your task. Thank you for the information you conveyed to the pilot. Godspeed. Your friend, Aaron.

Michael was devastated. Elif was a superb agent and a kindhearted woman. Nevertheless, he replied immediately to the Mossad officer he met several days ago in Tel Aviv.

My condolences, Aaron. She was a gifted officer and incredible human being. I am truly sorry for your loss. Will you please notify me where her memorial will be? I would like to pay my respects in the future. I hope our paths cross again soon. Shalom, Michael.

Michael turned his attention to Laura's text.

Hi Mike, yes, I am back. Great trip and many new contacts in the predictive analytics world. Lots to tell. It is unbelievable what some of the technology is allowing companies to do now. Get back soon. The French make wonderful food! I am happy to have met you as well. More than you know right now. Lol. Laura

Michael opened his laptop and soon began studying the files on the Kenema Mosque. Satellite imagery showed the square building sitting aside two streets, one to the north and one to the east. Either approach would work he thought, but the northern street was closer to the primary road just one hundred and twenty-five feet away.

The parking lot seemed small, but it was Kenema, so it did not need to accommodate many vehicles. Michael thought the lot was probably used by the staff, food delivery trucks, and maintenance crews.

There were four light fixtures atop the building that surrounded the Mosque. Michael wondered if they worked in the evening.

Langley also provided a dossier on Sheikh Cissi. A native of Sierra Leone, and born of the Jawei chiefdom in Gelehum, Sheikh Cissi's dossier was slim. A picture of Cissi accompanied the file. It was taken by a local photographer in 2003 and Michael wondered what he might look like now.

Michael read a few excerpts from public statements he made in Kenema. Cissi gave no speeches or interviews indicating support for Islamic State or any other terror organizations. The file contained few clues of the man's habits, nor was there a psychological profile written on him. Cissi was a man operating under the radar of the American intelligence community.

The report did indicate some references to his security. The Sheikh apparently traveled with one bodyguard and used several more to protect the Mosque at nights. Michael noticed the date of the paragraph to be November 2005.

He sighed and closed the file. The intelligence Michael received on the man was outdated and practically useless. This would complicate his strategy to gather actionable

intelligence and determine if the Ebola plot was genu a fabrication by Haris to flee the Islamic State.

He reminded himself of the Iraqi scientist who convinced German BND and CIA that Saddam Huss possessed weapons of mass destruction. What a blur that turned out to be for the agency, Michael though

Michael then examined the brief country report Sierra Leone. At the top of the threats he faced, Ebo criminal gangs concerned him the most.

The report included early symptoms of Ebola. However, he didn't learn much more than what was reported by various media outlets.

The report also characterized criminal activity critical. Foreigners and expatriates from the United were targets for robberies and break-ins due to perc affluence. Petty criminals also targeted many of th hotels in Kenema. The Capitol Hotel, however, ha superb reputation for security among its internatior clientele.

Michael finished browsing at geographic featu networks in and around Kenema, and weather fore the coming seventy-two-hour period. The remaind report provided nothing of significant tactical intel he might have needed.

Michael's cell phone rang.

"Mike, it's Doug. Where are you?"

"At the Capitol Hotel. Just reviewing the file, analysts sent. It is worthless. No current Intel exis

"Yes, Freetown will provide me an address in a few hours. You will get it as soon as we do. It's just outside Kenema and contractors are there now."

"Who are the contractors?"

"A group of mercenaries recommended by Freetown. They have been useful in the past and off the book."

"How many?"

"Four. They come highly recommended and I'm sure you will find them useful, if necessary. The group's leader is an ex Nigerian special forces officer. He recently worked with the French in Mali."

"Sounds good. I will let you know when I have him."

"Collect what you can. We are pressed for time."

Michael hung up. The long flight from Hatay made him hungry for local cuisine.

Hangha, Sierra Leone - November 8, 4:57 PM

The four men dressed in local clothing returned to the trailer sitting along the southwest side of the abandoned diamond mine. Hangha, a dusty and nearly abandoned village, once thrived when diamond fever hit the region. In fact, Queen Elizabeth of the United Kingdom visited Hangha in 1961 to witness the digging firsthand.

Hangha and many other parts of Sierra Leone suffered greatly during the country's civil war from 1991 until 2002. It was Revolutionary United Front (RUF) forces, together with Special Forces from Charles Taylor's National Patriotic Front of Liberia (NPFL), that took control of Hangha. The conflict would leave 50,000 people dead throughout eastern and southeastern Sierra Leone.

Control over alluvial diamond production lay at the heart of the eleven-year battle. Old treasure hunters and young single men dreaming of striking it rich made up the bulk of the remaining population.

"Okay, boys. It looks like we are ready to go. I will call our friends in Freetown. No one leaves unless I say so."

The middle-aged man pulled out his cell phone.

"Mr. Thompson. We are ready."

"You have everything you need?"

"We do. We just need a guest."

"You come highly recommended. You will follow all instructions given by our man on site, understood?"

"We always do, Mr. Thompson. Send the first half of the contract to the routing number I provided."

"Just sent. I will let you know when our man is close."

Capitol Hotel, Kenema, Sierra Leone - November 8, 5:55 PM

Michael returned to the hotel restaurant. Standing in front of the maître de was a young woman wearing a beautiful blue dress adorned with floral colors.

"I am sorry Ma'am. We have no tables now. All our guests this evening have reservations. Would you like to wait or come back in an hour?"

"Good evening. I am sorry to interrupt. My name is Michael Brennan. I believe you have a table reserved for me?"

"Yes, sir. We do."

Michael turned to the woman.

"Hello. Would you like to join me for dinner?"

Lucee agreed as she was impressed by the man's confidence and pleasant invitation.

"Thank you. Are you sure you don't mind?"

"I do not. I never enjoy eating alone."

"I am Lucee Ba."

Nice to meet you, Lucee. I am Michael."

The two sat down a few moments later.

"What brings you to the hotel, Lucee?"

"I work for Doctors Without Borders. I am just taking a few days off. It's been a long two weeks."

"What do you do?"

"I help them bring in people suspected of contracting Ebola. We find patients and transport them into field hospitals. I also try to educate villagers about its symptoms and how to prevent spreading the virus."

"I hear it's getting worse."

"It is. Each week the numbers get higher. It is crazy around here. Hundreds of people have died near Kenema. If the disease hits the city, it will get a lot worse. Just two days ago, someone came into one of the field hospitals and stole infected blood. How crazy is that?"

Michael moved forward.

"What do you mean? Someone stole blood from a hospital?" asked Michael.

"Yes, I cannot imagine why someone would do that."

"Where was the hospital?"

"About forty minutes north of us. A small village named Barma. What do you do for a living, Michael?"

"I am a freelance reporter from Atlanta, Georgia. I write mostly for CNN.com and the Economist. Now you have me curious. Has this ever happened before?"

"No. Never."

"Is the staff at Barma sure it was stolen? Maybe it was temporarily misplaced or simply lost?"

"They are certain. The procedures for handling infected blood are stringent. No one there would have a reason to take it."

"This could be a story, Lucee. Do you think the doctors in Barma would speak to me about this?"

Lucee paused for a moment.

"I'm not sure. There are some who are worried it will get out and cause panic with the villagers there."

"Lucee, I would really like to look into this. Could you possibly make an introduction with someone at Barma?"

"Sure. I can try calling the director at the field hospital. She might be willing to speak with you. However, you will likely have to promise the story is not published soon."

"If they confirm, I can hold the story for a month."

"Okay. I will leave you a message at the front desk in the morning."

"Thank you, Lucee."

About an hour into his dinner, Michael needed to excuse himself.

"Lucee, I have some work I need to finish. It has been a pleasure speaking with you this evening. I will look for a message from you in the morning."

"Likewise, Michael. I should have something for you by nine."

"Goodnight, Lucee."

**Kenema Mosque, Kenema, Sierra Leone -
November 8, 8:10 PM**

Michael arrived at the intersection where the Mosque
stood. He continued driving south and saw no signs of
activity. There were no lights were visible from the
building where satellite imagery captured the complex just
a few days before. Strange, he thought to himself.

He pulled into the abandoned parking lot. The only
sounds he heard were from nearby dogs howling at the
clear night sky. It was too quiet for Michael. The Kenema
Mosque was the largest Mosque in the city, and he fully
expected stragglers from evening prayers or organized
groups meeting inside the sacred dwelling.

Michael decided to exit his SUV and have a look
around. He was in unfamiliar territory and recalled seeing a
group of local men walking toward the intersection as he
passed by. Michael was on his own and had no support. He
wished Elif and Nanook were with him.

Michael turned around the corner of the building and
made his way toward the front entrance of the Mosque.
There, he passed through the beautiful *sahn*, a courtyard
filled with a water cascade which welcomed its patrons.
The water was symbolic for ritual cleansing before prayer.

Michael looked upward and saw the minaret, a tower
adjacent to the Mosque used to call for prayer. The spiral
structure served as a commanding reminder of the Islamic
faith. This was a beautiful place to worship.

The locked doors served as a clear indication that the Mosque was no longer open for business. Michael decided to knock on the door anyway.

Nothing. He knocked again. The door opened as Michael turned away. An older man stood at the door.

"Hello. I am sorry to disturb you this evening. I am a reporter and seeking an interview with Sheikh Sahr Cissi. Is he available?"

"I am afraid we are closed."

"May I return in the morning?"

"No, sir. The Mosque will remain closed for two days for renovations. You may come back Monday."

"Will the Sheikh be available Monday?"

"No, sir. He has meetings to tend to all week. Do you have a business card?"

Michael handed the man his card and the doors closed quickly behind him. Michael thought the timing of the Sheikh's absence to be unusual. If he was indeed aware of the plot or personally involved, now would be the time to slip away from public view for a few days. On the other hand, there was always the chance the Mosque needed renovation. Either way, the timing troubled him. Michael had to find the Sheikh quickly.

Twenty minutes later Michael returned to his suite. He pulled out his laptop and provided Langley with a quick update.

Sheikh Cissi does not appear to be at his Mosque. Apparently, the Mosque is undergoing renovation. Will return onsite tomorrow afternoon to confirm. Spoke with a

*local NGO representative earlier. She indicated that
several vials of blood which tested positive for Ebola are
missing from a field hospital in Barma. Source indicates
staff at Barma are certain it was not lost or misplaced.
Source appears reliable. Plan to check in the morning.
Request additional support from Freetown to determine
whereabouts of the Sheikh.*

Michael finished his summary and drifted to sleep. He
was still feeling the effects of the trip from Hatay.
Tomorrow, there would be much work to do.

Capitol Hotel, Kenema, Sierra Leone - November 9, 8:58 AM

The early morning sun radiated its light into the hotel's lobby. Michael exited the elevator and made his way toward the front desk. Guests mingled around the Capitol's lobby as they waited for their taxis. Michael discerned many to be medical professionals based on their wardrobe and baggage.

"Good morning, sir. Do you have a message for Michael Brennan?"

"Yes, sir. The lady is waiting for you over there."

Michael turned toward the restaurant and saw Lucee sipping a cup of local coffee. The fresh mango picked earlier in the morning was nearly finished. She smiled and motioned him to join her.

"Good morning, Michael."

"Hi, Lucee. Good morning to you as well."

"You have permission to speak with the hospital's director. You will meet her at ten-thirty AM. May I travel with you to Barma? I can tell you more about my wonderful country."

"I would like that very much. What about taking a few days off?"

"I am already bored. I will return to the pool this afternoon. The journey to Barma will not be long."

"Okay. Let's go."

The short trip north to the field hospital offered Michael a fresh perspective of Sierra Leone. The country, ravaged by Ebola and civil war, was actually plush with tropical rainforests, home to countless wild animals, and the beaches were some of the best in the world. Sierra Leone was an undiscovered paradise.

Until they arrived at Barma.

Lucee pulled the vehicle into the designated staff parking area. The slight breeze coming from the east drew the aroma of dead bodies with it. Michael noticed it right away. Up ahead, he detected the ambulance and four medical staff standing at the rear doors.

A mother and three children just exited the ambulance. The medical staff had to assist the woman, as she appeared weak and unable to stand on her own. Michael suspected she had Ebola, along with the children.

"Mr. Brennan. I may not have much time to speak with you. We are expecting several ambulances this morning and our staff is thin," said the director.

"Thank you, Dr. Engel."

Michael flashed his CNN credentials and the two sat down.

"So, Lucee tells me you are working on a story about Ebola?"

"Yes, we understand the virus continues to spread across the entire region. Why is this occurring?"

"There are many factors. First, there is a lack of education on exactly how the virus transmits from one person to another. People in rural areas do not understand the risks and factors associated with the disease. Another problem commonly found in rural areas is the tradition of touching the dead before burial ceremonies. We have employees like Lucee who comb the countryside informing people of this, but the vast distances make it nearly impossible to educate everyone with the staff we have. Finally, many rural villagers have limited access to drinkable water. When infection occurs, a person must be fully hydrated and in a hospital to have a chance."

"How large is your staff?" asked Michael.

"We have nine doctors here, including me. We lost several more to the disease in just the last few months."

"What do you need to have a chance to curb the spread of Ebola?"

"More staff to educate the villagers who are isolated by remote distances. We need more field hospitals. Sierra Leone does not have the infrastructure to handle the outbreak."

"Lucee mentioned you had several vials of blood go missing. Have you recovered them or are they lost?"

"It was stolen, Mr. Brennan. I would appreciate it if you did not include that in your report. It would cause undue panic here in Barma and spread to cities such as Kenema and Hangha."

"I can hold off for a few weeks, but this is an important development. Why would someone do that?"

"I have no idea. It makes no sense to me. If I had to guess, the person or individuals responsible, plans to sell it to a pharmaceutical company to develop a vaccine."

"Would someone have to steal it?"

"Yes. The protocols on handling infected blood are massive. Only a few companies would have access to it."

"Have you introduced new security procedures to prevent this from happening again?"

"Look around, Mr. Brennan. We have no funds for that and our focus is on patient care."

"Thank you very much, Dr. Engel. May I have a look around with Lucee?"

"Not today, we are too busy, and the entire staff is working with patients right now."

"May I return in a few days?" asked Michael, though he had no intention of following up.

"Let us see, Mr. Brennan. At the rate we are going, we may be too overwhelmed."

Michael and Lucee soon departed. He acquired the intelligence he needed. There was little doubt in his mind that Islamic State was likely behind the stolen blood. The pieces were coming together, but he required confirmation. Sheikh Cissi had to be found right away.

INR Headquarters, Washington, D.C. - November 9, 9:30 AM

"Leslie, can you come over to my office?"

"On my way, Joe."

Leslie arrived minutes later and heard the news.

"Good morning, Leslie. We got Intel last night that some infected blood is missing from a field hospital outside Barma, Sierra Leone. The source reported to a NOC at CIA that it is highly unlikely the blood was lost."

"Infected with Ebola?"

"Correct. CIA is going to confirm this morning and enter the information into the database. You should see the report as soon as it is released."

"So, it could be true? Islamic State may be trying to introduce the Ebola virus into the country."

"Maybe. We have to get confirmation first before we go further. Nevertheless, we have to prepare assessments and develop scenarios. You need to prepare for a possible briefing to the National Security Council as soon as we get confirmation, if at all."

"Will do. When do we expect the report to be ready?"

"No idea. I spoke to a colleague at CIA who said they would enter into the information into the database when they got the Intel. In the meantime, proceed as if the information is credible and confirmed."

"Yes, sir."

Leslie raced back to her office and assembled her analytical team.

"We may see a report this afternoon that confirms missing blood from a field hospital in Sierra Leone. The blood is infected with Ebola."

"Dear Lord in heaven," said Jeremy.

"Dear Lord is right, Jeremy. All our work going forward will focus on scenarios. I don't want any work done on the national intelligence estimate requested by DOD and no support for routine reports. The only thing I care about is how someone would deliver the blood to the United States. I want an update to your scenarios by eleven-thirty this morning. Jordan, order us some lunch. Here is my credit card."

Leslie ended the short meeting. Her team would now focus on the task of developing credible courses of action for Islamic State. She picked up the phone and called Kerry at NCMI.

"Hey, Kerry. I may have to brief NSC soon. Can you join me in case some detailed medical questions come up about Ebola?"

"Uh sure, I have to clear it with my boss. Do you have more information on that plot we spoke about?"

"Yes. I will have to get you cleared, first."

Kerry held a top-secret clearance with several code words as an analyst with NCMI. Leslie believed her boss would have no issues with the request.

"I will see you later; do not wait up for me."

Leslie hung up and began to red team. She promised herself she would examine all courses of action despite how insane they might sound to the NSC staff.

Office of Internal Investigations, NYC Police Department – November 9, 10:00 AM

Peter Marsico stood at attention and prepared to hear his fate.

"Officer Marsico. This panel has concluded your actions on November 6 were beyond your scope of responsibilities. The actions you took were reckless, and you should have waited for a negotiator. It is our belief that a negotiator would have calmed the individual down resulting in the release of his hostage. However, given your spotless record and selfless service to the police department and the community, we believe a short suspension is more appropriate. You will forfeit two weeks of pay, and return to full duty on November twenty-third. The infraction will go into your personnel file and will be considered upon any future promotions. This hearing is concluded."

Peter saluted the panel and promptly left the building. Maybe a two-week vacation will do him some good, he thought to himself. Peter felt betrayed by the panel despite the short suspension.

A daytime visit to McMahon's Ale House, a popular watering hole in Brooklyn, New York, was in order. He wondered how many fellow officers from the Brooklyn borough might be there.

**United States Embassy, Freetown, Sierra Leone –
November 9, 10:36 PM**

"Ma'am, I just received a report from one of our sources working at the Radisson Blu Mammy Yoko Hotel here in Freetown. A group of four men arrived yesterday afternoon. They are from Kenema. The credit card on file with the hotel is registered with the Kenema Mosque."

"Thanks, Pat. Any idea who the four men are?"

"He did not know. He just said it was the talk of the hotel. Apparently, the room has had many visitors, if you catch my drift?"

"Women, Pat?"

"Yes, quite a few of them and housekeeping said the place was a mess this morning."

Brittany Stonebridge, the deputy chief of station for CIA in Sierra Leone, was not surprised. What caught her attention, however, was the credit card used for the suite. This might be the information her boss was looking for.

Brittany, a career CIA officer, was on station in Sierra Leone for two years. After battling skin cancer for three years before the assignment, the strong woman, and mother of four children, resumed her duties and her career thrived.

"Pat, how long are they staying?"

"They booked an executive suite for three days."

"What is the suite number?"

"Five-nineteen."

Brittany left her desk and entered Zach Thompson's office. Zach, the chief of station for CIA in Freetown, welcomed her in.

255

"Zach, looks like we got possible Intel on the Sheikh."

"What do you have?"

"Looks like four men checked into the Radisson Blu Mammy on Lumley beach. The card used to pay for the room belongs to the Kenema Mosque. It is an executive suite."

"Interesting. Think Sheikh Cissi is located there?"

"No way to tell now, Zach. The executive suite fits the profile. We will have to take a team there and find out for ourselves."

Zach smiled.

"What are you waiting for?"

Brittany left the office and gathered two of her officers. The trip to the Radisson would only take twenty minutes unless the group got mired in traffic.

A short while later, Zach called Doug Weatherbee.

"Doug, we might have the Sheikh located here in Freetown. A group checked in yesterday and paid for the rooms via a credit card registered to Kenema Mosque. I have a few people heading there now to confirm. If he is here, what would you like us to do?"

"Grab him and get him to the site we spoke of. If it is him, I want my man to question him."

"Do we have authorization for a rendition, Doug?"

"Yes, I had it approved this morning, just in case."

"Is he still in Kenema?"

"Yes, he is looking into a few things. He was just at the Mosque last night, and it was empty."

"Okay. I will update you when I know something."

Zach picked up his cell phone and texted Brittany right away. It simply read, *capture the Sheikh if possible. Rendition authorized.*

Brittany's team arrived at the Blu Mammy Yoko hotel. It was a breathtaking beachfront luxury resort sitting on pristine beaches with sparkling sand and clear blue waters. The hotel catered to the wealthy and elite businesspeople traveling into Freetown.

She entered through the front and made her way to the escalator.

Brittany led her two officers as she made the left turn on the fifth floor. Room 519 became visible a few moments later and Brittany knocked on the door.

"Good morning, I am with the United States Agency for International Development (USAID) here in Freetown. One of our guests staying here said she thought she recognized Sheikh Cissi from Kenema. He is apparently a kind and generous man focused on ending poverty in the region. I was wondering if I could speak with him for a few minutes about a project we would like to pursue in Kenema soon?"

"The Sheikh is not here. He is in Kenema."

Brittany noticed an older man with gray hair sitting in the room watching television.

"Our guest was quite certain. I only need a few minutes of his time. Please, we have a good project in mind and think he would be a tremendous partner in Kenema."

"I am sorry, but…"

The Sheikh intervened. Cissi spoke Hausa and directed the man to let her inside.

"I am Sheikh Cissi. And you are?"

"Brittany Seacrest."

"Please, come here and have a seat."

Brittany sat across from the Sheikh while the three men assembled around her. Little did they realize that Brittany's men had gathered in the hallway.

"Who did you say saw me at the hotel?"

"One of our project officers at USAID. Her name is Kate Bush."

"Bush? Like your last President?"

Brittany smiled and said, "No relation, Sheikh Cissi."

"What is this project all about?"

One of the men standing to Brittany's left spoke in Hausa. He did not trust her and suggested Cissi should have her escorted outside.

Brittany spoke enough Hausa to understand the man's suggestion.

Brittany immediately reached into her purse and pulled out a Glock 9mm pistol. She pointed it toward the Sheikh.

Cissi's men reached for their weapons soon after.

"Tell your men to lower their weapons, Cissi."

"I will do no such thing."

Brittany moved directly in front of Cissi and placed the barrel directly onto his forehead.

"All I want to do is ask you some questions. Your men will lower their weapons in five seconds, or I will pull the trigger."

Sheikh Cissi stared into the woman's eyes and recognized her commitment. He doubted she was bluffing.

"Lower your weapons."

"Now tell them to place their weapons on the floor."

She circled the Sheikh and now stood behind him.

"You heard her. Do it, now."

"Sheikh Cissi. You will slowly walk backward toward the front door. My weapon is pointed squarely at the back of your head."

"Where are you taking me," asked Cissi.

He was now clearly distressed and his arrogance had faded.

"Do not worry about that now."

Brittany opened the door and quickly stood behind Cissi once again. She entered the hallway and issued instructions to her men.

"Tyler. Collect their weapons and stay inside. I will call you when it is time to leave. Drew, grab the car and pull alongside the hotel's side entrance. I'll use the stairs and wait for you."

Brittany and her team quickly departed the hotel for the Embassy. She texted Zach from the car.

We have him. Moving to the Embassy now. ETA fifteen minutes.

Zach immediately placed the first of two calls.

"Doug, we have him. Our team picked him up at a hotel in Freetown just moments ago. We have a jet ready to fly him to Kenema within the hour. Two of my agents will accompany Cissi."

259

"Excellent news, Zach. I will let my man know. Do you have an ETA?"

"Not right now. I will send it to you ASAP. Be in touch soon, Doug."

Zach hung up the phone and called his contractor in Hangha.

"Gideon. Your guest will arrive this afternoon. I will send you the ETA."

"Thank you, Mr. Thompson. We are standing by."

Hangha, Sierra Leone – November 9, 5:30 PM

Michael pulled alongside the trailer at the abandoned diamond mine. Gideon was waiting for him.

"You must be Gideon? Your team comes highly recommended."

"Thank you. You as well. How may I address you?"

"Michael is fine."

Michael reached into the passenger side of the vehicle and pulled Cissi to his feet. A nylon braid restraint encircled Cissi's wrists. The breaking strength of eight hundred pounds ensured Cissi remained under control during his trip to the dusty remote mine.

Gideon's men took hold of Cissi and escorted him into the trailer. They sat him down on a folding aluminum chair. Sheikh Cissi quickly noticed the sets of tools designed to inflict pain and suffering. He gazed at the pliers and wondered what purpose they served. The seriousness and appearance of Gideon and his men further intimidated Cissi. His heart began to race and his breathing intensified.

"I don't have much time, Sheikh Cissi. It is my understanding you are aware of a plan to deliver an infected person with Ebola into the United States. Are you aware of such a plan?" asked Michael.

"I do not know what you are talking about. This is preposterous. I am a Muslim Sheikh. You have no right to do this."

"Are you aware of a plan to deliver an infected individual with Ebola into the United States?"

"No. I am not."

"Are you affiliated with Islamic State?"

"Of course not. I am a peaceful man."

Michael determined the man had calmed down a bit as his breathing became more normal.

"Do you know anyone affiliated with Islamic State?"

"No."

"Sheikh Cissi. I am a peaceful and patient man. I do not embrace violence nor do I look for trouble. However, I hear otherwise. Someone close to Shirazi specifically mentioned your name in connection with the plot."

"Who would say such a thing?"

"A dead man, Sheikh. A credible man. What do you know of the plot?"

"Nothing. I told you that, already. I know nothing. You cannot hurt me. CIA has outlawed torture at the direction of your President."

"Do you see these men here? They do not work for CIA. They are private contractors and free from restrictions. They actually enjoy hurting people. Would you like to spend some time with them?"

"You cannot allow such a thing. You would be in violation of your President's directives."

"How do you know so much about my President?"

"I watch the news. I read papers. You are breaking the law."

"Which law, Sheikh Cissi?"

"I want to be released now. I demand you let me go."

"I will not. The only way you leave here is by being brutally honest with me. If you tell me what you know

now, I will return you to the Mosque unharmed. And you will never see me again."

"I cannot give you what I do not know."

Michael motioned for Gideon to join him outside.

"Let's soften him up a bit tonight. Use white noise and stress positions to keep him awake. Nothing physical tonight. I am staying in Kenema and will return in the morning. If he talks, call me right away."

"Will do, Michael."

Cissi's first night in captivity was not as bad as he feared. The annoying sounds of continuous white noise and bright lights burning toward his face only prevented him from sleeping. At one point, Gideon forced the man to get on his knees and keep his back straight with his hands tied behind his back. The stress position became too difficult as the weight of his body pressed onto his knees directly in contact with the rigid floor. Gideon and his men spent much of the night taking turns to ensure the Sheikh remained awake.

Michael returned the following morning.

"Has he said anything yet, Gideon?"

"No, but he has been awake all night."

Michael walked into the trailer and asked that Gideon and his men leave. Michael wanted to speak with the man and establish rapport.

"Sheikh Cissi. How long have you lived in Kenema?"

"Since my childhood."

"Do you have a family?"

"A wife and two daughters. My son died after birth from complications."

"I am sorry to hear that. Where is your family now?"

"Why would I tell you such things? You will just take them."

"You have my word, I will not. Do they reside with you in Kenema?"

The Sheikh did not respond.

"What do you enjoy doing with your family?"

Silence. Sheikh Cissi recognized Michael's attempt to personalize the situation.

"If I had a wife and two children I would do anything to be with them," said Michael.

Still nothing.

"Why are you not answering my questions? I am simply trying to get to know you, Sheikh Cissi. Why do you not want to talk?"

"Would you want to talk with me if I were sitting there?"

"Probably not, but I would tell you everything I know. I would want to return to my family."

Sheikh Cissi remained quiet.

"What if I could guarantee safe passage to the west for you and your family? You could start a new life and be free from the Islamic State. All I need to know is if someone with Ebola is attempting to enter the United States. Has this person already left or are they still in Kenema?"

Still no response from Sheikh Cissi.

"I am going to have these men gather some food for you. They will bring you water, and I will tell them to let you sleep. How does that sound, Sheikh?"

The Sheikh looked into his eyes and still said nothing. Michael recognized the bitterness in his eyes, but the prospect of sleeping appealed to the man.

"I'll let you think on it for a few hours, Sheikh Cissi."

Michael went outside and gave Gideon his instructions.

"Gideon, allow him to rest until one o'clock. Give him some food and plenty of water."

The kidnapping of Cissi from Freetown was not an extraordinary rendition, defined as the transfer of an individual without due legal process to a foreign government for the purpose of interrogation or detention. Cissi now belonged to Michael and his group of Nigerian contractors. The situation Michael found himself was still in the gray area of CIA's legal restrictions under President Obama. Up to this point, Michael only questioned the man and did not intend to harm him. He just wanted to scare Cissi and convince him to give up the information.

Renditions were widely used in the Bush administration following the 9/11 attacks. President Bush and his senior foreign policy advisors were shaping a new world order and implementing aggressive tactics to combat international terror groups. Michael participated in his first rendition in June 2002. There, he managed to capture a top leader in the Abu Sayyaf, a militant group in the Philippines. His detention and interrogation led to the rescue of three North American citizens, two of which were American missionaries.

"Michael, are you staying or heading back to Kenema?" asked Gideon.

"No, I'll be here most of the day. I have two, maybe three days to get the Intel. He needs to start talking soon."

Michael returned several hours later to the trailer and found himself alone with the Sheikh.

"Sheikh Cissi. Have you given any more thought to what we spoke about earlier?"

National Security Council Deputies Committee, Washington, D.C. – November 10, 9:00 AM

Leslie, along with several other guests, arrived at the White House at 8:30 AM. She passed through screening at the east entrance and was escorted to the situation room by an assistant to the National Security Advisor.

Attending today's National Security Council Deputies Committee meeting were the deputy director at CIA, the Under Secretary of State for Political Affairs, the Deputy Secretary for Homeland Security, and Deputy National Security Advisor. Several civilian assistants and military advisors surrounded the group.

Leslie had the good fortune of starting the briefing.

"Sir, it appears the possibility that Islamic State plans to introduce the Ebola virus into the United States may be credible. We have confirmed reports from CIA that Shirazi approved the plan and directed a man named Sheikh Sahr Cissi to execute it from his Mosque in Kenema, Sierra Leone. We have since then received additional information that several vials of Ebola-infected blood are missing from a field hospital in Barma, Sierra Leone. The director of the facility is sure it was not an error on their part. They believe someone outside the facility stole the blood. CIA has…."

"Leslie, let me cut you off right there. How long ago did the blood go missing?" asked Jason Clancy, the deputy national security advisor.

"Approximately five days ago."

Clancy turned to Kerry at NCMI.

"Is it feasible for someone to do this and not be infected themselves?"

"Quite feasible, sir. All the individual has to do is use a high-quality transport device to secure the vials. With the proper equipment, and cooling temperatures regulated, it would be quite safe."

"Go on, Leslie."

"CIA has an operative on the ground and is attempting to extract the information from Sheikh Cissi."

Clancy turned to CIA.

"Do I want to know what we are doing with him?"

"All legal. We are following the law."

"So, let's say this is legit. How could Islamic State inflict a significant number of casualties? Ebola is treatable, and our medical facilities could deter any outbreak. Leslie, help me out here."

"Sir, you are correct. Our medical facilities could probably contain any infections. However, the problem I see is with timing."

"How so?"

"If this is true and the virus is introduced into the United States, imagine if the infected individual wandered around a large city. Take the District, for example. What if an individual rode along the subway and simply spent the day coughing and sneezing? In theory, the infection could spread to several passengers over the course of a few hours or days. Due to the time of the year, some infected individuals would likely deal with early symptoms as they would with the common cold. Those people could, in turn, ride the subway and continue infecting others. The contagion could spill to hundreds of people within days. There would be panic. The psychological blow Islamic State could deliver would be massive."

Clancy sat back in his seat.

"How would they do it, Leslie?"

"There are multiple scenarios here, sir. I believe the most likely course of action is for Islamic State to introduce the virus via a cargo ship or a private transatlantic vessel. The cargo ship is a possibility but a smaller ship is more likely, something like a yacht perhaps. They could enter at any of the hundreds of marinas along the east coast. The vessel would probably have the capability to keep the blood at the required temperatures."

"How long can the blood be stored, Kerry?"

"At least thirty days if cooled at ten degrees Celsius."

"Leslie, do we know when this Sheikh Cissi put the plans in motion?"

"No sir, the individual may already be here in the United States."

"Ben, any idea when your man will get the information?"

"This could take days, weeks or even months. I have no idea how long it will take to get the information."

"Okay. I do not think we have enough to alert the President right now. However, I want to reconvene in a couple of days or as soon as the information is collected. Take care everyone."

The situation room cleared within a few short minutes. Jason returned to his desk and pondered the briefing. He prayed the hypothesis was false and the intelligence community was stretching its imagination. However, something inside him felt uneasy concerning this potential threat to the homeland. Its sheer insanity and simplicity are what actually gave it credibility.

Hangha, Sierra Leone – November 10, 1:05 PM

"What kind of guarantees can you provide me if I talk?" asked Cissi.

The Sheikh just made a major miscalculation. He all but admitted he was a full participant by asking for assurances. This would allow Michael the opening he needed if partial torture or enhanced interrogation were necessary. Any information provided by the Sheikh, under those circumstances, would become less credible due to the physical mistreatment.

"That depends on what you give me, Sheikh Cissi," said Michael.

"What if I knew the individual that was planning to enter the United States?"

"Then I would want to know that information, Sheikh Cissi."

"What would I get in return for his name?"

"Nothing. I will need his full name, any aliases, recent photos, and where he is right now."

"I do not know where he is now."

"Who is he?"

"I need assurances you will get me and my family out."

"No, I already told you that."

Michael immediately stood up and stared into the Sheikh's eyes.

"I gave you an opportunity, Sheikh Cissi. I want you to remember that. Gideon, come inside."

Michael walked toward Gideon standing at the entrance of the trailer. He whispered in his ear. The gesture had the intended effect.

Gideon turned to one of his men standing outside and motioned him to come inside the trailer.

"Rough him up a bit," said Gideon as Michael stepped outside.

The young man began slapping Sheikh Cissi in the face with his hands while keeping his fingers spread apart, also known as an "insult slap." He did not exert all of his strength on the elderly Sheikh for fear of hurting him too quickly. The Nigerian then proceeded to conduct a series of facial holds and attention grasps, techniques the CIA could no longer perform. The Sheikh suffered for approximately thirty minutes.

"Move away and return outside. Bring in our friend," said Gideon.

"Sheikh Cissi, who is the person you directed to the United States," asked Michael.

"I will give you his name. First, I need a signed letter from your government assuring my family's safety. Once my family and I board a plane, I will give you his name."

"Where is the individual now?"

"That I do not know. He left the country four days ago. He is on a ship."

"What ship?"

"I am not aware of its name, but I know where it is going."

"Where and when will it arrive?"

"Jamaica. I will not say more until I receive my guarantee."

"Where is your family now?"

"Somewhere safe in Kenema. You will not find them. If I get the letter and we are safely on a plane, I will tell you everything I know."

Michael became annoyed at the Sheikh's bravado. He was not used to bargaining with evil men. However, under the circumstances, he considered the Sheikh's proposal.

"Gideon, please come inside," shouted Michael.

"Yes?"

"Find his family. They are in Kenema. Do what you have to. Bring them here. Go to the Mosque first. They are probably there."

Michael reached a point of no return. Time was critical and tactics that were more intimidating became necessary. He did not intend to harm the Sheikh's family, but the psychological impact of their capture might discourage the Sheikh's resolve.

"All right Sheikh Cissi, let me see what I can do to get you out. The information you give me must be confirmed first."

"Why have you sent those men to Kenema?"

"Time to relax, Sheikh Cissi. Would you like some water?"

"No."

Michael returned to his car and reached for his bag. Within a few minutes, he was back in the trailer and securely connected with Langley.

273

In Hangha with the Sheikh. Plot confirmed. An individual left Sierra Leone four days ago via ship. Destination is Jamaica. No further information available at this time. Will update when more details emerge.

"Did you send your superiors a message to get me and my family out?" asked Cissi.

"Yes. This type of request will have to go through many offices. It will likely take several days, Sheikh Cissi. Time which I do not have," said Michael.

"Then how will I know if I can trust you?"

"You can. It is the men looking for your family that you should be worried about. They are contractors and only paid for specific services. They will listen to me only as long as they are assured we will pay."

"Would it help if I gave you the name of the boat they are using?"

"Very much, Sheikh Cissi. Look, I do not know or care why you agreed to help the Islamic State. Maybe they threatened your family. Maybe they paid you large sums of cash. On the other hand, maybe you just believe in the Caliphate. Either way, I do not care. All I want to do is stop the individual traveling to my country."

"Your country has caused many people to suffer in the past."

"You are right, but I don't care about that right now."

"Maybe you should?"

"Sheikh Cissi, I am not a politician. I do not engage in policy decisions. I only care about my mission. I am sure you understand."

Michael continued to converse with Sheikh Cissi for much of the afternoon. He had established rapport and got the Sheikh talking. He was convinced if Gideon found the Sheikh's family he would give up everything he knew.

Atlantic Ocean - November 10, 4:20 PM

Foday and Manjo sat inside the galley of the Black River. Fallubah was at the helm of the boat where he had been for much of the trip. The advanced autopilot system aboard the yacht allowed the man to squeeze in much-needed naps and several hours of sleep at night. Fallubah bore the brunt of the difficult crossing as Foday and Manjo remained below deck focused on their mission.

The winds blowing along the frigid Atlantic waters remained calm while the salty sea air made its way inside the yacht. The Black River swayed violently the previous evening from a storm which blew over from the south. However, today the seas were calm, and the group was moving at nearly twenty knots.

Foday dialed his satellite phone and called Dayo, who remained at the Errol Flynn Marina in Jamaica.

"Dayo, we have crossed the halfway point. I think we will arrive in three to four days depending on the conditions. How are things there?"

"Good, Foday. You are all set to refuel, and I have the provisions for the rest of your trip."

"Have you spoken to Sahr?"

"Every day as he instructed, except yesterday. He did not answer his phone."

This unexpected bit of news displeased Foday.

"You tried his cell and office?"

"Yes, both, many times. I also called today and nothing. Is there something wrong, Foday?"

"Maybe not, Dayo. I will call again tomorrow and check in with you. This is not like Sahr."

Foday turned to Manjo.

"Manjo, you have probably been wondering why we are aboard this ship. It's time I tell you the mission."

"Okay, I have wondered but figured you would tell me when you were ready."

"What have you read from the Quran today?"

"I read from the Quran, 9:5."

"And what do you remember?"

"Slay the idolaters wherever ye find them, arrest them, besiege them, and lie in ambush everywhere for them. Prophet! Make war on the unbelievers and hypocrites! Hell shall be their home, an evil fate."

Foday smiled at Manjo and simply nodded his head as if he approved.

"You and I are going to the United States, specifically to New York City. Once we arrive in New York, you will spend several days along the subway trains scouting out potential targets for bombings. I will give you the routes and trains to ride once we settle in. Fallubah will assist with the planning and build the detonators for the bombs. This will not be a suicide mission for you Manjo. Rather, the start of a jihad in the United States against the country responsible for our troubles."

"We are going to New York City? I hear surveillance there is very good."

"Yes. The best in the world. They will never expect us. New York has become comfortable since 9/11."

277

"What will we do after we bomb?"

"We simply travel to another city and do it again. Allah willing, we will conduct many attacks."

Foday set the first part of his plan in motion. Manjo became excited and optimistic the plan could work.

"Thank you, Foday, for giving me this honor."

"The honor is ours, Manjo. Many brothers around the world will speak your name. Return to your studies. I am going to get some air and talk to Fallubah."

Hangha, Sierra Leone – November 10, 5:30 PM

"We have them, Michael. It was not easy. I lost one of my men. You were right, we found them inside the Mosque guarded by two men," said Gideon.

"Good work, Gideon. See you soon."

Michael turned to Cissi.

"The men found your family, Sheikh Cissi. They are bringing them here now."

"Are they harmed?"

"Of course, not. Now please tell me what you know."

"Not until I know we are leaving."

"That is not what I wanted to hear. Do you not trust me, Sheikh Cissi?"

"Right now, I trust no one."

"Who is the man you sent? Where is he going?" Michael's pace and intensity increased.

"Not until my family and I are safe."

"Sheikh Cissi. I do not think you understand what is going on here. You will not leave until I am satisfied you have given me what I need. Do you want to give those men a reason to harm your wife or children? I will not be able to stop them. They require fees for their services."

"You wouldn't dare do such a thing."

"No, but I cannot guarantee what they will do."

Sheikh Cissi sighed and sat back in his chair. The moment he feared arrived. His family would be joining him soon. He ran out of time and imagined what might happen, if he remained silent.

"The man's name is Manjo. I do not know his last name. He only arrived at the Mosque ten days ago. We trained him, and he is going to Jamaica."

"Where in Jamaica?"

"You promise my family will be safe?"

"Yes."

"They will arrive at the Errol Flynn Marina in a city called Port Antonio."

"What is the name of their boat?"

"Black River."

"How many men are traveling with Manjo?"

"The boat's captain is Fallubah Owusu."

"Is he part of the plan?"

"No. He is simply transporting him there and returning home."

"Anyone else on board besides Manjo and Fallubah?"

"No, not that I know of."

"Is someone waiting for them in Jamaica?"

"Yes, a man named Dayo. He is only gathering provisions and coordinating for fuel."

What is Dayo's last name?"

"Tinibu."

"Where is Dayo staying?"

"The Trident Hotel in Port Antonio."

"Where are they going?"

"New York City."

"How do they plan to release Ebola into the population?"

"I do not know."

"Sheikh Cissi. Think of your family. Be very careful here."

"Fallubah is going to infect Manjo. Fallubah did not give me the specifics."

"Where will he go?"

"I do not know. He was given instructions to choose targets and locations of his choosing."

"You are sure?"

"I am."

Michael sat back. The Sheikh's body language, tone and demeanor indicated he told Michael everything he knew.

A short while later, Gideon and his men returned to the trailer. Cissi's wife and children were with the Nigerian mercenaries. Their faces spoke of sheer terror. Gideon's men clearly made an impression. Michael joined them outside and motioned Gideon to walk with him.

"I believe I have the Intel I need and you probably won't be seeing me again. Keep the family and Sheikh Cissi here until Freetown calls with instructions. They are not to be touched for now. You and your men did a good job."

"Okay, Michael. How long will we wait? My men and I will need payment soon."

Michael was not pleased with Gideon's demeanor.

"Until Freetown calls you."

"My men and I are not babysitters, Michael."

"Give Freetown a few hours, okay Gideon?"

"A few hours, but not much longer. I have other contracts waiting."

Michael entered his car as Gideon and his men bustled the family into the trailer. Michael was not pleased with how they handled the children. Despite their father's failings, the siblings were innocent victims. As the door behind them closed, he heard a shriek coming from Sheikh Cissi's wife. One of Gideon's men yelled at her to move away. The cries from Cissi's children grew louder.

Michael stormed into the trailer. He had his weapon drawn and noticed Gideon's men were manhandling Cissi's wife. Their intentions were clear, and the loss of one of their men probably added to their vicious behavior. One of the men turned toward Michael and began drawing his weapon. Michael immediately reacted and fired off two quick shots. Both of Gideon's men fell to the floor. Gideon reached for his sidearm, but it was too late. Two rounds entered his chest, and the Nigerian mercenary hit the ground. Chaos ensued as Cissi's children began crying loudly.

"Calm them down, Sheikh. Tell them they are safe now," said Michael unemotionally.

Michael quickly called Freetown with the news. No one was pleased, but Michael felt he had little choice. He made a deal with the Sheikh, and his family was off limits.

"Michael, I can get a team there in a few hours."

"Good. I want the Sheikh and his family taken to the Embassy. They will remain there until Doug gives you instructions."

Several hours later, Brittany and her team from Freetown arrived. They took hold of the Sheikh and his family, while two men remained to clean up the mess.

Michael returned to his car and sent another message to Langley.

The ship is called the Black River. Port of destination is the Errol Flynn Marina in Port Antonio, Jamaica. Target's name is Manjo. Last name unknown. The boat's captain is Fallubah Owusu. A man named Dayo Tinibu is staying at the Trident Hotel in Port Antonio. Sheikh Cissi cooperated and will move to Freetown this evening. Request he and his family be relocated to the US or destination of their choosing. This assumes Intel is good and confirmed. Need travel arrangements to the nearest airport to Port Antonio tonight or tomorrow morning.

Michael sped off. His drive to Kenema would be short, and Laura occupied his attention for the first time in several days. He was anxious to reach out and send her a message.

Lying in bed, he wrote his new love.

Good evening Laura. Wow, the last few days have been busy! Still unsure when I can get the heck out of here. So looking forward to seeing you soon. Been brushing up on my French cuisine. How does a Marjoram roasted rack with Morel Panna Cotta and Fava beans sound to you? How are things at work since your conference? Are you planning any more trips soon? Michael

Michael turned his attention to Jamaica as he drifted closer to sleep. He visited the country once before for a short assignment in 1994. There, he conducted a reconnaissance against drug lords with ties to Haitian street gangs. During the assignment in support of Operation Uphold Democracy, he collected valuable information supporting US military forces. Their mission was to restore order to the ravaged country. Michael wondered if this trip would lead to similar success.

The hunt for the Black River would begin in the morning.

Atlantic Ocean – November 11, 7:45 AM

"Good morning, Dayo. Have you heard from Sahr?"

"Still nothing, Foday. I am worried."

"As am I. We need a change of plans. Can you find another marina on the island?"

"I'm sure I can, but we are all set here."

"We cannot risk detection. We must assume our enemies are aware of our plans. I want you to begin preparations for a new entry point. Do you still have plenty of cash on hand?"

"Yes, Sahr provided extra for contingencies."

"Good, find another hotel. I will call again tomorrow morning. We are moving closer, and the winds are in our favor."

"Okay, Foday. Safe journey my friend."

"You as well, Dayo."

Foday thought to himself for a while. The Sheikh's sudden and unexpected silence was clearly worrisome. Nevertheless, Foday's decision to alter the plan was correct. Islamic State and the Sheikh would not care of tactical considerations. Their only concern was the successful delivery of the virus. Foday and Dayo would be the only men aware of the new marina.

St Margarets Bay, Jamaica – November 11, 3:30 PM

Michael debarked from the private Lear jet on loan from Freetown. He was well rested and soon began the short twenty-minute trip to Port Antonio. The magnificent drive along Highway 4 reminded Michael of the Caribbean's mystique and natural beauty. Halfway into his trip, he looked north toward Orange Bay and gazed at the white sandy beaches and tropical trees. The seas were calm, and he wondered where the Black River might be.

"Good afternoon, please transfer me to Mr. Dayo Tinibu's room," asked Michael from inside the cab.

"I'm sorry sir, he checked out this morning," said the hotel's front desk clerk.

"Did he mention where he might be going?"

"No sir, he was scheduled to spend several more days with us, but he left unexpectedly."

"Thanks. Do you have a room available?"

"Yes sir, we do."

"My name is Michael Brennan. I will be there in just a few minutes."

"How long will be you be staying with us, sir?"

"A week."

Michael hung up and placed a call to Doug.

"Doug, our lead here in Jamaica has left his hotel."

"Where are you now, Michael?"

"In a cab heading to the hotel. I should be there in a few minutes."

"The Black River is still a day or two away depending on the conditions. Let me see what I can do to get some additional assets down there. I already passed on the data associated with the Sheikh's cell phone. It should not take NSA long to identify his recent calls. With a little luck, they will determine Dayo's location quickly. In the meantime, see if you can track this kid down. I will send you an update tonight or tomorrow morning regarding additional coverage."

"Sounds good, thanks."

Dayo Tinibu had become one of the world's most wanted men.

Joint Interagency Task Force South (JIATS-S), Key West, Florida – November 11, 8:45 PM

"Sir, we have a request from CIA for aerial coverage over Jamaica," said Olivia Bell, a young intelligence analyst with the Joint Interagency Task Force in southern Florida.

"What are they looking for?" asked Lieutenant Commander Lance Fuller, a career officer with the United States Coast Guard.

"They are asking for drone support. They are searching for a ship called the Black River, which departed West Africa five days ago. They estimate it will reach Jamaican waters in the next couple of days or so."

"They say why, Olivia?"

"No. Only to know which port or marina it goes to."

"Do they realize we only have three drones on the books? We are drowning here looking for drug shipments throughout the Caribbean region, and they want us looking for one ship somewhere in the ocean?"

"The request is high priority," said Olivia.

Joint Interagency Task Force South was one of the most successful intelligence sharing agencies within the United States government. The agency's focus is to detect and monitor transnational organized crime groups operating in the Caribbean region. JIATF-S used a sophisticated array of classified intelligence gathering systems as it alerted Coast Guard cutters, naval ships and allied partners to intercept suspected narcotics traffickers.

"I'll need to run this by Commander Hunter in the morning. I suspect we will have to figure out how to support the request before someone tasks us. CIA usually gets what it wants."

"Does CIA call us often?" asked Olivia.

"I have been here four years now and only aware of one time. They called about a drug shipment from Brazil last year and wanted to know the names of the crew. Apparently, one of the individual's names we captured went missing from the initial report. They simply wanted to fill in the gap."

"So, this is probably important then?"

"I imagine so. However, we only have three drones and many requirements. Commander Hunter and the CO will have to speak with J2 to figure it out. Some of our customers may be upset, but it is CIA after all. I will set up the meeting."

Lieutenant Commander Lance Fuller and Olivia Bell resumed their night duties. Both imagined why CIA made the rare request.

The Black River, Eastern Caribbean Sea - November 12, 8:00 AM

"Dayo, have you found a new location?"

"Yes. The Grand Hotel in Port Royal. There is a Marina there and has everything you will need to finish the journey."

Dayo's choice was fitting. Port Royal, a picturesque town steeped in pirate folklore used to be known as "the wickedest and most sinful city in the world." Founded in 1518, the city was ideally located to interdict Spanish shipping lanes all the way to Panama. Infamous buccaneers ranging from Captain Henry Morgan to Captain John Davis staged their attacks from Port Royal. Booty from successful raids and assaults on Spanish settlements were spent on women and alcohol. Today, Port Royal is a thriving community ripe with tourism and eager archaeologists.

"Will customs be an issue?" asked Foday.

"No. I do not think so. If you refuel quickly, it probably will not come up. I will have the provisions you require and load them while you wait."

"Have you had the opportunity to observe their security?"

"Yes. It appears minimal, but I have only been here one day. I will continue to assess them."

Foday hung up and joined Manjo in the galley. It was time to prepare the young jihadist for his mission in New York City.

"Manjo, when the time comes I will purchase several tickets for you to ride the metro train in New York. On the first day, you will take the N metro line from Brooklyn all the way to Queens. I want you to make four stops. You will stop at Atlantic Avenue/Barclays Center/4 Avenue. Your second stop will be Canal Street, and your third will be Times Square/42nd Street station. This location will have many police officers, but I want you to find several stalls that might be useful for a bomb. I want you to find the bathroom closest to the center of Times Square. If there is no suitable bathroom, make a mental note. You will get back on the train and make your last stop at the Queensboro Plaza. Look for large gatherings of people in coffee shops and restaurants. Once again, you will return to the train and finish up in Queens. You will simply ride back to Brooklyn and meet me in Coney Island. I want you to study the map in front of you. Each station has a circle. Memorize them. We will look at the second day later."

"How can I remember everything, Foday?"

"You will have to do your best, Manjo. You cannot risk being seen taking notes or looking suspicious. If you do, the police will question you which could jeopardize the mission."

"I will do my best, Foday."

"I know Manjo, I know you will. I will be back in a few hours to test you. Study well."

Foday returned to the deck. The cool winds from the Caribbean Ocean swayed the Black River. He turned to Fallubah.

"We have a new port. Plot a course for Port Royal, Jamaica. The Grand Hotel there has a Marina where Dayo will meet us."

"Okay, Foday, but we have a possible storm approaching from the Gulf of Mexico. We may be delayed depending on the conditions."

"How long if the seas remain calm?"

"Thirty-two hours, Foday."

With a new course plotted and entered into the ship's navigation system, the Black River set its sights on Port Royal. Ebola was making its way to the United States.

Trident Hotel, Port Antonio, Jamaica – November 12, 8:30 AM

Michael sat alone at Lucky's outdoor restaurant, a casual spot along the beach. He prepared for his day while eating his usual breakfast entailing fried eggs, bacon, and toast. Freshly chilled orange juice and local coffee added to the delicious meal. Today's task was to search for nearby marinas. Michael anticipated Dayo would likely remain on the island, but find a nearby port within a few hours' drive. His sudden departure would require reconnaissance and Dayo had few opportunities to travel the long distance to Jamaica's west coast on such short notice.

"Good morning, man. Are you Mr. Brennan?"

"Yes, may I help you?"

"Doug sent me. May I sit down?"

"Doug who?"

"Your friend from Virginia."

"Please, sit down."

"My name is Ashani Brown. A pleasure to meet you."

Ashani looked the part. A native of Jamaica, he wore flip-flops, baggy tan shorts, and a bright yellow t-shirt. His dreadlocks reached past his shoulders, and his accent left little doubt he was a local.

"Hello, Ashani. So, Doug sent you?"

"Yes, man. I have known Doug for a long time. We go back almost thirty years. I provide information from time to time."

"You are with the company?"

"Oh no, man. Just a contractor."

"What did Doug ask you to do?"

"To take you around the island. I believe you're looking for a yacht?"

"Yes."

"Well, you can forget about the maps you are looking at. There are only a few marinas on Jamaica capable of housing a yacht. How big is it?"

"No idea. Probably forty feet at least."

"Then let's go. Would you like to head east or south?"

"What do you suggest?" asked Michael.

"South. There are two marinas near Kingston. And I have friends at both."

An hour into their drive, Michael and Ashani entered the Blue Mountain State Park. The park is home to the Blue Mountains, one of the largest mountain ranges in the Caribbean. Crowded with wildlife and mysterious foliage, the mountains give off a bluish color due to constant mist along its trails.

Ashani's cell phone rang.

"Hello, man. You have something for me?"

"Maybe. A man was at the Grand Hotel Marina this morning asking questions about fuel. I've never seen him before, and he sounded African."

"Did he give his name?"

"No. But he asked some unusual questions."

"Like what?"

"Like how quickly he could refuel a ship. He also asked questions about the marina's security. He seemed a bit anxious to me, Ashani."

"It could be who I'm looking for. Thank you, man. Are you there now?"

"Yes."

"Good. I will see you in about two hours."

Ashani turned to Michael.

"We may already have something, Michael."

"What did you find out?"

"An African was at the marina in Port Royal. He asked some strange questions."

"That sounds like a good lead to me, Ashani."

Michael gazed into the thick treeline along highway B1. Who needs the NSA and satellites, he thought to himself. As usual, good old-fashioned human intelligence collection did the trick.

Michael and Ashani arrived at the Port Royal Grand Hotel approximately two hours later. Michael marveled at its pristine location along the shoreline. They quickly made their way to the marina.

"Hello, man. Good to see you."

"You too, Ashani. Who is your friend?"

"This is Mr. Brennan. He is my guest for the next few days."

The young man speculated who Michael was but never asked. He was an acquaintance of Ashani and that was enough. Ashani was a trusted friend and paid well for information.

"You say this man is African?" asked Ashani.

"Yes. I have met many Africans here at the marina. I am certain of it."

"Did he say when he would be back?"

"Today. He said sometime after lunch."

"Sounds like we have time to eat, Michael," said Ashani.

Michael and Ashani sat at the Red Jack restaurant with a superb vantage point of the marina. Both men were enjoying some local burgers and fries. Ashani proved to be an interesting man and shared his talents during the meal.

"I've lived here all my life, Michael. I know the names of the harbormasters and their families."

"What kind of work have you done for Doug?"

"Information. Doug and I met in Kingston when your country began its war on drugs in 1986. I became a source for him and mostly focused on street gangs and shipments of drugs into the ports and marinas. I remained his source after he left. He still calls from time to time, but not as much lately. Is your focus now on the Middle East?"

"Yes, the Middle East. It's very complicated there now."

"Have you spent much time there?"

"No, I don't travel much."

Ashani might have worked with Doug in the past, but Michael was not about to give the stranger more information.

"What do you do for Doug?" asked Ashani, now curious.

"I provide information, like you," said Michael with a smile.

Michael noticed a man walking nearby.

"Is that someone walking toward your friend?"

"I believe so," said Ashani.

"This could be our man. Please confirm with your friend after he leaves. I'll follow him to see where he goes and return to pick you up," said Michael.

Dayo approached the marina's office as his eyes scanned the surrounding area. Ashani stood up from his chair and made his way toward the small strcuture. Michael, convinced of Dayo's unease, flipped open his wallet, placed cash on the table, and waited.

Michael studied Dayo's every move as he neared the entrance. He noticed the position of his shoulders as his arms swung forward, and the length of his steps. The man was walking faster than the average person would.

Ashani finally arrived at the front door of the office. Michael hoped he would not spook the young African. He noticed Dayo exiting the office while Ashani smiled at him and wished him a good day. Dayo did not return the pleasantry. Moments later, Ashani exited the office and gave Michael a thumbs-up. Michael quickly snapped a picture of the man for his next update to Langley. He now had a clear mark and turned his attention on following him.

Dayo returned to the lobby of the hotel and made his way to the elevator. He looked back toward the lobby's entrance as Michael peeled off to the front desk.

"May I use your phone? My cell is dead," said Michael.

Dayo entered the elevator and gave it no thought. Michael soon left the lobby and met Ashani on the dock leading to the office.

"That's him, Michael," said Ashani.

"Can you find out his name? It looks like he is staying at the hotel."

Dayo Tinibu was within reach and continuous surveillance of the man would start right away.

Michael made his way to the car while Ashani conversed with the front desk clerks.

"Good afternoon, Tara and Claire."

"Ashani, have you come to ask me out again?"

"No, Claire. You have broken my heart too many times. Has an African checked in the last couple of days?"

"Yes, why?"

"I heard from the harbor master he was looking for a tour guide to Kingston tomorrow. Can you tell me his name?"

"You know I'm not supposed to do that, Ashani."

"I know, but I really need the money. Please, can you help a poor man earn a living? Have I ever let you down or harassed one of your guests?"

"I guess not old man."

"Thank you, ladies. I would sweep you both off your feet if I were fifteen years younger."

"Don't be silly, Ashani, but I like your charm and effort," said Claire.

"He checked in under Dayo Turay. Please do not ask for his room number, Ashani," said Tara.

"I won't. Thank you very much. I will call later and ask you to transfer me to his room. I will bring you both flowers the next time I come back."

Ashani rejoined Michael in the car.

"He checked in as Dayo Turay."

"First name matches what I'm looking for. He's probably using a fake last name. This is our man, Ashani. Do you have friends we can use to watch him if he leaves?"

"Yes, I know plenty of people in Kingston."

"How fast can you get them here?"

"Give me an hour," said Ashani.

"Have you worked with them before?"

"Yes. They can be trusted and they owe me some favors."

Ashani's men arrived as promised. The three men pulled alongside Ashani's car, as he flashed them the picture of Dayo.

"This is the man I want you to keep an eye on. Let me know when he leaves the hotel. Your job is to follow him and keep me informed. We will be in Kingston for a while and return at lunch. Any questions?"

Ashani and Michael left the hotel parking lot and began the short trip to Kingston. There, the two men would find a hotel and wait. Michael knew the Black River was nearby.

The Black River, Caribbean Sea - November 12, 10:04 AM

"Have you had a chance to study the map and plans for surveillance, Manjo?"

"Yes, I think I have it."

Foday proceeded to question Manjo and after several minutes felt the young man was ready for more.

"Good, Manjo. Now let us look at the second day."

"May I ask where I will be staying, Foday."

"Sure, I have a place in Brooklyn ready to go. I have a friend there that will allow you stay at his apartment during the mission."

"We will not be staying there together?"

"No. I will be somewhere else. It is safer for us to remain apart. Now let us look at day two. Here, you will take the N train again to Times Square. There you will change trains and go to the red line, number 1. This train will be the Broadway, 7 Avenue Local. It will take you north to the Bronx, another borough in New York City. There, I want you to make two stops. Your first stop will be 137 Street/City College Broadway exit. I want you to walk a few blocks and look for areas where there are large concentrations of people. Get back on the red line. Your second stop will be the last station in the Bronx called Van Cortlandt Park 242. This will be your secondary target if security is too tight in the other locations. Keep looking at the maps this morning, and we'll discuss a few more details in the afternoon."

Foday returned topside.

"Fallubah, how does it look?"

"We should be there around six o'clock tomorrow unless the weather changes."

"You think he's up to it?"

"Yes. He is still angry over his father and appears ready. I still need to determine exactly how to inject him with the virus. What do you think about doing it while he sleeps?"

"Good idea. We need that anger to fuel his focus. He might wake up. Have you thought about just telling him?"

"I have but am concerned it will be too much for him. His father's slow death must have been gruesome, and I cannot imagine him going through that."

"Convince him to martyr himself then, Foday. Does he think the both of you will conduct more than one attack? Tell him the request comes from the Caliph directly. That should motivate him enough, I think."

"Maybe, Fallubah, but my concern is that the moment he feels symptoms he will panic and ask to be martyred earlier. The only chance this will work is if he is on the metro trains for at least two days. We cannot even be sure he will infect a single person. If we fail, the Caliph will be disappointed."

"Does that matter now, Foday?"

"No. I suppose not. You are probably right, Fallubah. I'll go below and speak with him."

"Manjo, Fallubah and I have spoken. There is something else I have not told you."

"What is it, Foday? Are you worried about my dedication to the mission?"

"No, Manjo. I know you are committed. You must do something else before you begin the reconnaissance aboard the trains. I am not sure you will be as enthusiastic."

"I am ready for anything, Foday. I want to strike at the Americans."

"Inside my cabin, there is a refrigerator with several vials of blood. They contain Ebola. Your true purpose is to remain on the trains and attempt to infect as many people as you can. Allah willing, the virus will spread. Once you become too weak to travel, then you will carry out a suicide attack and martyr yourself."

Manjo sat back in his chair. The prospect of Ebola frightened him and conjured images of his father. Was he ready to die so soon, he asked himself? Foday waited for the information to settle in.

"I will not suffer, Foday?"

"No, absolutely not. As you know, the early symptoms are similar to the common cold and flu. Once you become weak, you will check in with me, and I will give you instructions. Your vest will already be in the apartment. When you are ready, you will wear it and go to one of the designated targets."

Manjo thought some more. He always figured this was a one way trip. His eyes turned toward Foday and his head slowly began nodding up and down.

"I can do it. I will do it. I am ready."

"Our brothers will speak of this until the end of days, Manjo. The Caliph will be proud of you. Sheikh Cissi will be proud. This honor is yours."

"How will I become infected?"

"Leave that to me, Manjo. Return to your bunk and get some sleep. I will remain top deck with Fallubah."

Foday rejoined Fallubah.

"You were right. He is willing to do it. I thought we might have to resort to other measures."

"Excellent. Think he has any idea of his true purpose?"

"No."

**JIATF-S Headquarters, Key West, Florida –
November 12, 10:30 AM**

"Sir, we got a request from CIA last night for drone support," said Lieutenant Commander Hunter.

"What does CIA want to know?" asked Rear Admiral Christopher Tobin.

"They want us to look for a ship called the Black River. Apparently, it's making its way to Jamaica."

"When is the ship scheduled to arrive in Jamaican waters?"

"Sometime today or tomorrow."

"From which direction?"

"Coming from the east, sir."

Rear Admiral Tobin turned to his senior intelligence officer. Captain Michele Griffin, a career officer with the United States Coast Guard since 1995, was a rising star in the Intelligence Community.

"Michele, can we spare a drone to support this?"

"We could, sir, but the tasking order for the next couple of days has our drones over the Dominican Republic. According to DEA, there is a suspected shipment of cocaine going to a marina near Santo Domingo. The tasking calls for continuous surveillance."

"What about our third drone?"

"In maintenance. The onboard GPS system failed during its last mission. Technicians are looking at it now."

"How long before they can fix it?"

"No idea, sir. You know how these things go. It could be within hours or days depending on what parts are needed and what they have in stock."

Tobin turned to his DEA liaison.

"Eric, what's the anticipated size of the shipment?"

"Small, sir. Source reporting suggests between ten and fifteen kilos."

"That's not too small. Commander Hunter, can we send more cutters to Santo Domingo?"

"I can call Miami and let you know ASAP, sir."

"Okay, let's do it. CIA would not be asking if it was not important. Michele, redirect the drones to Jamaica for the next three days. After that, they go back to Eric's people, assuming he still needs them. Eric, let your people know and have them call Michele if there are any complaints. I suspect someone will not be happy with me this morning."

"Will do, sir. If we can get an extra cutter that might be enough."

Within the hour, the first drone began its flight toward Jamaica. The hunt for the Black River was on.

The White House, Washington, D.C. – November 12, 11:30 AM

"Good morning everyone. Leslie, get us started," said Deputy National Security Advisor Clancy.

"Good morning sir. A lot has happened since we spoke two days ago. First, we know the name of the vessel. It is the Black River, a fifty-foot yacht registered in Freetown, Sierra Leone. It departed Freetown on November 6 and is heading for Jamaica. Second, the original port of entry was Port Antonio along the northeastern coast. However, CIA is reporting the man scheduled to meet the Black River suddenly checked out of his hotel. We believe he is currently looking for another marina or port to link up with the crew."

"In Jamaica or somewhere else?"

"Probably Jamaica, sir. I do not think he has enough time to find another location. CIA and other analysts I've spoken to agree."

"Can the Black River really make it across the Atlantic in seven or eight days?"

"Yes, if they average twenty knots, it's very possible due to the ship's design. Good weather is also a must."

"So, let's say the crew makes it to Jamaica. What next?"

"If we are unable to stop them, my assessment is that they will make their way to Miami or a marina off the west coast of Florida. They could try to make their way to New Orleans, but Florida is the quickest route to get off the ship and travel north using a car or other type of transportation."

"Who are the passengers?"

"Two men. Fallubah Tinibu is the captain and a man called Manjo. We do not know his last name and he is the individual who will infect himself."

"Should we assume they have fake passports or visas?"

"No sir, research indicates most terrorists use legitimate passports. Very few are fake."

Clancy turned to Homeland Security.

"How quickly can we add these two names to the terror watch list and get their names to state and local authorities?"

"Already done. CIA shared the Intel, and we have passed it on to all the fusion centers up and down the east coast. By this afternoon, every law enforcement agency will have their names. If the analysts are correct, we should be able to pick them up if CIA fails."

"If word of this gets to the press, we'll have a panic on our hands. Let's do this as discreetly as possible. Leslie, who else can we think of that has a need to know?"

"Do we know if JIATF-S has been updated?" asked Leslie as she turned to Homeland Security.

CIA chimed in, still reeling from Homeland Security's insinuation they might fail.

"We requested they provide drone support along Eastern Jamaica. I am confident they will execute the mission. We should be able to spot them before they even hit the port, wherever that might be."

"What is the plan if we find them?" asked Clancy.

"We'll send the coast guard to pick them up and arrest them, that simple."

"It's never simple, Mark," said Clancy.

"Leslie, what if we fail to find the Black River or the individuals on board?"

"Sir, I recommend you wait two days. If we cannot find her or the crew, then we have to notify NYPD. This will at least give them time to assess the situation and prepare their hazmat teams. We should probably ask the hospitals in the city to submit their current Ebola preparedness and risk mitigation plans."

"Why not now?"

"You could, sir, but if word gets out that Homeland Security is asking hospitals for Ebola preparedness plans, it might leak to the press. There will likely be a lot of questions."

"We'll have to take that chance. If they land in Miami, they could be in New York within a day. I'll update the President."

Clancy turned back to Homeland Security.

"Let's notify NYPD this afternoon. Who is responsible for notifying the hospitals?"

"We'll take care of that as well, Jason."

Clancy then turned to CIA.

"I want all Intel on this shared with Leslie in real time. Is that going to be an issue?"

"No, not all."

Clancy concluded the meeting and asked Leslie to remain in the room.

"Leslie, do you have a secure cell?"

"Yes, sir."

"Give me the number in case I need to reach you. I'll need your insight if this thing spins out of control."

Kingston, Jamaica – November 12, 1:30 PM

Michael and Ashani checked into their rooms.

"I'm going to run downtown for a few minutes, Michael," said Ashani.

"What for?"

"Art, man. After this mission is over, I am going to spoil myself with a painting. This artist is amazing and will ensure my retirement is fully funded."

"Good for you, Ashani. Let me know if your boys see our man leave."

"Of course, Michael. I will be back shortly."

Michael reached into his bag and opened his personal cell. A message from Laura awaited.

Great choice for dinner, Michael. That sounds wonderful. What did you have in mind for dessert? Yes, heading to Chicago next week for another conference. Same topics just different players. When do you think you will be back? I leave Thursday and return to DC on Saturday afternoon. So excited for dinner. I even bought a new dress for the occasion! Hope you like blue. Stay safe. Laura

Michael felt special; something he had not felt in a very long time. Laura genuinely made him feel this way, and he still could not believe how quickly he fell for her. This mission could not end soon enough, he thought to himself. He hoped to catch a flight to D.C. in the coming days. Michael turned his attention to Langley and called Doug.

"Doug, we found Dayo here in Kingston. It looks like the Black River will arrive at the marina of the Grand Hotel in Port Royal. Ashani's men are watching him now. By the way, thanks for sending him. He seems like a good man."

"He is a good man and glad he could help. I put in a request for drone support so we should be able to give you a few hours' notice before the Black River approaches. With just two men on board, this should be easy for you."

"We'll see, Doug. I assume the Coast Guard or Navy will have a ship nearby?"

"Yes, the Coast Guard will remain in international waters. I will send over their position later so you can rendezvous with them."

"How are Sheikh Cissi and his family?"

"They are still in Freetown. It won't be easy securing their visas."

"Good. I made a deal with the man, but his Intel still needs to check out."

"Agreed, what is your assessment of the man?"

"He got in over his head. I think Islamic State put pressure on him and they probably paid him very well. He might have told me everything, but we will know for sure when the boat arrives. I cannot help thinking he may have withheld something. Have you run his finances?"

"Yes, there was a large deposit in his Mosque's account in Freetown. It originated from a bank in Damascus. However, there was a large withdrawal the day before the Black River left."

"How much?"

"One hundred thousand dollars in cash."

"Who withdrew it?"

"Someone by the name of Foday Bello. He's made withdrawals before but never this much."

"Who is this guy?"

"A member of the Mosque. Freetown is checking it out."

"Think this guy delivered the cash to the Black River?"

"It's a good bet, but Sheikh Cissi has used large sums of cash to fund local projects in Kenema. I will send you an update if we get anything."

"Will the drone feed go into the operations center?"

"Yes, we are coordinating for the links now."

"Good, it might come in handy. Thanks, Doug. I'll be in touch."

Kingston, Jamaica – November 12, 2:35 PM

Ashani arrived at the Studio 174 art gallery in Kingston. A group of talented locals ran the gallery, which included exhibits from some of the hottest artists in the metropolitan area. It was also home to many inner-city youth who used the gallery to escape the violence and street gangs of Kingston. One of its more notorious and lethal gangs included the Shower Posse. Ashani had caused the imprisonment of many of its members and risked confrontation each time he visited. He did not care. Ashani was a mentor to many of the kids there and popular with the staff.

A vehicle with three passengers drove up as Ashani made his way back to the car. He instantly recognized them as members of the Scare Dem street gang, a rival to the Shower Posse. Scare Dem was battling Shower Posse in Kingston's west side for control over the lucrative cocaine business. Cocaine distribution was exploding on the island as the United States had conducted successful seizures and high-profile arrests in Puerto Rico and the Dominican Republic. Kingston was a war zone.

"Ashani, how's it kickin, man?"

"Curtis, what do you need? Still living by the gun?"

"Live by the gun them say or dead by the gun. You're powerful you know… next to God, and when people hear it they backup, you understand?"

"Yeah, man. I get it."

"Me going to do you a favor, Ashani. Shower Posse is looking for you. They have people all around the ghettos. They are looking for jungle justice."

"Why are you telling me, Curtis?"

"I owe you. My cousin said you vouched for him in court. I wanted to thank you. Now we are even."

"Thank you, man."

Ashani returned to the Jamaica Pegasus Hotel, a four-star resort with seventeen floors in downtown Kingston and a popular destination for business travelers from throughout the Caribbean. Michael waited in the lobby, as the two would soon make their way back to the Port Royal marina. Michael requested they return for additional reconnaissance.

Michael turned to Ashani soon after they departed.

"You see it?"

"The blue sedan about four cars back? Yes, I see it, man."

"Friends of yours?"

"Not hardly. They could be Shower Posse."

"Are they a local gang here?"

"Yes and no. They are a transnational syndicate. They operate all over the island, in the United States, Canada and throughout the Caribbean."

"How did they get their name?"

Suddenly the sedan pulled up alongside the rear of their vehicle and sprayed a volley of bullets. The rear window of Ashani's SUV shattered into hundreds of pieces and several bullets narrowly missed the two men. Both men ducked as Ashani slammed his foot on the accelerator pedal. Bullets continued to fly around them from Israeli Uzis, a preferred weapon of Shower Posse. The ensuing chase down Highway 4 gave Michael the opportunity to draw his weapon.

"Stay ahead of them and get to the left side of the road," shouted Michael.

Michael lowered his window and looked back. He fired his weapon several times and the driver of the blue sedan began to swerve. Michael continued shooting while aiming for the front tires. Out of bullets, he slammed another clip into his weapon and continued firing.

Finally, one of the rounds hit the front right tire, and the driver lost control. The car made a violent right turn and flipped several times along Highway 4. The chase ended as quickly as it began.

"What the hell was that about, Ashani?"

"Now you know how Shower Posse got its name. They spray their enemies with bullets from automatic rifles."

"That doesn't answer my question. What did they want?"

"I gave Kingston police some information about one of their leaders last month. They were trying to recruit one of the kids at the galleries I visit. I could not let that happen."

"Just recruit?"

"They wanted him to sell cocaine on the streets, man. The kid's life would have been ruined."

"You have any more surprises for me, Ashani?"

"Not that I can think of, Michael. Let's get the vehicle back to the city. I know where we can get another."

Ashani's cell phone rang.

"The man just left the hotel and took a short drive to Danny's Marina. Looks like he is getting lunch."

"Good, let me know if he moves."

**Caribbean Sea, fifty miles southeast of Jamaica –
November 13, – 5:25 PM**

Fifty miles from Jamaica's southeastern coast, the
Black River was nearing the end of its voyage. The choppy
seas and heavy rains made for a challenging approach to
Port Royal. Fallubah and Foday were unaware of the drone
approaching overhead.

The MQ-1 Predator drone, initially flown in 1994 and
still in service, included a variant of the AN/AAS-52 Multi-
spectral Targeting System. It also carried a day-TV camera,
and a variable aperture thermographic camera used for low
light conditions and nighttime surveillance. The drone
flying overhead the Black River did not include any
missiles, as JIATF-S did not engage targets within the
scope of its missions.

"Fallubah, how close are we now?" asked Foday.

"About fifty miles. You should go below. Call Dayo
and get him ready."

Foday entered the galley. His clothes were soaking wet
from the storm's pounding rainfall. A few minutes later, a
break in the clouds gave CIA and JIATF-S their first
glimpse of the Black River. Their version of the MQ-1
Predator was older and not equipped with a synthetic
aperture radar capable of detecting targets through the thick
clouds below.

"Target acquired. Finally. Black River confirmed,"
said the pilot.

"These clouds are going to make it difficult to stay
with her," said the co-pilot.

317

"Yes, but at least we have a positive identification and direction of movement. I hope this sucker gets to his port quickly so we can get out of here. Plenty of drug boats to hunt. Why the heck did the tasking order get changed so quickly?"

"Ha, good question bud, but it doesn't matter. As soon as the boat reaches the dock, we are out of here. I see one man at the helm."

"Let's circle around to his stern and see if we can get a better look."

The pilot made a slow right turn, as the camera remained focused on the Black River.

"You see anything else besides the skipper?"

"Nope."

"Okay, let's see where she goes."

Foday made his way back to the galley. A fresh set of clothes did him some good. Time to call Dayo, he thought to himself.

"Dayo, we are fifty miles from the marina. Are you ready to meet us?"

"Yes, I am ready to go. Let me know when you are twenty miles away."

"Are you expecting any surprises?" asked Foday.

"None."

South Beach Cafe, Kingston, Jamaica – November 13, 5:50 PM

Michael and Ashani were enjoying an early dinner at the South Beach Cafe in downtown Kingston. The restaurant and sports bar boasted it was the only daiquiri bar in Jamaica. Michael listened as Ashani recalled his first encounter with Doug in 1986.

"Yes, Doug is a good man. I was a young, stupid kid running cocaine for one of the gangs here in Kingston. The local police let me go a few hours after my booking. Doug came to the police station and spoke to me in one of the holding rooms. He convinced me to provide him information."

"How did he do it?"

"Money, of course. He paid me close to what I was making selling the powder. I had to learn how to hustle and build relationships with people around the ports. It was far less dangerous, man."

"How are you making your money now?"

"I get by. I do odd jobs for friends of mine but miss the money I made before 9/11. Since then, CIA's only focus has been the Middle East. No one cares about drugs anymore."

"I bet DEA would beg to differ. Ever work with them?"

"No, it's been years since anyone has called me."

Michael sensed a bit of frustration in Ashani's voice. The fact that he was not making as much money anymore clearly bothered the Jamaican. He also seemed to have lost purpose. Michael thought these were lousy combinations. His cell buzzed.

"Mike, how are things with Ashani," asked Doug.

"Just talking about you. Guess you saved his butt in 86. Any news?"

"Yes, a drone just spotted the Black River. It is about fifty miles off the coast in choppy waters. It appears to be heading for Port Royal or somewhere along the southeastern shoreline. The drone is having difficulty keeping eyes on the boat due to the storm. Before you ask, it is an older model. It could be morning before it makes its way to the Grand Hotel marina. I read your report this morning, and the plan looks good. The operations center will send you a text when it's within five miles."

"How far away is the cutter?"

"Just off the coast in international waters. Once you secure the boat, call the operations center. They will contact the ship's captain letting them know you are on the way. They have a hazmat team on board, in case things get dicey."

"Thanks, Doug. This thing should go down quickly."

"You have news, Michael?" asked Ashani.

"Yes, they found it. It's about fifty miles off shore and heading for the Marina. Let's finish our dinner and go. If the storm passes, they could be here before midnight."

"We've got time, man."

"I want to be ready several hours in advance, Ashani. I don't want any surprises."

Grand Hotel Marina, Port Royal, Jamaica – November 14, 6:45 AM

Michael gazed into the harbor from the Red Jack restaurant and spotted a yacht approaching the marina. He was certain it was the Black River. Michael turned to Ashani.

"If I were a betting man, that's it, Ashani. They were five miles out a while ago. The timing makes sense."

"Give it a few minutes, Michael. Maybe it's another ship coming in from the storm."

"Now I am certain. There it is. The Black River. You have the radios prepped?"

"Yes. They are fully charged."

"One thing is troubling me, Ashani?"

"What's that, man?"

"Where is our friend Dayo? He should be here now or at the fuel station. I don't see him."

"Maybe he's asleep, Michael. I am sure they plan to rest and refuel."

"Yes, but Dayo should be here. Your guy has not seen him since last night?"

"No, he would have called."

"Okay. Let's wait for them to tie down their ropes and secure the boat. I'll start moving then."

Fifteen minutes later, Michael Brennan sat up and began moving toward the dock where the Black River lay moored. Walking at a brisk pace, his attention now focused on the two men working around the boat. His eyes stared right through them. His job now was to secure the men, get

321

them below deck and link up with the awaiting Coast Guard cutter offshore. Simple enough he thought.

Michael came within fifteen meters before Fallubah noticed the man. Both men's eyes locked onto one another. At first, Fallubah was unsure of the man's purpose. Michael's pace and penetrating eyes left little doubt about his purpose as he came to within ten meters.

"Manjo, go below," said Fallubah.

"Good morning, is this the Black River?" asked Michael.

"Yes, sir. We have made our way from Freetown, Sierra Leone. Is the fuel station open?"

"No, it won't open for another hour."

Michael drew his weapon and pointed it toward Fallubah.

"What is your name?" asked Michael.

"What are you doing, sir? Why have you pointed a gun at me?"

"Let's go below deck. I have some questions for you."

Fallubah stepped into the galley and looked at Manjo. He signaled him to remain seated.

"What are your names?" asked Michael.

"I am Fallubah, and this is Manjo. Who are you?"

"My name is Michael. Where is the blood?"

"What blood, sir? We have no blood."

Michael reached into his back pocket and called Ashani on the radio.

"Come on in. They are secure."

"On my way, Michael."

322

"Where is your friend Dayo?"

"We know no one by that name."

"I'll ask again, where is Dayo?"

"We do not know anyone by that name." Ashani joined Michael in the galley.

"Ashani, keep an eye on them while I take a look around."

"You got it, man."

Michael found the cooler in the second berthing room with a temperature set at ten degrees Celsius. He pulled on the handle and opened the door. It was empty. He cursed Sheikh Cissi to himself. The man had double-crossed him. Furious, he quickly stood up and turned back toward the narrow opening.

He found Ashani standing at the door with his pistol drawn.

"I'm sorry, Michael."

"What the hell are you doing, Ashani?"

"Walk slowly to the galley, Michael. Please, no heroics, man."

"Mind telling me what you're doing, Ashani?"

"I met Dayo many days ago in Port Antonio. It was by coincidence, but he needed help. I was able to offer it."

"At a good price, I hope."

"Very good, man. This will be my last job."

"Tie him up, Manjo," said Fallubah.

A few minutes later, Fallubah and Manjo left the Black River. Michael stared at Ashani as he sat inside the galley.

"There's still time for you to change your mind, Ashani. You can't possibly think you'll get away with this," said Michael.

"I can and I will, Michael. I already have a place in Brazil lined up."

"When this is over, I will come for you, Ashani."

"I doubt that, Michael. Once we depart, we will make our way to the Bahamas. You will never see me again. No more talk, man, just relax, we will be underway shortly."

Langley, Virginia – November 14, 10:30 AM

Doug entered the operations center. He should have heard from Michael by now based on the Black River's arrival.

"When was our last feed, Larry?" asked Doug.

"The drone departed at six-fifty-six AM after the Black River moored."

"Show me the feed; back it up five minutes before we lost it."

"Is that Michael walking along the dock?"

"Yes. At this point, the camera shifts to another angle and our feed goes dead."

"Damnit, something is wrong. Michael should have given us an update by now. Can you get me a direct line to the drone pilot?"

"Sure, we made contact with them when the tasking began."

Larry dialed the number for the ground control station.

"Pilot, this is Larry again. I have someone who would like to speak with you."

"Go ahead."

"Pilot, this is Doug Weatherbee from Langley. I need you to return to Port Royal."

"Mr. Weatherbee, we finished that tasking earlier this morning."

"Who am I speaking with?"

"First Lieutenant Chuck Stansby, sir."

"Lieutenant Stansby, I need confirmation the Black River is still at the marina."

"Sir, I have my tasking. Our orders were to track the vessel and move off station when it docked."

"I understand that Lieutenant Stansby. However, we have lost communication with one of our officers on the ground. I need to know if the Black River is still there."

"I'll have to get approval for that, sir."

"How long will it take?"

"It could take hours, sir."

"We don't have that kind of time. Where are you flying now?"

"I can't divulge that, sir. We're flying for another customer now."

"Lieutenant Stansby. I am the deputy director for Operations here in Langley. We have a national security issue on our hands. If we lose that boat and its contents, there may be an attack on the homeland that could kill dozens, if not hundreds, of people. It could even get worse than that. I need you to get back on station and confirm the boat is still there."

Stansby thought to himself for a moment. He was in a precarious position. As a young officer, he felt uneasy about moving the drone away from his current observation point and track. These decisions can end careers. On the other hand, he recognized the urgency in Doug's voice. He assumed the man would not have called if it were not urgent. He did not know much about CIA but knew the DDO was a senior position within the organization.

"Stand by, sir."

"How long before we could get back to Port Royal?" Stansby asked as he turned to his co-pilot.

"In these conditions, no more than twenty minutes. Why?"

"Langley's on the phone. The customer wants us to go back and confirm if the Black River is still there."

"What about our current requirements?"

Stansby thought some more. The hell with it. He thought of John Paul Jones and his famous line, 'those who will not risk cannot win.'

"Get our bird over Port Royal. I'll take whatever heat comes down."

"Turning now."

"Mr. Weatherbee, we should have eyes over the marina soon. Have your operator re-establish the satellite link."

"Thank you, Lieutenant Stansby."

Nearly twenty minutes went by before the marina came into focus. Doug peered into the screen as the camera zoomed in. The Black River was gone.

**Caribbean Sea, 2 miles southwest of Pilon, Cuba –
November 14, 9:30 PM**

"Take him back to the rear berthing room, Ashani.
Manjo, join me topside. I need help with one of the sails,"
said Fallubah.

Ashani pulled Michael up by his right arm, and the two
slowly walked through the narrow hallway. Michael
stopped and turned to Ashani.

"Did you know these guys are Islamic State, Ashani?"

"No way, man. They are smugglers. They're just trying
to get product into the United States."

"Did you ask them where they're from?"

"No, I know they're African. So, what? Lots of
Africans come through Jamaica to move product."

"You really think Doug sent me here to screw around
with a few drug dealers?"

"I don't know, Michael. I do not care. You said you do
not travel much. What do you know anyway? For all I
know, you've been assigned to Jamaica."

Michael had him talking. That was the goal for now.
He waited patiently for the moment to strike.

"Ashani, I lied to you. I have had many assignments in
the Middle East. These people are trying to get Ebola into
the United States."

"Man, stop talking crazy."

"Look, I get why you helped these guys. One final
payoff to retire. I get it, but they are not who they say they
are. You are helping terrorists transport a virus. A deadly
virus that is probably going to kill many people. There will

328

be no place on earth you can hide. You will be a dead man, Ashani."

Michael's opportunity to strike finally came as the boat rocked upwards from an approaching wave. Ashani stumbled forward just enough for Michael to execute a vicious head butt. Ashani's body stumbled backward as Michael raised his front leg and struck Ashani in the gut rendering him to the floor. With a swift follow-up kick to the side of the head, Ashani was out cold. Michael raced into the galley and scanned for a knife or sharp instrument to cut the rope holding his wrists in place. Nothing. He found a drawer and pulled it open. Michael found a knife and was free within ten seconds.

He returned to the narrow hallway and grabbed Ashani's weapon, a fully loaded .38 special revolver located on the floor. He then dragged Ashani into the rear cabin and locked the door. Michael was pleased to see his bag on top of the bed.

Michael now shifted his attention toward the steps leading to the upper deck. Manjo and Fallubah were somewhere up above. Michael slowly moved through the galley and patiently climbed the stairs. His targets were now visible.

"Fallubah. You and Manjo will join me below, now!" exclaimed Michael as he pointed the .38 revolver in their direction.

Fallubah was stunned. He did not expect to see the American again. After failing to reach Sheikh Cissi, Foday altered their plan to ensure he and the blood were safe in case the Black River was lost. Dayo performed superbly by acquiring the boat within twenty-four hours of Foday's instructions.

Michael used the extra rope he found up top and tied the two men to the galley chairs. He returned to the helm and examined the console. The first thing he noticed was the satellite phone. It would come in handy shortly. He looked for the waypoints entered into the ship's navigation systems and stumbled to find the Black River was on autopilot. This was good for Michael, as he had not sailed in many years. Black River's destination was set for Gran Parque National Sierra Maestra, along Cuba's southern coastline. A cove near Marea del Portillo appeared to be the final waypoint.

Michael reached for the satellite phone.

"Doug, it's Michael."

"Michael, where the hell are you? What number are you calling me from?"

"My cell might be in the waters off the marina right now. I am on the Black River. The blood was not here when I searched earlier this morning. There must have been another passenger or two aboard."

"What's your situation?"

"I'm at the helm and have control of the Black River. Looks like I am just along Cuba's southern coastline. Manjo and Fallubah are down below in the galley. Your man, Ashani, turned against us, Doug."

"What the hell happened?"

"Exactly what it means, Doug."

"We'll deal with that later. I am sorry. I thought he could help."

"Doug, the ship's navigation system is set for Marea del Portillo, Cuba. We have any satellites overhead?"

"It's Cuba, I will try. You think the virus is there?"

"Yes, there's no reason why these guys are going to a cove off Cuba. They had plenty of time to refuel in Port Royal. The virus will be there. I'm sure of it."

"How far are you from the location?"

"About three miles. I should be there shortly."

"Take care of yourself, Michael. No telling how many were on the boat."

"One or two tops, Doug. There was not room for more than that. I will be in touch."

Michael returned to the galley.

"Fallubah, why is the boat heading for an area off the Cuban coast?"

Silence.

"Fallubah, I will not ask again. Why?"

Silence.

Michael fired a round toward his left knee. Fallubah began screaming in agony. The bullet pierced his patella and severed the anterior cruciate ligament. Michael became emotionless as he had so many times in his career. He calmly asked again.

"Fallubah, where is this boat heading and why?"

"I curse you and your family!" yelled Fallubah.

Michael immediately fired a second round toward his left knee once again. Manjo cursed in his native tongue as

Fallubah continued screaming. Michael sat back in his chair.

"Fallubah. You have forced me into this position. The Ebola virus is nearing my country. I will not allow it to enter. You understand?"

"Yes," yelled Fallubah as he continued breathing deeply.

"I do not want to continue hurting you, but I will. Where is this damn boat going?"

"To meet up with our friend."

"Who is that?"

"Foday."

"Is he carrying the virus with him?"

"Yes."

"How does he plan to enter the United States?"

"I do not know."

"Fallubah, I will shoot the other one."

"I do not know. I swear it. Why would he tell me?"

"Will anyone else be with him at the location?"

"Yes, Dayo."

Michael found some bandages and stopped the bleeding the best he could. Either way, the man would never walk normally again. Fallubah would have to pay the price for his participation in the evil scheme. He sometimes hated these kinds of aggressive tactics, but his targets always deserved it. Why should he care if a crazy terrorist cannot walk if it saves the lives of countless individuals?

"Where exactly are you supposed to meet them?"

"At the front of the cove. They are expecting us soon."

"What will they expect when we arrive?"

"Nothing, Foday and Dayo will board the ship."

"Good. Does he expect a phone call from you?"

"He does, as soon we get to the entrance of the cove he expects a call."

"Let's make sure we forget that, Fallubah," said Michael.

"If I don't call, he will figure something is wrong and may not board."

"I'll worry about that Fallubah."

About an hour later, the Black River entered the quiet cove. It was a beautiful night as the moon's light bounced off the cold Cuban waters. At the helm, Michael easily controlled the thrusters guiding the boat. Just prior, he placed painter's tape on the mouths of Manjo and Fallubah. Ashani remained unconscious in the berthing room.

Michael dropped the anchor and went below as the Black River came to a near stop. The insects and other various animals in and around the cove made their presence known. Chirping and buzzing, they seemed to sing in harmony.

Foday and Dayo arrived within minutes of Michael laying the anchor. They approached the Black River in two boats. Foday would rejoin their brothers on the Black River while Ashani would take one of the boats and his cash with him.

"Look, Foday the Black River is safe. This is good news. The mission can continue."

"Maybe Dayo, but where is Fallubah? He should be at the helm waiting for us. I do not like it. It's too quiet."

"Stop worrying, Foday. You will soon be back on the open seas. We are safe. You will be in America in a couple of days. Your mission will be successful, and the Caliph will be pleased."

The men piloted their boats alongside the Black River. The insects and local animals continued their harmonious singing. Foday called out to Fallubah. Nothing. Then again. Nothing. The Black River was dead silent.

"Dayo, grab your weapon. Let us board together and make our way slowly to the stairs. You lead down to the galley, understand?"

"Okay Foday, but this is not necessary. There's probably a very good reason why Fallubah is below."

"Whatever the reason, Dayo, it does not matter. He should have called and that makes me nervous. Let's go and remain quiet."

The two men carefully entered the Black River. Their weapons drawn, Dayo led them down the steps into the galley. Michael noticed the feet of the approaching man. From his angle, it appeared he was seconds from noticing Manjo and Fallubah. Michael waited patiently in the corner of the galley and leaned forward. He was ready to strike.

Foday placed his left hand on Dayo's right shoulder as they neared the bottom of the steps. Foday shook his head, but Dayo continued.

"Stop right there," shouted Michael.

Dayo crouched his upper torso down, turned to his left and attempted to fire two rounds. It was too late. Michael Brennan already had his weapon pointed at the man as his body came into view. Dayo fell forward and took his last breath.

Foday stepped back and up one stair. He crouched his body down to see into the galley and finally saw Fallubah and Manjo. The walls and his angle of view prevented him from seeing the rest of the galley, but he saw Dayo fall.

Foday stared at Fallubah. Fallubah could see the sadness in his eyes as he pointed his weapon at him. Fallubah attempted to smile and gave Foday the nod as if giving his friend the approval to fire. The two men were lifelong friends and grew up in the same village northeast of Kenema. This would not be an easy task for Foday, despite his propensity for violence. Fallubah was his friend and he condemned the man who put him there. A few seconds later, Foday pulled the trigger and placed a single round into his forehead. A sudden feeling of anger and sadness befell the man. His heart genuinely wept for Fallubah and he nearly became enraged. Manjo would be far less difficult. Foday turned to Manjo and the young farmer would die the same way. Fallubah and Manjo's jihad were over. Foday would now have to accomplish the mission by himself.

Michael stepped forward as he saw Manjo's head move backward. Turning upward and to his right, he looked up the steps leading to the Black River's upper deck. Michael and Foday stared into one another's eyes for

335

at least two seconds. Foday lurched his weapon to the left and fired, but Michael had already quickly moved as the two rounds found the galley floor.

Foday stood up and raced to the ship's stern. He jumped into the first small speedboat and removed the keys. Foday then quickly jumped to the second boat just ahead of him. With the turn of a key, he started the engine. Propellers turned, and into the Caribbean he went.

Michael followed and made his way topside toward the sounds of the engine. He saw Foday speed off and jumped into the boat alongside the Black River. Almost instantly, Michael realized the key was missing.

Michael watched as Foday slipped further into the darkness. His disappointment showed, but there was one consolation. Michael Brennan had a good look at the man and there were few places to hide.

Guantanamo Bay, Cuba – November 15, 10:08 AM

"Doug, it's Michael."

"About time you called, are you at Gitmo now?"

"Yes, thanks for the support last night. The Coast Guard came through and are holding Ashani. What are you going to do with him?"

"Nothing until this operation is over. He will stay at Gitmo. I am arranging for transport to get you to New York tomorrow morning. If Foday makes it into the country, I want you there to stop him."

"Got it. The Sheikh did not give us all the Intel, Doug."

"I know. You made that clear last night when you called the operations center. Freetown is going to release his family today, but Cissi is moving to an offsite for further questioning."

"Have the analysts found any pictures of Foday?"

"None, but they are looking at all sources. If we find one, it will probably come from open source. That analyst I told you about at INR is already running queries. Her team is looking for any pictures using social media and newspapers from the region. I have put a request into NSA to see if they can get into the bank's video surveillance system, but that may be a long shot. I do not think they have much infrastructure built there. He's got to be on camera somewhere."

"At least I've seen him. Can you make contact with INR and give her my number?"

"Sure. Did you really get all your equipment back from Port Royal?"

"Yes, Ashani must have come back for it before we left Port Royal. I'm not sure why, but I have everything, and it looks in order."

"They probably had plans to try and break into some of your equipment to find out what you know. Expect to hear from her this afternoon. Keep the operations center in the loop, but feel free to share mission data with her."

"What is her name?"

"Leslie Parson. She's good; use her if possible."

"What do you think of the maps found in the Black River, Doug?"

"Probably useless by now. I cannot imagine the routes are still a viable option for Foday after the Black River's compromise. He may develop a brand-new course of action. What worries me is how much, if any, additional support he has in New York?"

"I'm betting he's all alone on this. The planning was quick, and I believe the Sheikh left him off in case we intercepted the Black River. Sheikh Cissi's infrastructure is relatively small, and according to your last report, he has no known networks or sympathizers in New York. I think if we find Foday, we find the Ebola and end this."

Michael hung up and now turned his attention to Laura. It had been three days since he heard from her and he wanted to reach out.

Hi, Laura. A trip to Chicago sounds good. Stay warm and hope it goes well for you. A blue dress? Awesome. I love blue. It is my favorite color. I cannot wait to see you wearing it. Things are winding down over here, and I am hoping to be back in a few days, but do not hold me to it, please. Reference dessert, let me think on it and surprise you. Have a safe trip. Michael

Intelligence Division, New York City Police Department – November 16, 1:55 PM

"Good afternoon, Mr. Brennan. I'm Tony Carlucci, director of the Intelligence Division."

Tony Carlucci had been the director of the Intelligence Division since March 2014. A veteran intelligence analyst with the Defense Intelligence Agency, he resigned over what he described as apathy coming from the Obama administration regarding the rise of Islamic State. Tony believed the President's national security team ignored DIA's assessment in order to fit a political narrative. However, there were others in the intelligence community who believed he and his analysts did not provide enough evidence to warrant a policy change.

"Hello, Tony. Thanks for the hospitality. Were you able to get INR on a secure link?"

"We are setting it up now; your video teleconference is scheduled for two-fifteen PM. You will be using our executive conference room. I spoke with Langley, and some of my analysts will join us."

A short while later, Michael and Tony arrived in the conference room. Two intelligence analysts were waiting for them, along with a network administrator responsible for establishing the link with INR.

"Do we have INR on the line, Terence?"

"Yes, sir. Ready to go."

"Good afternoon everyone, I'm Tony Carlucci. I am here with Michael Brennan from CIA. Who are we speaking with?"

"Tony, I am Leslie Parson, and this is my analytical team."

"Hi, Leslie, good to finally see you. How far back were you able to find pictures of the Sheikh?" asked Michael.

"Hey, Michael. We looked as far back as ten years. Most of our efforts have gone toward social media sites where we looked for followers of the Sheikh. We did not find anything useful except an occasional single image of the Sheikh or him posing with people who posted to their Facebook or Twitter account. We found very few of these. However, we did find a few pictures of the Sheikh at local charity events surrounded by some members of the Mosque. I will show those to you in a minute. We also found a few images from the local press in and around Kenema. They are not very good, but it is the best we could do in the time constraints we are working in."

"Okay, Leslie. Can you start bringing them up on the screen?"

Leslie and the team slowly began enlarging each picture within the collage which they downloaded onto their computer. They timed the duration of each frame at five seconds so Michael could get a good look. One by one, each photo crossed the large sixty-inch screen monitor, and Michael saw no one resembling the man from the Black River. Finally, on the twenty-sixth frame, Michael saw a possible match. There, Sheikh Cissi and several men from the Mosque posed in front of a new school outside the village of Hangha.

"Hold that one, Leslie. Can you zoom in on the man on the far left?"

"Sure, give me a second."

"That's him, that's the man I saw on the Black River. What is the name of the press release?"

"According to the story, he is listed as Kossi Mensah."

"That's our man, Leslie. Do you have the capability at INR to enhance the image?"

"No, our team doesn't have that capability."

"Michael, we can do it. We have the equipment here in the office. We could have an enhanced image within an hour," said Carlucci.

Carlucci was referring to the process of Digital Image Interpolation, which resizes images based on surrounding pixels. The Intelligence Division in New York had the technology fully implemented into its offices in 2008. With several software upgrades, coupled with technological advancements, Foday's picture would become sharp and easily visible to law enforcement.

"Good, we'll need to get that to Homeland Security for distribution. He may or may not have gotten into the country by now. Maybe we'll get lucky, and CBP or TSA will identify and apprehend him," said Michael.

"Leslie, do you think Foday will change his routes at this point?"

"Anything is possible, but my first inclination is to say yes. I am betting he stays in the city and blends in for a few days to conduct surveillance of several trains."

"Why, would it matter where he got onto a metro train? Would it not be enough to just hop on one and take his chances? The longer he stays in New York, the more risk he assumes."

"Sure, Michael, but I suspect he will want to get on a crowded line. If he jumps on a train with fewer passengers, the chances for widespread infection will decrease. I seriously doubt he knows which lines are going to have the most people. Though he knows you saw him, he will probably assume he can easily blend into the city and conduct the required surveillance."

"Tony, do you have access to the camera feeds at each metro station?" asked Michael.

"Yes, we can also alert each station manager on duty and send his photograph. Unless he completely changes his identity, we should be able to spot him and isolate him on one of the trains."

"Let's hope we can catch him during his reconnaissance," said Michael.

"Leslie, great work on getting his photo. It must have taken your team many hours of work. Thank you very much," said Michael.

"Just get this guy, Michael. Even if only a few individuals are infected, the psychological damage to the country will be enormous."

"We will catch him, Leslie. Thanks for everything. I will be in touch if I have any questions."

Michael turned to Tony.

"What kind of net can we cast over the city?"

"Once we have the enhanced image, Michael, every police officer on every shift in all five boroughs will have seen his photo. We will repeat it every day until we find him. I will also alert the hazardous materials teams to remain on standby. He won't be able to move around the city without us knowing it."

"I'm worried he may already be here," said Michael.

Langley, Virginia – November 16, 3:11 PM

Doug Weatherbee sat at his desk. He was reviewing reports from other intelligence officers deployed throughout Africa, and one high priority update captured his attention. It came from an officer operating in Lagos, Nigeria. CIA had dozens of non-official cover officers there over the previous decades. However, its current strategic importance to the United States was due primarily to oil production and the rise of Boko Haram, a radical terror group and transnational organized crime syndicate in Africa.

The report read, *asset reports he received a request from a client in Freetown, Sierra Leone to transfer the sum of fifteen thousand dollars to a Bank of America account registered in Brooklyn, New York City. The transfer occurred on November 3 to Jesse Sane. Asset reports this is the first such request from a client to transfer dollars to the United States. The client is a member of the Council of Imams in Sierra Leone.*

Doug called Michael right away.

"Michael, I may have a lead for us. One of our officers in Nigeria is reporting an asset of hers indicated a wire transfer of fifteen thousand dollars from a client in Freetown to Brooklyn. It could be nothing, but probably worth looking into until we get more Intel. I'll send you whatever information we can collect on the account in Brooklyn."

"It's something, Doug. I just finished here at the Intel division. We have Foday identified from photos that Leslie

Parson's team provided. NYPD is enhancing the image as we speak and will distribute to all the agencies and officers in the city. They are listing him as a person of interest."

"We needed that. With any luck, there will be a connection with Foday and the transaction. I imagine things are going to move quickly from this point. Find this person, Michael. NYPD thinks you're an analyst so keep them in the loop where possible."

"Of course, Doug. Do me a favor and send Leslie the Intel on the client in Freetown. She may be able to put more pieces together if we run into any roadblocks here."

"I already plan to, Michael."

McMahon's Ale House, Brooklyn, New York – November 16, 7:45 PM

Peter Marsico sat at the table along with four fellow police officers at McMahons Ale House. None of the officers included members of his elite Hercules team, rather local patrol officers from inside the Brooklyn district. Peter enjoyed the local watering hole and routinely visited the locale several nights each week since his entire team was married. After seven days of suspension, boredom had officially kicked in. He wondered if he should have gone on vacation but needed the money to visit his family on the west coast. Christmas was on the horizon, and he had a new niece to spoil.

"Peter, you hear about the guy whose picture hit the entire department this afternoon?"

"Nope, who is he?"

"A person of interest. Rumors are he is some terrorist trying to enter the city."

"Who issued the alert?"

"Homeland Security."

"What is he? Al Qaeda, or from some domestic group?"

"No idea. We're just speculating."

"You got his picture handy?"

"Sure do, right here on the cell."

"Text it to me."

"You're still on suspension bud. I do not want to get an ass-kicking from the chief if he finds out."

"C'mon, Sal. Just give it to him already. Chief won't know a thing," said the man to his left.

"Peter, by some freak chance you see this guy while you're on suspension you call us first. Fair enough?"

"He won't, Sal. This guy won't get within a mile of the city."

"Fair enough, Sal," said Peter.

The group of officers continued to enjoy each other's comradery for several hours while watching a New York Mets baseball game. Peter glanced at his cell several times to ensure he had the man's face memorized before leaving the smoke-filled pub. Peter Marsico had something to occupy his attention until the suspension expired.

The 66 Rockwell, Brooklyn, New York – November 16, 11:05 PM

Foday and Jesse Sane arrived at the lobby of the 66 Rockwell Apartment Complex. The forty-two-story luxury high-rise building had breathtaking views of New York and was conveniently located close to several hot spots including Barclays Center and the Brooklyn Academy of Music. A short walk one block away offered its residents access to the coveted New York Metro Transit system. It was the ideal location for Foday to conduct his reconnaissance.

"Thank you again, Jesse, for providing me a place to stay for a few days. Do you have the money we transferred to your account?"

"Yes, it's in the drawer by the computer."

"You know why I came to New York?"

"I have no idea, Foday, but I do not care. When I left Kenema, I came to make a new home here in the United States. You are only here because my father is an acquaintance of Sheikh Cissi."

"You appear to have done well for yourself, my old friend. Are you still managing that restaurant?"

"I am. I have enjoyed living here for the past nine years. Hard work and some luck has paid off."

"Why did you leave Jesse? You would have made a good life for yourself in Kenema. The Mosque has grown tremendously the last few years. We have more members than we could have ever imagined."

"When Sheikh Cissi began publicly supporting Al Qaeda I could no longer remain in Kenema. That kind of thinking is why Muslims are still struggling all over the world. The senseless killing of civilians only sets us back. We might as well be in the middle ages. My father asked me to house you for a few days. I will honor him but do not ask me to join in whatever craziness you have planned. Let us make the best of it."

"You know, Jesse, I see you here in a nice apartment surrounded by all these Americans. What are they doing to help us in Kenema as Ebola ravages our people?"

"I understand your frustration, Foday. I really do. We have both lost family during previous outbreaks. You may have even lost some now. America cannot help everyone, but its people are good, and they help where they can."

"Why then do they not help us, Jesse?"

"They are too busy fighting terrorists around the world for starters. At least they are helping those who cannot help themselves. Many American doctors and nurses have traveled to Sierra Leone to help. Could America do more? Sure, but that is not for me to decide."

"Have you heard of the Islamic State?"

"I heard something recently in the news. They want to create a caliphate. So, what?"

"Have you been practicing our faith here in the United States?"

"Every day, of course. I am welcome here, and a Mosque is just a few miles away. There are thousands of us in the city, Foday."

"That is good, Jesse," said Foday as he reached for the pistol inside his bag.

Foday fired several rounds into Jesse's chest. The man slumped forward and fell to the ground. Jesse Sane was dead. He might have been useful for a few days if not for the Black River's compromise. Like any operation, no plan survives without the ability to exert flexibility. Foday was demonstrating that yet again. He simply did not need the man, only his apartment as a location to stage the attack. In a few days, it would be over, and no one would miss Jesse.

He entered Jesse's bathroom and opened the thick sliding glass door. He placed his hands into the armpits of Jesse and carefully slid him into the bathtub. Foday returned to the living room and opened his backpack. He reached in and pulled out the vials of blood still cold from the frozen ice packs surrounding them. Walking into the kitchen, he placed the vials into the refrigerator. Turning to his left, Foday walked toward the balcony's door. With a gentle pull, he slipped onto the terrace and sat down. As he gazed into the bright lights of New York City, he wondered if he had the courage to do what he came for. An hour later, he decided the citizens of New York would experience the fear and horror of Ebola as his fellow compatriots back home.

The following morning, Peter Marsico decided to go for an early morning run. Today, he would take the L train on his way to Central Park and enjoy the cool temperatures and clear blue skies. These were ideal conditions for any runner regardless of their ability or commitment. He looked forward to crossing the thirty-six bridges and arches that welcome millions of tourists each year. Situated on eight hundred and forty-three acres of landscaped beauty, Central Park was the ideal location for Peter to go and keep himself busy.

He pulled his keys from the indigo-painted walls and opened the door to his nineteenth story furnished studio apartment. The lucky son of one of the principal investors of the 66 Rockwell apartment building, he enjoyed a steeply discounted monthly rent commensurate with his salary from the New York City police department. Peter Marsico was the only public employee he knew who resided in the swank complex.

Dressed in long black sweat pants, and a short sleeve yellow t-shirt composed of lycra fabrics, Peter walked out of his apartment and closed the door. He decided to leave his sweatshirt at home since the long run would be difficult enough without the added heat it would bring while worn.

This morning, he took the stairs, a ritual he adopted years ago while going for a run on a wet stormy day. He hoped taking the stairs would deter the insanity of running in cold, wet conditions with winds blowing onto his exposed skin. On that day, he had his best workout, and the routine stuck with him ever since.

Peter began descending the stairs along the eastern side of the building. As he passed the fourth floor, he ran into Mrs. Honeyrider, a widowed British woman who still walked the stairs to her sixth-floor apartment. At seventy-five years young, the woman retained her stamina through daily walks with her black fifty-two-pound labradoodle, Sunny.

As Peter approached the second floor, he noticed a man walking up the stairs. He had never seen him before, but he was only able to see the top of his head. After the stranger turned left, he and Peter walked right past each other. Peter observed the stranger looking down, a clear indication he did not want to be recognized. However, he quickly turned around and looked upward as the man continued his slow walk alongside the Russet stairwell walls.

Peter Marsico realized he was staring at the man whose photo he saw last night at the McMahon Ale House. The stranger's pace picked up as if he knew Peter's stare was more than a curious look.

Peter waited a few seconds until the man disappeared behind the stairwell. He then turned around and began moving up the flight of stairs. His instincts told him to simply go to the lobby and call his blue brothers at the 77th Precinct in the northern portion of Crown Heights in Brooklyn. If the man did not suspect anything, he would surely remain in the building, thought Peter. However, Peter's bravado would get the best of himself and he went where the action took him. Rather than showing discipline, the appeal of assisting with the apprehension of New York's top person of interest was too great.

As Foday approached the seventh floor, he considered whether the stranger below was following him. He did not wave in his pace and rapidity as he continued climbing the stairs. Foday determined it was best to continue up to the nineteenth floor. The remaining flight of stairs allowed Foday to think of contingencies for at least a few minutes longer.

Foday arrived at the nineteenth floor and quickly entered the hallway leading to the apartment. Room 1912 was only a few steps away and adjacent to the stairwell. He could feel the stranger just a few seconds behind him. He had no doubt the man was dangerous, but, as far as he could tell, had not made any phone calls or communications.

Peter Marsico entered the hallway and turned to his left as the stairwell door opened to his right. Just ahead, he saw one of the apartments unsecure with the red door slightly open. He did not see the person of interest but expected he was inside the apartment. It did not matter.

As soon as he glanced in the direction of the apartment, the door came crashing behind him. The violent strike hit Peter in the back of the head and knocked his body forward into the open hallway. Foday immediately positioned himself behind the stranger and applied a vicious neck hold while strangling the man. Foday's momentum put both men at the entrance of the apartment.

Peter fought back, but the stranger's grip was too strong. He even attempted to execute a reverse head butt; however, Foday's position prevented a successful strike to the face. Peter then tried to slam his attacker backward into the wall, but Foday hung on. Foday feared the ruckus would bring curious dwellers.

The situation then turned in Foday's favor. As he bounced off the wall and pushed his legs forward, he used his weight to pull Peter into the apartment. Peter's ability to resist began to fade as the lack of oxygen took its toll on the police officer. He motivation to fight faded quickly.

Peter Marsico would lose consciousness within a minute. Death followed shortly thereafter.

Ten minutes later, Foday moved toward the refrigerator. The time to act was upon him. He pulled open the refrigerator and removed the vials of blood stored in the plastic container. His first priority was to assemble the supplies he needed to begin. Foday had identified the likely venipuncture site and he placed the tourniquet around his arm and tightened it. He then took the empty needle and carefully placed the tip into the first vial filled with blood. Slowly, he pulled back the plunger and filled the needle with the infected blood. He felt as if he could already feel the Ebola virus moving through his veins.

Foday was a cold and calculating man, never shy of being incredibly unforgiving and brutal. Nevertheless, this was by far the most challenging task he had ever attempted. The man took a deep breath, satisfied his veins were ready for the puncture. Foday carefully stuck the needle into his vein and depressed the needle's plunger.

Foday now became a weapon of mass destruction.

It would take several days before he felt the effects of the disease. By the time it became unbearable, it would not matter.

He would spend the next several days riding on the trains in New York hoping to infect anyone he met or shared space with on the train. Tonight, he would prepare his suicide vest for a massive detonation near Times Square. This final act of jihad would allow him the opportunity to kill more Americans, resulting in a surefire and swift death.

The full effects of Ebola would never come to fruition Foday thought to himself, but his place in Islamic State history would soon be secure.

Hampton Inn, Manhattan Grand Central Hotel, New York – November 17, 7:10 AM

Michael sat inside the hotel's restaurant sipping coffee and reading the New York Times. A traditional newspaper with ink was still his preferred choice for keeping abreast of current international developments. He always enjoyed the depth and intense research often found within its articles and opinions, as did the millions of readers around the world. An article on Ebola captured his attention as the journalist proposed for further US action in the region to combat the deadly outbreak. After his trip to Sierra Leone, he agreed with the woman's assessment. Then his phone rang.

"Good morning, Michael," said Doug.

"Good morning, Doug."

"We finally got the Intel on that account in Brooklyn. It belongs to a man named Jesse Sane. He is a former citizen of Sierra Leone and has lived here for nearly a decade. It looks like his father has a connection with Sheikh Cissi."

"What is the connection?"

"His father was the site manager who oversaw the construction of his Mosque."

"Good. Where does this Jesse Sane live?"

"He resides at the 66 Rockwell Apartment Complex in Brooklyn. I imagine you are just a few miles from there. His apartment number is 1912. We'll send you the address right away."

"What else do we know about this guy?"

"By all accounts, he appears to be a law-abiding citizen. We found no criminal history or financial problems. There are no purchases of firearms or liquids and materials to create explosives. He pays his taxes and does not even have a parking ticket. He appears clean."

"How does he earn his living?"

"He manages a restaurant in Brooklyn."

"Have we contacted NYPD?"

"Not yet."

"Give me an hour to find out what I can, Doug."

"You have it. I cannot hold on to this information longer than that. The Director will have my ass if we do not share this Intel with New York. If you see the locals moving in, you need to leave, Michael. You're now on US soil."

"Understood, Doug. I'm heading there now. I assume the address is 66 Rockwell?"

"Yes."

"Who is the onsite manager for the complex?"

"Not sure, but I can have the operations center text you the name."

Michael quickly exited the restaurant and found the valet.

"I need a cab right away."

"Yes sir," as the man motioned for a cab alongside the circular entrance.

Fortunately for Michael, the traffic moved, albeit slowly. Michael received a text shortly after the cab departed.

The manager is Raymond Hurt. Ack receipt.
Received. B

Michael arrived at the complex and met the
apartment's concierge.

"Good morning, my name is Michael Brennan. I have
a meeting with Raymond Hurt. Where can I find him?"

The valet checked his folder and found no such
meeting.

"Sir, I have no record of a meeting with Mr. Hurt this
morning. He usually comes in at eight AM."

"Are you sure? He was very adamant about meeting
him here at seven-thirty."

"I am sure, sir. I have no record of a meeting."

"There must be a mistake. Can I at least go inside and
wait in the lobby?"

"Why are you meeting Mr. Hurt?"

"I am with the Bergeson agency. We are the company
that just secured the marketing contract with Mr. Hurt. I am
meeting him to discuss some proposals we have in mind for
the holidays."

"I suppose it would be okay to wait in the lobby.
Please go inside and make yourself comfortable. There are
plenty of sofas and chairs."

"Thank you."

Michael sat closest to the elevator waiting for the
opportunity to jump in. He would give this course of action
only a few minutes and hoped a distraction to the valet
occurred. It finally came when Michael heard the chimes of
the elevator. He sprung off the chair and walked briskly to

the doors. The young couple, dressed in workout gear, exited, gave Michael a smile, and wished him a good morning.

The ride up to the nineteenth floor allowed Michael a few moments to prepare for a possible encounter with Jesse Sane. What would he ask him? How would he establish rapport with a man who apparently lived a normal life free from radicalization? How quickly would he confront him about the fifteen-thousand-dollar-transfer? How would he deal with the valet on his way out? Michael would soon get his answers.

Upon exiting the elevator, he moved swiftly down the spacious corridor toward the apartment. Nothing seemed out of the ordinary, except for a picture frame near apartment 1912. It was slightly crooked. Probably nothing, Michael thought to himself as he arrived at the front door.

Michael knocked several times, as he maintained a watchful eye to his left and right. A professional spy never likes being in confined spaces as his or her options become limited.

Michael knocked a second time and still nothing. It was early in the morning, and he fully anticipated the man to be home due to his profession as a restaurant manager. Michael finally realized that no one was going to answer. He reached into his left suit pocket and pulled out an advanced rake pick developed by CIA. Using a tradecraft technique he learned at his initial training, Michael carefully maneuvered the pick into the keyhole and unlocked the front door.

He then reached into his hip holder and removed his trusted Ruger LCP. Michael Brennan was prepared for anything.

Michael slowly opened the front door and entered Jesse Sane's apartment. It looked clean and well maintained, he thought to himself. The bright colors emanating from the floral walls added a sense of calm and serenity. As he walked into the living area, he noticed the hallway to his right. Michael slowly entered with his pistol drawn at the ready.

Michael glanced into the bathroom and saw two dead bodies in the bathtub. Michael guessed the man at the bottom was Jesse Sane; however, he had no idea who the man on top of him was. Probably an innocent bystander, he thought to himself. Michael knew Foday was nearby.

"Doug, I'm here at the apartment. Two dead bodies. I am certain one is the tenant, Jesse Sane. Not sure who the other one is but he has not been dead for very long."

"Any sign of the blood, Michael?"

"Going to look in the refrigerator now. Stand by."

Michael looked inside and found a blood-shipping container. He carefully removed it and only saw five vials of blood inside.

"Only five vials, Doug. The sixth one is missing."

"Damnit. Foday either has it with him or has used it."

"Yep. I am going to call Tony Carlucci and let his people deal with this. They will have to get a Hazmat team here right away and secure the vials."

"Understood. Where do you think Foday went?"

"He's probably already on a train doing his reconnaissance, unless of course, he injected the blood days ago. My bet is he did it very recently, if at all. Either way, we have a potential mess on our hands."

"Agreed. I will update the Director right away. What are your plans, Michael?"

"I'm calling Leslie. Maybe she can give us insight where he might be. I'll be in touch when I can, Doug."

"Let me call her, Michael. You focus on Tony."

Michael dialed Tony.

"Tony, I've got two dead bodies at 66 Rockwell Place apartments here in Brooklyn. The apartment is 1912. Five Ebola vials are here. One is missing. Recommend you get a hazmat team here right away and some detectives at the crime scene. I will leave the door unlocked. How fast until you can get a team here?"

"What the hell are you doing there, Michael?"

"I'll explain later. How fast can you get your people here?"

"They should be there in fifteen minutes. Are you planning to stay until they arrive?"

"No. Unless you can get someone here within ten minutes."

"Okay. I'll have a patrol car from Brooklyn there in minutes to secure the site."

Michael waited for the officer to arrive. As soon as he entered the apartment, Michael gave the officer instructions on where to find the bodies. The vials were on the kitchen counter, and Michael explained the blood was not to be touched until Hazmat arrived. He then quickly departed the apartment complex through the garage on the lower level.

INR Headquarters, State Department, Washington, D.C. – November 17, 2:52 PM

Leslie and her team scoured through intelligence reports. They could find nothing linking Foday to anyone in the New York region, except for Jesse Sane. Utilizing all metadata collection techniques, nothing turned up. Foday was operating in New York like a ghost and no indicators existed on where to search next. It would take a random police officer or gate attendant at one of hundreds of metro stations to spot Foday, if at all. Then her phone rang.

"Leslie, it's Doug from DO."

"Hey, Doug. We are finding nothing to connect Foday with anyone other than Jesse Sane. I feel like it will take dumb luck to find him."

"You may be right. Listen, I am here on a conference call with Michael and Tony at NYPD Intel. We have a couple of questions for you."

"Leslie, earlier today we found Jesse Sane dead in his apartment. If Foday did it, do you think he will return sometime this evening after conducting reconnaissance? Or do you think he'll attempt to find a new location?" asked Tony.

"I think he'll return. He has no reason to think we are onto him. He assumes we found the maps in the Black River, but he is betting on anonymity due to the size of the city. Unless he thinks he's been spotted, he will follow the plan."

"Why do you believe that? Would it make more sense to go to another city? Say D.C., Boston, or Philadelphia?"

"It is certainly possible, Tony. An attack inside New York would have enormous propaganda value for Islamic State. He has a plan, and nothing indicates he would deviate from that now. Unfortunately, we have no psychological profile on him now, and I know of no other agency tracking him. So, we must assume he will stick with his original plan."

"Leslie, it's Michael. If Foday has injected himself with the infected blood within the last twelve to eighteen hours, how long will it be before he can spread the virus?"

"Research suggests it could be immediate. If he shares bodily fluids with anyone, it might transfer. I am not aware of any conclusive evidence to indicate otherwise. If he did recently infect himself, it could take several days before he shows visible symptoms such as coughing or sneezing."

"Thanks, Leslie. We really appreciate your thoughts on this. We will be in touch if we have any more questions," said Doug.

Michael, Doug, and Tony remained on the line.

"Tony, how would you feel if I went back to the apartment and waited for Foday? I know it would screw up the crime scene, but we have no leads," said Michael.

"You mean just sit there and wait?"

"Yes. If he returns, we can end this at the apartment away from public scrutiny."

"And if he doesn't, Michael?" asked Doug.

"Then the NYPD will have to catch up with him. The more he goes out the more likely someone spots him."

"Michael, I'm not opposed, but the Chief will have to be informed. Screwing up the crime scene complicates things for the lawyers. There are going to be questions among the officers there now," said Tony.

"We need to keep this from as many people as we can, Doug. The fewer people know, the better. How about if NYPD hangs back from the complex? We keep everything as is---door attendants, security, etc. This should give Foday a sense of normalcy when, or if, he returns. What do you think Tony?"

"It's going to be a hard sell, Michael, but I can probably convince the Chief. Doug, can we get support from the Director on this too?"

"I will be going to his office immediately after we are done. Why don't we schedule another conference call in thirty minutes to get everyone on board?"

The three men concluded their conference call. Within an hour, the Mayor and Chief of Police of New York City approved the contentious plan. Both men quietly hoped their police force would find and capture Foday. Crime scene investigators, with whatever evidence they were able to collect, including the bodies, left the apartment complex. Michael Brennan would soon arrive in the apartment and wait for his chance to strike.

Capitol Hotel, Kenema, Sierra Leone - November 8, 2:10 PM

Michael reached for his cell phone after finally waking up from a deep sleep. There were two messages. He read Aaron's first.

Michael, Elif did not make it. She died this morning. Thought you should know. I pray for a successful conclusion to your task. Thank you for the information you conveyed to the pilot. Godspeed. Your friend, Aaron.

Michael was devastated. Elif was a superb agent and a kindhearted woman. Nevertheless, he replied immediately to the Mossad officer he met several days ago in Tel Aviv.

My condolences, Aaron. She was a gifted officer and incredible human being. I am truly sorry for your loss. Will you please notify me where her memorial will be? I would like to pay my respects in the future. I hope our paths cross again soon. Shalom, Michael.

Michael turned his attention to Laura's text.

Hi Mike, yes, I am back. Great trip and many new contacts in the predictive analytics world. Lots to tell. It is unbelievable what some of the technology is allowing companies to do now. Get back soon. The French make wonderful food! I am happy to have met you as well. More than you know right now. Lol. Laura

Michael opened his laptop and soon began studying the files on the Kenema Mosque. Satellite imagery showed the square building sitting aside two streets, one to the north and one to the east. Either approach would work he thought, but the northern street was closer to the primary road just one hundred and twenty-five feet away.

The parking lot seemed small, but it was Kenema, so it did not need to accommodate many vehicles. Michael thought the lot was probably used by the staff, food delivery trucks, and maintenance crews.

There were four light fixtures atop the building that surrounded the Mosque. Michael wondered if they worked in the evening.

Langley also provided a dossier on Sheikh Cissi. A native of Sierra Leone, and born of the Jawei chiefdom in Gelehum, Sheikh Cissi's dossier was slim. A picture of Cissi accompanied the file. It was taken by a local photographer in 2003 and Michael wondered what he might look like now.

Michael read a few excerpts from public statements he made in Kenema. Cissi gave no speeches or interviews indicating support for Islamic State or any other terror organizations. The file contained few clues of the man's habits, nor was there a psychological profile written on him. Cissi was a man operating under the radar of the American intelligence community.

The report did indicate some references to his security. The Sheikh apparently traveled with one bodyguard and used several more to protect the Mosque at nights. Michael noticed the date of the paragraph to be November 2005.

He sighed and closed the file. The intelligence Michael received on the man was outdated and practically useless. This would complicate his strategy to gather actionable intelligence and determine if the Ebola plot was genuine or a fabrication by Haris to flee the Islamic State.

He reminded himself of the Iraqi scientist who convinced German BND and CIA that Saddam Hussein possessed weapons of mass destruction. What a blunder that turned out to be for the agency, Michael thought.

Michael then examined the brief country report on Sierra Leone. At the top of the threats he faced, Ebola and criminal gangs concerned him the most.

The report included early symptoms of Ebola. However, he didn't learn much more than what was widely reported by various media outlets.

The report also characterized criminal activity as critical. Foreigners and expatriates from the United States were targets for robberies and break-ins due to perceived affluence. Petty criminals also targeted many of the upscale hotels in Kenema. The Capitol Hotel, however, had a superb reputation for security among its international clientele.

Michael finished browsing at geographic features, road networks in and around Kenema, and weather forecasts for the coming seventy-two-hour period. The remainder of the report provided nothing of significant tactical intelligence he might have needed.

Michael's cell phone rang.

"Mike, it's Doug. Where are you?"

"At the Capitol Hotel. Just reviewing the file, the analysts sent. It is worthless. No current Intel exists. The only thing relevant was the imagery of the Mosque and his picture."

"I know. It's all we had. His name was not found in many of the database queries we ran."

"Probably because he has not been targeted."

"Yeah. Sierra Leone has never been a high priority for collection."

"What does Freetown know?" asked Michael.

"I spoke with them earlier. They are going to give me something tomorrow."

"Okay. I plan to scout the Mosque tonight and see what security measures I can find. Can you get Freetown to look into any cell phones he may be using? He may not even be here right now."

"I'll pass it on. Mike, DI continues to believe the plot is ludicrous. They are no longer looking at it as a viable threat. I am getting some pressure to either confirm this or move on. I need you to get to Cissi in a day or two. Not sure if the Director has the stomach for more guessing. He's been asking why you are not in Libya."

"Any analysts you know taking this seriously?"

"I think one is. Apparently, INR has an analyst still looking at scenarios. She seems fiery and taking the threat seriously. I hear she is very good."

"Okay. I will push forward with the recon tonight and make a play for Cissi tomorrow. Any word back yet on the off-site?"

Apartment 1912, 66 Rockwell Complex, New York – November 17, 9:20 PM

Michael sat alone in the empty apartment. He remained alert in the nearly pitch-black room with some light penetrating the blinds. Jesse Sane clearly enjoyed his solitude after spending daylight hours sleeping to prepare for his evening duties. Bored, Michael continued thinking if he and Doug made the right decision. Waiting patiently was something Michael learned to do over the years, but his intelligence then was more clear and highly predictable. Not knowing Foday's whereabouts irritated the professional spy. However, he knew he had few options.

He recalled a time in 2004 where he awaited the arrival of an asset in India who claimed to have information on Usama Bin Laden's location in the tribal region of Waziristan, Pakistan. The mountainous region, often believed to be the location of Usama Bin Laden after his escape from the Battle of Tora Bora, seemed the likely location according to most experts in the Intelligence Community. While in Mumbai, he waited for twelve hours in an upscale hotel for a meeting that never took place. His asset never showed, and Michael learned a short while later that Al Qaeda operatives learned of his betrayal and ordered his execution.

There were a handful of unmarked sedans filled with members of the NYPD counterterrorism unit near the apartment. Hazmat teams were also nearby. NYPD did not add additional resources for fear of alerting Foday.

Everything had to look just like it did the past few days. Then the moment Michael awaited for had finally arrived.

The sound of the key entering the door meant one thing. Foday was returning to the apartment. He opened the door slowly and turned on the lights. The apartment appeared as it did earlier in the day and so he took two steps inside. Foday left the door ajar. He was ready for anything, and his careful observation of the apartment did not settle his nerves. After all, he was operating in unfamiliar territory on foreign soil.

Michael sprung to attention from behind the counter with his pistol in his left hand. Foday instantly reacted and fled to the hallway racing toward the stairwell as Michael pursued him. Foday slammed the stairwell door open, and began rapidly descending the stairs. He continued to evade Michael all the way to the garage level of the complex.

Foday exited the stairwell and knew his pursuer was only a few seconds behind him. He felt the dash across the open and lighted parking complex was pointless. He knew the man he saw on the Black River was probably a professional and expert sharpshooter. Turning to his left, he decided to confront the stranger as he came through the door. He stood along the wall and prepared to strike.

Michael made his last turn down the stairs. In front of him, the only door leading to the garage remained closed. He lifted his right leg and violently kicked it open. Peering his head around the corner, he saw no signs of Foday. Nevertheless, Michael decided to quickly enter the garage and continue his pursuit. As he passed through the entrance, he felt the powerful blow on his left arm followed by a strike to the forehead. Momentarily weakened, Michael regained his footing and landed a powerful punch to Foday's chest.

For the next several minutes, the two men engaged in hand-to-hand combat inside the garage complex. Neither man gained an advantage until Michael finally postured his body behind Foday and placed him into a chokehold. His strength overwhelmed Foday who attempted furiously to escape Michael's clutch. Foday's elbow punches landed more infrequently, and after several minutes, his resistance began to fade. Michael continued to strangle Foday's neck until the men reached the concrete floor. He continued to hold Foday until he was sure the man was dead.

Michael let go and stood up. Foday's lifeless eyes stared at him.

"Tony, it's over. Foday is dead. Bring your people into the garage."

A few minutes later, without any sirens, flashing lights or public spectacle, the New York Police Department and its biological hazard team arrived. They quickly placed Foday's body in the ambulance and sped off to an undisclosed location to examine the body. Michael would join them for observation for several weeks to ensure no signs of the virus existed.

The time spent in the hospital allowed Michael to reflect on his recent mission and thank those who supported him. It also offered him an opportunity to speak with Laura and make plans for dinner. During his mission, he could not wait until he saw her again. Her beautiful smile, long black hair, and warm personality captured his attention even during the most dangerous times throughout the operation. In just a few days, he and his new love would be in Georgetown, Washington, D.C. where dinner would finally come at last.

Acknowledgements

To those I had the honor and privilege to serve with, thank you for your selfless service to our great nation and the sacrifices you endure to keep us safe. To my parents, thank you for being great role models and always being there when I needed you. To my late wife, Sharon, thank you for being an incredibly loving mother and showing me what true courage is. Rest in peace.

To my children, Sarah, Shane, and Sean, live life to the fullest and never stop dreaming. To my publishing team, Barbara, Carol, and Marc, thank you for your expertise, patience and support and for giving an unknown author an opportunity to share a story. Finally, thank you to my current love, best friend and partner, Laura. Your faithful support means everything.

Author Bio

Lieutenant Colonel Michael Brady, USA, (RET), earned his MS in Strategic Intelligence from the National Intelligence University in Washington, D.C. in 2003. His classified thesis focused on the current and emerging issues confronting China and Taiwan and Taiwan's ability to retain sovereignty into the future. He was published in the Military Intelligence Professional Bulletin (MIPB) in July 2000 where he focused on the critical tasks an intelligence officer must perform to excel and be an integral member of a combat team. He has performed a wide variety of tactical and strategic intelligence functions including long-range surveillance, interrogation, intelligence analysis, collection management, emergency operations, and intelligence production. He served as the Director, Presidential Emergency Operations Center in the White House from January 2001 until July 2002 under President George W. Bush.

LTC Brady is a 1990 graduate of The Citadel, Marine Corps Command and General Staff College, Joint Forces Staff College, US Army Airborne School and US Army Ranger School.

His areas of expertise and research include threats to the homeland, intelligence collection systems and programs, intelligence analysis, and intelligence support to national policy making.

Michael currently lives in Charleston, SC and teaches graduate and undergraduate courses at The Citadel. He also lectures at FSU, a constituent institution of the University of North Carolina. Michael spends most of his free time in Jacksonville, Florida. He is also the proud father of three children - Sarah, Shane, and Sean.

Michael Brady can be found on:

Twitter - @profmbrady.

Facebook – Into The Shadows

Please visit his website michaelbradybooks.com to sign up and learn more about upcoming novels, release dates and book signings.